# TARO

# 太郎

*by* BLUE SPRUELL

---

*Illustrated by* MIYA OUTLAW

# TARŌ

*Blue Spruell*

Tarō is a work of fiction. Names, characters, places, and events are either the product of the author's imagination or used fictitiously. Any resemblance to actual persons, living or dead, places, or events is entirely coincidental.

Published by Out of the Blue Productions, LLC
315 Sycamore Street
Decatur, Georgia 30030
info@outoftheblueproductions.llc

Cover Design: Miya Outlaw and Blue Spruell
Illustrations: Miya Outlaw
www.miyaoutlaw.com



ISBN: 978-1-7357292-1-3

TO MY MOTHER

*who inspired me on so many adventures, imaginary and real*

AND MY WIFE

*who inspired me on this adventure*

## ACKNOWLEDGMENTS

This book would not have been possible without the support of my family, friends, and mentors. Authors Terry Kay, Roshani Chokshi, and Christopher Vogler deserve special thanks for their guidance and encouragement, and I am grateful to Madison Bernath and Dusty Socarras for their proofreading. Collaboration with my family—my wife and son for cultural and creative inspiration, my daughter for her enchanting illustrations, and my mother for her editorial eye—was the most enjoyable part of telling this story, but I am also grateful for masterful historical accounts by Stephen Turnbull, Danny Chaplin, Mitsuo Kure, Harry Cook, David Miller, Nelly Delay, Anthony J. Bryant, the works of Lafcadio Hearn and Akira Kurosawa, and the legacy of myths and legends that captured my imagination and inspired me to celebrate all I love about the magical, mystical folklore of Japan.

# CONTENTS

3 Faces of Taro

# INTRODUCTION

*Blue Spruell*

Tarō is the quintessential hero of three timeless Japanese folktales: *Kintarō* (Golden Boy), *Urashima Tarō* (Island Boy), and *Momotarō* (Peach Boy). Each legend stands alone, bearing no relation to the others except in name.

Some years ago, I saw a parallel between the personalities of Japan's three Great Unifiers and Momotarō's animal companions, the pheasant, monkey, and dog. I thought it might be amusing to write a short story drawing on this comparison. What began as a little excursion became a grand adventure. While the rest may not be history *per se*, I hope the reader will enjoy this new yarn as much as I enjoyed spinning it.

Many of the people and places in this story are real, although the circumstances are fictitious and bear no intentional resemblance to any locations or persons, living or dead. This story reimagines the pivotal period in Japan's unification, *sengoku jidai*, the age of the country at war.

In the sixteenth century, feudal Japan was a collection of warring provinces, nominally affiliated with the imperial family, which wielded little to no real power. For all intents and purposes, the sword of the *samurai*, the warrior class, ruled the realm. The three great warlords of Japan were, in order of their preeminence, Oda Nobunaga, Hashiba (Toyotomi) Hideyoshi, and Tokugawa Ieyasu. Each *daimyō* demonstrated qualities critical to Japan's unification. Oda was notoriously ruthless and cruel; Hashiba, cunning and manipulative; Tokugawa, diplomatic and patient.

A famous Japanese poem about their respective, formidable methods translates:

*If the cuckoo does not sing, kill it.* [Oda]
*If the cuckoo does not sing, coax it.* [Hashiba]
*If the cuckoo does not sing, wait for it.* [Tokugawa]

Another famous verse describes their roles in the history of Japan's unification:

*Nobunaga pounded the rice.*
*Hideyoshi kneaded the cake.*
*Ieyasu ate.*

Quite naturally, each of these men possessed legendary personalities. Oda was infamously mercurial but surprisingly liberal in his adoption of Western influences, most notably the matchlock gun, as well as his patronage of the arts, especially *chanoyu,* the tea ceremony. Unlike his contemporaries, Hashiba had not been born to the warrior class but rose through the ranks from his appointment as Oda's sandal-bearer and ultimately succeeded his lord who, ironically, had cruelly nicknamed his vassal "little monkey" because of his slight frame and reputedly ugly face. Tokugawa claimed birthright to the hereditary title of *shōgun*, a de facto military dictator, and ushered in three centuries of peace when he secured his title following the decisive Battle of Sekigahara in 1600.

Another contender in this celebrated conflict deserves special mention, Takeda Shingen, the warlord whose death Akira Kurosawa popularized in his superb film, *Kagemusha*, the "shadow warrior." A contemporary of the three Great Unifiers, Takeda was an exemplary *samurai* and military tactician. Had his life not been cut short, who knows how high he might have risen in the annals of Japan? As a final introductory note, before Takeda received his Buddhist name of Shingen, his family called him *Tarō*.

---

| | |
|---|---|
| *Swift as the wind* | 疾如風 |
| *Quiet as the forest* | 徐如林 |
| *Fierce as the fire* | 侵掠如火 |
| *Firm as the mountain* | 不動如山 |

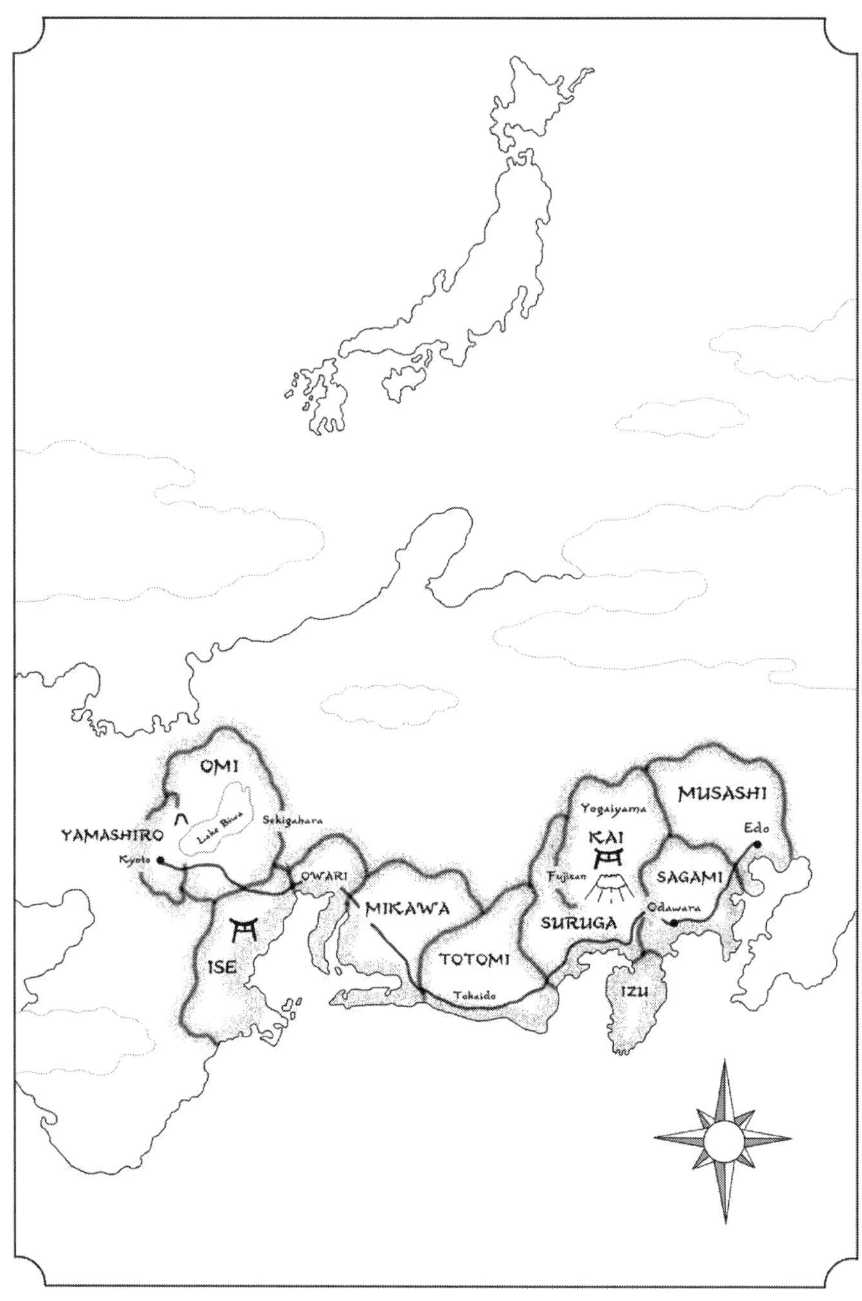
OMI
YAMASHIRO
Kyoto
Lake Biwa
Sekigahara
OWARI
ISE
MIKAWA
TOTOMI
Tokaido
SURUGA
Fujisan
KAI
Yogaiyama
MUSASHI
Edo
SAGAMI
Odawara
IZU

Nihon

# PART ONE

---

## KIN TARŌ

## 金太郎

# Kin Taro

# 1

## SWORD OF THE SAMURAI

*Kai Province*

*New Year's Day, Year of the Monkey*

"Once upon a time—" the story began.

The boy cradled the loosely bound book in his lap, enchanted by a brush-and-ink drawing of the full moon rising over majestic Mount Fuji. Tiny figures stood in the foreground, a humble woodcutter discovering a princess in bright, flowing robes in the middle of a feathery bamboo forest. In Japanese script the title read, *Tale of the Bamboo Cutter.*

"Tarō!" a woman's voice called to the boy, disturbing the cold quiet around him.

Tarō hunched over his book. He did not want to be found. Cold as it was, he had thought to hide himself outside and fled the warm confinement of the castle in search of a peaceful place to read—his secret retreat—for stories carried him away, far from the harsh life to which he had been born. In a time ruled by the sword, Tarō read books as the horseman gallops and with a marksman's focus that far exceeded his practical ability in such skills as were to be expected of a boy of his birth and age. He longed for greatness only in a boyish way, naively, effortlessly, and often out of spite when he growled how he would show his father someday.

"Be careful what you wish for," his mother warned whenever he ran off in protest, but Tarō paid no heed.

Climbing into the wintry sky, the sun had just crested the castle wall. The air frosted his breath and made him shiver in his light robe. He slid across the veranda to a warm patch of sunlight. One hand in salute, he shaded his eyes from bright Amaterasu as the Sun Goddess melted the shimmering snowfall over the stone garden. Camellia trees with dark green, waxy leaves and bright red blossoms grew along the castle wall and around the garden, the crimson heads of their fallen flowers littering the borders. Four massive rocks, the centerpiece, marched across a rippling sea of glittering, snow-laden gravel. When Tarō winked, a trick of the eye fused the four stones into one.

*"Smaller stones will sink beneath the Sea, but one great stone may withstand the tide," his father once said.*

At the time, his father had been speaking to his vassals. Tarō crept close to the audience chamber to listen—but not too close, so the stalwart guards at the closed doors did not see him.

*"Lord Oda holds too much influence over the young Emperor," his father continued his rant. "He abuses his position to sanction his brazen conquests, and these petty rivalries among the provinces only weaken the country, exposing all of us to his devilry. And Hashiba, that scheming sandal-bearer—"*

"Tarō!" the voice came more sharply than before from somewhere within the castle quarters, recalling him from his daydream. He glanced over his shoulder, frowning as the voice drew near, accompanied by the sound of footsteps hurriedly thumping on the wooden veranda.

"Tarō! Wake up!" his mother said sharply. "What are you doing out here in the cold—you'll catch your death!"

Tarō turned as his mother shuffled up to him, her elegantly patterned *kimono* of richly colored silk whispering around her feet as she fought to keep her trailing gown from tripping her up. She was already out of breath, but she did not stop. She grabbed his shoulders gently but firmly and gave him a reproachful shake as a prelude to a real scolding, but he hung his head to save her hand.

Looking him over, she could not resist a smile. She adored her boy, thinking him so handsome with his bushy eyebrows and thick, black bangs. She pinched his pudgy cheek, and Tarō winced.

"Wake up now, this is a big day! No time for daydreaming," she said, taking him firmly by his arm. "What will your father say!"

She led him off the way she had come, while Tarō protested, dragging his feet as she shuffled down the paneled corridor, pulling on him with one hand and doing her best to keep her unruly *kimono* at heel with the other.

"Why do we have to go *now*?" he groaned.

"Tarō, now don't be difficult," she chided, tugging on his arm. "This is an important day, your *seventh* birth day,[1] and we must go to the shrine, and that is that."

Tarō's mother ushered him into his room where his nurse was busily arranging his clothes for the big day. A sumptuous *kimono* of golden silk, a matching jacket with a golden, brocade clasp, and handsome, pleated *hakama* trousers lay spread upon the *tatami* floor. The room smelled grassy from the *tatami* mats.

"There you are!" his nurse said upon seeing him. She bowed to her mistress. "Off hiding with a book again? I've never seen such a bookworm!" she said, taking his treasure and setting it aside. "Just a moment and I will have him ready for you, my Lady."

Tarō's mother gave him another reproachful look, then disappeared to attend other matters in preparation for the big day.

---

[1] Child mortality was common, and children were considered offspring of the gods until they attained age seven, so a vital rite of passage for *samurai* boys included visiting a shrine to expel evil spirits and pray for a long, healthy life.

Tarō liked the look of the golden silk, and he marveled at the matching brocade *obi* sash his nurse unfurled for him. His dour matron stripped off his checkered robe and quickly draped him in a light undergarment before clothing him in his golden *kimono*.

"Hiding yourself away again," she scolded, "Lord Takeda won't be pleased, you know!"

Tarō fussed and fidgeted as she bound him with the golden sash, frustrating her pains to dress him in his finery. The more she tugged and tucked, the more Tarō growled like a tiger cub.

"If you don't stand still—" his nurse complained, suddenly warning, "Yama Uba will come for you for sure!"

At this, Tarō stopped fidgeting, not for fear but because he loved his nurse's stories.

"Tell me!" he demanded.

"Oh, she's a terrible witch," his nurse said, as she tugged and tucked on his *kimono*, "with wild white hair and black eyes. She just loves plump, undisciplined little boys! She will steal you away and carry you off to her lair, and then fatten you up and—" she paused for effect, pinching his cheek, and teased, "eat you!"

As Tarō yowled and rubbed the sting from his cheek, she ordered, "Now, off you go! You must not keep your father waiting any longer or he will have your hide—and my head!"

"Where is my son?" Lord Takeda roared.

With a furrowed brow, Tarō's father rapped the low table with his bamboo *sensu* folding fan, rattling the slate inkwell in front of him. Seated on a *zabuton* cushion on a raised portion of the floor overlooking the room, Lord Takeda wore his formal Buddhist *kesa* draped over his *kimono*. His squire sat in silent attendance behind him.

Only a little natural light filtered through the cypress transoms, but tall *ikari* candles lit the corners, their shadows falling across the *tatami* floor and upon the plastered walls and sliding doors partitioning the room. A magnificent painting of a tiger decorated the wall in the alcove behind them, its eyes glowing fiercely in the candlelight. A stack of two *kagami mochi,* "mirror" rice cakes, food of the gods, topped with a small, bitter orange, sat on the shelf in the alcove as an offering to the New Year.

An attendant bowed nervously at his Lord's displeasure, humbly displaying his tonsured bald spot and topknot as he backed away to investigate, but when the nervous fellow pushed aside the sliding door, Lady Takeda was already seated just outside the room, her two ladies-in-waiting and Tarō's nurse behind her. She knelt beside the door, carrying herself as if she had been there for some time, and bowed her head so elegantly that Lord Takeda quickly forgot himself. Although they had been married nearly eight years, his consort was still pleasant to behold, her porcelain face delicately framed by the long black tresses of her hair.

"Ah! My lady," he sighed. "Where is my son?"

Tarō appeared from behind his mother, jumping forward to strike a confident pose in his golden *kimono*, legs straight and arms raised as if he were about to somersault into the room.

"Yesterday in rags, today in gold brocade," Lady Takeda quoted the old saying, thinking herself witty, but it fell flat on her husband's ears.

Lord Takeda inspected his son for a tense moment until Tarō forgot himself. He was small, and his father was an imposing figure, even without his armor and sword. Tarō wore his hair in a ponytail since he had not come of age to shave his head and wear a topknot, nor did he have the nearly perpetual scowl that only aggrandized Lord Takeda's fearsome appearance, but anyone could see where Tarō got his bushy brows and piercing eyes.

*"Kin Tarō!"* Lord Takeda said at last in an equally fearsome voice, as he beheld his golden boy. "Already seven years old?"

Tarō nodded timidly.

"Then what are you thinking?" his father roared suddenly, slamming his fist on the low table, the inkwell rattling once again.

Tarō flinched. The servants quickly bowed their heads.

"Always idle," Lord Takeda blustered, "always absent-minded, sticking your head in books when you should be training with the General! Well? What do you have to say for yourself?"

"My Lord—" His wife tried to speak, but he cut her off.

"Nothing! Not a word! You should attend my son better!"

His stab hurt her deeply. She quickly bowed her head and tugged on Tarō's *kimono*, prompting him to do the same. Tarō immediately complied, kneeling with his head bowed so it touched the floor. His backside knew well what came of non-compliance.

"Tarō is the heir to Yōgaiyama Castle and the whole dominion of Kai Province," Lord Takeda pressed his rant. "He should be attending his training, and you should not be filling his head with all your books and stories. Fairy tales! Nonsense! You are both soft! A soft *samurai* will not do!—" He beat the table again, rattling the inkwell once more. "Not in these times," he trailed off, muttering and shaking his head. For reassurance, he glanced at his *katana,* the sword on the rack beside him.

Following an awkward silence, Lord Takeda waved for his son to come to him. Cautiously, Tarō slid forward, keeping his head down until he sat next to his father. After a tense moment and another flinch from Tarō, Lord Takeda pulled his boy into his arms, feeling guilty for having lost his temper. Lady Takeda smiled and relaxed.

"Are you ready to go?"

"Yes," Tarō lied for he knew better than to fight the Tiger.[2]

---

[2] Lord Takeda's given name was Nobutora [信虎], "Trusty Tiger."

"Good!" his father growled. "But first—" he added, reaching beneath the low table to find a long, slender package wrapped in purple crepe.

Tarō's eyes grew big and round at the sight of it.

"Congratulations on your birth day!" Lord Takeda grunted, intending to keep his son humble as he handed him the gift.

"Is it a scroll?" Tarō asked eagerly but his question fell flat.

"A scroll?" Lord Takeda repeated, frowning at his wife.

Lady Takeda averted her eyes. Her husband exhaled noisily.

"Go on," he said, prompting Tarō to open the package.

Tarō tore at the knotted cloth, which fell away to reveal a handsome short sword with black and gold lacquered fittings. He gasped. Although neither expected nor desired, the sword was no ordinary gift. Lord Takeda glanced at his wife just long enough to perceive her displeasure and smiled smugly.

"It's okay," he said, urging Tarō with a nod.

Tarō held the sword close for a better look. Then, remembering his lessons, and surprising both of his parents, he cradled the sword as if making an offering. Holding it up, he bowed his head reverently. Although it barely showed on his stern face, Lord Takeda gleamed with pride to see his son behave with such martial maturity. Only his wife could have detected it, but she took no notice, too busy hiding her sad recognition that her son would soon outgrow her when he assumed the harsh mantle of manhood.

The sword was short, a *wakizashi* or *shōtō*, in keeping with the custom, since Tarō would not receive a longer matching *daitō* until his *genpuku*, the coming-of-age ceremony when he attained fifteen years of age. The gold lacquer sheath shone like polished mirror inlaid with the Takeda family *mon* in black lacquer—four separate diamonds arranged in a single unified diamond crest, their coat of arms. A cord of woven black silk attached to the scabbard. Tarō took hold of the hilt, which had been wrapped tightly in ray skin and braided black silk

Taro and the Tiger

and fitted with an iron handguard wrought with a gilded dragon. The scabbard held the blade as snugly as a glove. He had to pull harder than expected, so the sword surprised him when at last he managed to free it.

"Careful now," his father cautioned, as Tarō unsheathed the razor-sharp blade.

Lady Takeda bit her lip. She knew better than to challenge her Lord's pleasure openly, but she could not help but worry for her boy, while Lord Takeda studied his son with high hopes for the *samurai* he would become.

Tarō held up the naked blade, all the elements—earth, water, fire, and wind—masterfully forged by hammer, anvil, and the skill of the swordsmith and his guiding spirit, into the supreme physical and spiritual embodiment of the *samurai.* Tarō marveled at the temper line, delicately wrought to resemble floating clouds.

"Every sword must have a name," his father said. "The smith Masamune named this one Murakumo no Hoken, the Gathering-Cloud Treasure Sword, just like the one Susanō no Mikoto the Storm God hewed from the dragon's tail."

Tarō's eyes grew large in amazement for he knew the story well. As he turned the blade in his hand, the edge caught the candlelight, and a mystical flash made him blink. He thought he heard a faint whisper, as if the sword were calling his name, *"Tarō!"*

"That's enough now, put it away," Lord Takeda said.

Tarō nervously sheathed the blade, thinking he had somehow displeased his father again. Taking the sword and pushing to make sure it was secure, Lord Takeda tucked the prize neatly in the folds of Tarō's brocade sash so only the hilt showed. Tarō felt awkward, uncertain of how he should carry himself.

Lord Takeda slid the inkwell on the low table to one side. He took up a strip of pure white cloth and spread it on the table.

"Today we will present you to Hachiman no Kami, the God of War, and pray that you grow up big and strong to serve your Emperor and your clan honorably," Lord Takeda said, reaching for a stick of charcoal and grinding it purposefully in the inkwell until he produced a dark pool of ink.

Tarō watched, his eyes riveted to his father's hands as Lord Takeda took up a brush and dipped it into the inkwell. His father raised the brush, poised over the pure white cloth. Then briskly, in just a few confident strokes, he wrote in elegant *kanji* script:

日本一

*"Ni-hon Ichi,"* Tarō read the words aloud.

"You will be a great leader someday, first in all Nihon."

"Foolish woman, do not tempt the gods! That is not what it means," Lord Takeda snapped. "You will fill his head with dangerous thoughts! Tarō is *samurai*, born and bound to serve and protect his Lord and his Emperor unto death."

Lord Takeda took up the cloth and tied the auspicious *hachimaki* around Tarō's head. He admired his son for a moment, reseating the sword in Tarō's sash and tugging sharply on his *kimono*, as if dressing his boy in a suit of armor, checking to make sure it was straight and secure.

As Tarō rolled his eyes upward, trying to get a look at his cloth crown, Lord Takeda leaned close.

"The Takeda family was meant to unite this land," he whispered. "It is your destiny."

Lord Takeda paused thoughtfully, then corrected himself.

"Only the gods can see your destiny," he said aloud. "On your birth day, this auspicious New Year's Day, we will ask their blessings at Fuji Hachiman Shrine."

Not prone to indulgence, Lord Takeda dropped his guard for an instant, exchanging a look of quiet pride with his Lady, while Tarō thoughtfully rubbed the handle of his new sword, trying to look the part of a *samurai.*

In the Hour of the Snake, drums beat a resounding command, echoing across the massive stone walls that stood guard over the impenetrable sanctuary of the castle courtyard. Here and there around the quadrangle, several braziers on tall iron tripods threw flame and thick black smoke into the frosty air. Fifty of Lord Takeda's *samurai* had assembled there to escort the family to Fuji Hachiman Shrine.

In full armor except for his helmet, Lord Takeda stood above the assemblage, surveying his retainers from a parapet overlooking the courtyard. Below him, his fearsome General Toramasa shouted commands to the contingent.

Lady Takeda stood silently behind her Lord, her ladies-in-waiting and Tarō's nurse behind her, but Tarō crept from her side to stand on tiptoe at the parapet, transfixed by the commotion. Catching sight of him, Lady Takeda grabbed his golden sleeve to hold him at a safe distance, but it did little to curb Tarō's fascination with the bustling activity below as Lord Takeda's men-at-arms mustered for the journey. Tarō grinned with delight, as the General's black steed stamped impatiently just below the parapet.

The courtyard air was still and cold, and the snow was deep in shady corners. The men and horses' cloudy breaths only added to the formidable look of the *samurai* in their red-lacquered *dō-maru* armor, the General himself wearing the more elaborate but similarly blood-colored *oyoroi* scaled armor over his torso and limbs, although his fanned helmet hung from his saddle. Frosty breaths punctuated his commands as the General shouted from horseback until the escort finished forming ranks, their red *sashimono* banners proclaiming the black composite diamond of their Takeda heraldry as they danced at their backs like insect wings.

Four footmen brought forward Lady Takeda's palanquin, and she took Tarō by the arm to follow her Lord from the parapet to the courtyard below. As they stopped to greet the General, Tarō eyed a steaming lump of *kuso* the General's steed had just dropped on the flagstones, his nose wrinkling when he got wind of it.

"My Lord!" General Toramasa shouted as he dismounted, his bearskin boots crunching on snow underfoot.

The General knelt, bowing low to his Lord, who nodded. The General stood and bowed to Lady Takeda, and she returned his favor.

Although much bigger than Tarō, the General was a squat man with a round face obscured only by sideburns and a mustache as bushy as a tiger's mane and whiskers. He was not wearing his face guard, and the red-devil *menpō* hung at his neck, staring back at Tarō with blank eyes as the General bent to greet his pupil.

"What a handsome *samurai* you look!" the General said. Catching sight of Tarō's *wakizashi*, he teased, "And that's a handsome knitting needle!"

Tarō reached for his sword and drew it, raising it proudly.

"Young Master!" the General said quickly and with some embarrassment for his pupil, "What did I teach you about drawing a sword?"

"If you draw the sword, you must use it," Tarō parroted bashfully, re-sheathing the blade.

"Well, at least he looks the part—" Lord Takeda said, quietly reproaching his tutor, "even if he still has a lot to learn."

"Do you think it wise to travel with so light a guard?" the General asked politely.

"It's fine," Lord Takeda said with a wave of his hand.

"Lord Oda has spies everywhere—" his General pressed.

"It is enough!" Lord Takeda snapped, annoyed at having his orders questioned. "It is but a day's excursion."

"Very well, my Lord," the General nodded sharply, bowing low, for he knew when to obey, even when his Lord chose to ignore wise counsel.

Lady Takeda and Tarō stepped into the palanquin, a cramped lacquer box with vertical slats for windows, but at least it was warmer inside, and there were cushions to ease the journey. Sumptuous gold leaf and paintings of crimson peonies in full bloom decorated the walls. Tarō slid into a corner, and his mother arranged the cushions for the two of them. A retainer closed the sliding door to shut them inside. Lady Takeda's ladies-in-waiting, Tarō 's nurse, and Lord Takeda's closest retainers rode separately.

Lord Takeda put on his impressive *kabuto,* his helmet decorated with white horse hair and stag's antlers so he resembled some mythical monster. Mounting his black stallion and surveying the ranks, he gave the command.

Slowly, to a resounding drumbeat, the Takeda retinue began its winding descent through the snow-laden streets toward the main castle gate, the horses' hooves clopping noisily on the stones in the road. All the while, Tarō peered through his window.

Sunlight dappled the cobblestones. The castle had been awake for hours, its citizens busying themselves about their daily affairs, but now those residents not accompanying Lord Takeda to the shrine had gathered to honor the procession. Craftsmen, gardeners, servants, and soldiers, all charged with protecting the castle in Lord Takeda's attendance or absence, all bowed low, some prostrate, as the procession made its way through the winding main street, kicking up muddy snow beneath the footmen's *waraji*-sandaled feet and the horses' hooves. When the procession had passed without further ado, all the castle folk went about their usual business as if their lives depended on it.

Tarō stared out his window at the sloping stone walls that flanked the street, the walls growing ever taller in his eyes as the cavalcade descended through the labyrinthine castle complex to the echoing drumbeat accompanying their march. The castle's chief defense was the maze of streets, passages, gates, walls and baileys that led to the main keep. Regular switchbacks in the steep and narrow pathways intended to frustrate navigation, the whole fortress having been laid out so as to confuse an attacking army, forcing it to wind its way through the fortifications to approach the keep, all the while exposed to the castle's formidable defenses.

Tarō spied the countless defensive loopholes, grinning black chutes angled in the face of the fortress walls from which the defenders could strike at attackers with spear, arrow, or musket ball. He shivered at their exposure as the palanquin jostled back and forth along the winding cobblestone road.

Watchtowers with upturned eaves punctuated the walls, one for each compass point, and countless other fortifications lined the way between the keep and the citadel's twelve gates, including not one but two protective dry moats, each over one hundred feet wide and taller than two men. As the procession passed beneath archways along the route, each arch, each gate proudly proclaimed the diamond crest of his clan, although Tarō took for granted this emblem of Takeda hegemony.

When the procession reached the outermost Tiger Gate, the drums ceased. Lord Takeda and his General having already crossed the drawbridge, they checked their mounts to allow the procession to pass, their horses stamping impatiently. Tarō watched his father through the slatted window at his side, then shifted to get another look through the rear window as the palanquin passed. Just when it seemed as though the procession might leave his father and the General behind, Lord Takeda suddenly spurred his horse to a gallop, followed by the General, and they quickly outpaced the plodding steps of the procession.

"How far is it?" Tarō asked, looking at the sword in his sash and touching it, as if to confirm he had not dreamed it.

"Tarō, don't start—" his mother said. "It will take several hours to get there."

Tarō rolled his eyes. With a sigh he slunk into his corner of the palanquin, looking back listlessly as the mountain castle retreated from sight.

"Here," Lady Takeda said, producing her *bentō*, a small lacquered lunchbox filled with pressed balls of brown rice sprinkled with sesame seeds. Tarō eagerly took one and chomped into it, his nose wrinkling when he discovered the pink pickled plum hidden inside. Recovering, he shoved the rest of the rice ball in his mouth so his cheeks bulged.

"More?" Tarō asked with his mouth full.

Lady Takeda shook her head and teased, "A wise man's belly is never full."

Tarō frowned, puzzled.

"It means you should always be hungry, for knowledge."

"Tell me a story!" he mumbled with his mouth still full.

"Oh, Tarō," Lady Takeda sighed. "Why don't you take a little nap instead?"

"The crab and the monkey!"

"Really?" she groaned. "You've heard it so many times, you could tell me the story!"

"Once more!" Tarō begged.

"Oh, alright," she conceded, making herself comfortable.

She offered Tarō a drink of water from a burnished brown gourd decorated with red cord and an ornate stopper, then took a drink herself to wet her mouth before beginning her tale.

"A very long time ago, a crab was foraging for food when she found a rice ball in a ditch. She was considering her good fortune when a sly monkey came along and chattered away until he charmed her into trading her rice ball for a persimmon seed."

As the palanquin jostled along their route to the shuffling steps of the footmen and the sound of the horses' hooves striking the frozen road, Tarō listened and watched the castle recede, his eyes following the elaborate flight of castle parapets rising above the snow-laden crest of Mount Yōgai, half a league above sea level, its sinewy arms descending into a peaceful countryside of foothills terraced with snow-laden rice fields bounded by bamboo plumes heavy with frost. Lady Takeda paused, smiling fondly at her inquisitive little boy.

"Then what?" Tarō chided, shaking her from her reverie.

"Well," she said with a smile, amused at his persistence, "when the crab realized she could not eat the persimmon seed, at first she was upset, but then she planted the seed, and soon a tree grew in its place, and the crab was very pleased with the abundant fruit it bore. When Monkey saw the tree he slyly told her, 'If you will let me climb the tree, I will pick the fruit for you,' so she agreed, but Monkey ate all the fruit instead of sharing it with her, which made the crab very angry."

Lady Takeda used her hand like a crab claw to pinch Tarō's arm and made him squirm.

"When she protested, Monkey threw little hard, unripe persimmons at her, and one struck her right between the eyes and killed her," she said, poking Tarō between his eyes so he blinked, "but just before she died, she gave birth to four baby crabs."

"Why didn't the monkey kill the baby crabs too?" Tarō asked, surprising her.

"I don't know," she said, troubled by Tarō's violent thought, then with a smile she wittily replied with the proverb, "Even monkeys fall from trees."

Tarō made a face.

"Do you want me to tell the story or not?" she parried, to which Tarō nodded quietly.

"Well, when the crab babies grew up, they decided to take their revenge on Monkey for killing their mother, so they armed themselves with a prickly chestnut, and a stinging wasp, and a smelly cow dung, and a heavy hammer, and they went to Monkey's house in the middle of the night. One crab crept into the house and hid the chestnut beside Monkey's bed. One hid the wasp in Monkey's water bucket. One hid the cow dung in front of the entrance, and one climbed onto the roof to place the heavy hammer just above the door."

Still listening, Tarō yawned and sank into his pillow as his eyes grew heavy. Lady Takeda smiled, pleased to think her story might charm her boy to sleep and give her some peace.

"When Monkey woke the next morning," she continued, "he tried to get out of bed and stepped on the prickly chestnut, which made his foot bleed terribly. Then, when he tried to wash his wound with water from the bucket, the wasp stung him terribly. Monkey tried to run out of the house, but he slipped on the cow dung and fell, and just then, the heavy hammer dropped from the roof onto his head, crushing and killing him. The crabs rejoiced, waving their little claws triumphantly—"

No sooner had she finished her story than Lady Takeda realized Tarō was fast asleep. She smiled to see him quiet and caressed his head. Then she too allowed herself to shut her eyes and rest to pass the time until they should arrive at the shrine.

Ascent to Fuji Hachiman Shrine

2

## THE MONKEY AND THE WITCH

*Kai Province*

*New Year's Day, Year of the Monkey*

The sun had begun to sink from midday when the procession arrived at the snow-laden approach to Fuji Hachimangū, the ancient *Shintō*[3] shrine nestled in the forested foothills of majestic Mount Fuji, wreathed in ragged snow clouds slithering like dragons through the giant cryptomeria trees guarding the sanctuary. Lady Takeda nudged Tarō from sleep.

"Listen, Tarō! Do you hear the river?"

Tarō rubbed the sleep from his eyes and yawned. Hearing the sound of rushing water and the muffled thunder of some great waterfall nearby, he pressed against the slatted window, straining to get a glimpse of what lay ahead. The procession approached the gentle arch of a red-lacquered bridge spanning the narrowest part of

---

[3] *Shintō* [神道], "the way of the spirits," an indigenous faith in the connection between the natural and supernatural worlds.

an immense gorge, where a great river cut its course from immortal *Fujisan* to the sea.

Tarō shifted for a better view. The vermillion bridge and its polished metal ornaments shone brilliantly against the snow and the dark forest of cryptomeria trees.

The procession neared the bridge, and the sweet cedar scent of the forest filled Tarō's nose as he peered through the window. Only the rushing river and the distant thundering cascade disturbed an otherwise frozen, sacred silence around them.

"This is where Hachiman no Kami crossed the river on the backs of two giant snakes on his pilgrimage to Mount Fuji," his mother told him, which immediately piqued his interest. "The shrine was built to honor the powerful spirits that dwell here."

Lord Takeda checked his horse for a moment, then spurred it across the threshold of the scarlet bridge, his mount's hooves clopping across the rising wooden planks. The General followed, his steed snorting restlessly.

As the bearers carried the jostling palanquin over the bridge, Tarō took a deep breath through the slatted window. The cold mountain air stung his face and froze his nose hairs. He craned his neck, trying to get a look at the mighty river rushing beneath them.

Once over the bridge, the procession made its way through another grove of tall cypress trees that flanked a wide, well-tracked path on its ascent to the shrine. A blanket of sacred snow covered the ground, unsullied by the footsteps of any profane intruders. The path wound gently upward, away from the great, rushing river, but the muffled thunder of the nearby waterfall could still be heard, announcing the spiritual power of this place.

At length, the procession passed through the massive arched *torii,* the gate between the profane and sacred worlds, its vermillion posts and curved lintel bright in the sunlight that dappled the snowy stone forecourt. An explosion of color greeted the procession, the shrine buildings decorated with elaborate carvings, all gilt and richly colored, a lavish, ornate feast for the eyes, set in the vast green swath of towering cypress trees surrounding the shrine.

A wide flight of broad stone steps led to the dazzlingly gilt Twilight Gate, flanked by drum and bell towers of similarly sumptuous design, guarding the entrance to the main hall and oratory. Here the procession halted, and Lord Takeda and his General dismounted, giving their horses to their squires who led the steeds to nearby stables. A footman opened the door to the palanquin, and Lady Takeda allowed Tarō to exit, assisted by his nurse, while her ladies-in-waiting attended their mistress.

"Careful now," his mother warned as Tarō stepped into his *zōri* sandals, "the ground must be slippery."

Tarō stood blinking in wonderment at the sunlight slipping through the surrounding cedar trees. Forgetting his earlier complaints about visiting the shrine, he drew another heady breath of the frozen forest air. Over the muffled thunder of the nearby waterfall, he heard the hollow plunk of a bamboo water hammer from somewhere within the shrine compound.

Lord Takeda looked around. At the moment, he could not imagine a more peaceful scene as lay before him. Snow covered the flagstone forecourt and shrine buildings. To the left stood the sacred reservoir and several shrine buildings behind it. At some distance to the right, a storehouse formed the forecourt boundary, and between the flagstone court and the storehouse a small park lay beneath a pristine mantle of snow, bordered on three sides by twelve venerable cherry trees praying silently in their frozen chapel. The shrine appeared deserted, quiet in its hibernation, forgotten in the ancient snow-laden forest below Mount Fuji.

One of three hallowed shrines dedicated to the God of War, Fuji Hachiman was the wealthiest in all Nihon, its construction spanning nearly eight hundred years of consecration and imperial patronage. Its size and extravagance intended to humble and instill in its observers a sense of awe at the wealth and power of the imperial family, which was not lost on Lord Takeda who had long studied the political upheavals of prior eras as well as his own time. The shrine had blessed—and cursed—over one hundred years of feudal strife among the provinces, crowning emperors and unseating warlords with divine indifference. Even so, the hopeful sought benediction here year after year. The Takeda clan regarded Hachiman no Kami as its own patron and guardian. Lord Takeda himself had dedicated a small fortune to the shrine in his years as *daimyō* of his clan. He thought it ironic that so sacred and peaceful a spot as this could have so influenced a thousand years of bloodshed, all in the name of the Emperor.

Lord Takeda shook himself from his dark thoughts. It was cold, and they had come for a purpose. General Toramasa and a handful of retainers and servants accompanied their Lord and his family to the sacred reservoir. A number of snow-laden stone lanterns marched along the shrine buildings behind the covered well. A luxurious roof, gilt with gold leaf and fanciful architectural decorations, sheltered the rectangular stone pool, all manner of colorful beasts staring down at the penitent. As he stepped up to the basin, Tarō fixed on the elaborate iron spout wrought in the likeness of a dragon, water spilling from its gaping mouth to splash into the pool.

Tarō watched as Lady Takeda took one of the bamboo ladles and filled it with water falling from the dragon's toothy grin. With ritual deliberateness she poured water over her hands to wash them, then filled a cupped hand with a little water and raised it to her lips. She sipped but did not drink, rinsing her mouth as daintily as she could manage in the company of others. Before returning the ladle to its resting place, she filled it once more and raised it slowly, allowing the water to run down and wash the handle. She gave Tarō the ladle and bade him do likewise. Lord Takeda, his General, and the others observed the same ritual before they made their way to the shrine, pausing at the bottom of the steps to the Twilight Gate.

Standing at the foot of the stairs, Tarō looked up at the imposing structure supported by twelve columns, two stories taller and wider than six men standing with arms outstretched. The formidable likenesses of Fūjin and Raijin, the Gods of Wind and Thunder, stood sentinel beneath the roofed gate, guarding either side of the entrance, staring down at Tarō with fiendish grins and gleaming eyes. As he met Fūjin's gaze, Tarō's heart skipped a beat.

Tarō longed to run up the stairs ahead of everyone, but he knew better. He waited impatiently as General Toramasa, accompanied by a squire, climbed the staircase to announce Lord Takeda's arrival to the abbot of the shrine.

Disappearing beneath the Twilight Gate, the General called out, but there was no answer, or perhaps he found the abbot's residence and went inside, but all was quiet except for the steady muffled thunder of the waterfall, still hidden from view by the forest, and the staccato hollow plunk of the bamboo water hammer from somewhere within the shrine.

Tarō fidgeted for the General's return, and Lord Takeda appeared equally impatient. He paced for a time, called out for the General, and then with a grunt he directed Lady Takeda and Tarō to follow, with her maids, Tarō 's nurse, and Lord Takeda's closest retainers close behind them as they mounted the stairs to the Twilight Gate.

At the top of the stairs, Tarō stood transfixed before the massive, colorful effigies of the gods leering back at him with glowing, inlaid crystal eyes. Both equally terrifying in size and demeanor, with muscular, humanoid forms and fierce, frozen expressions, Fūjin wore a leopard pelt over his green skin, his red hair waving wildly from some invisible gale he harnessed with a large sack carried over his shoulder, while a blue *fundoshi* loincloth swaddled white-skinned Raijin, who also wore a green kerchief around his neck and appeared poised to leap from the clouds beneath him as he beat his hammers, one in each hand, upon the halo of thundering *taiko* drums around him.

"Cover your belly button," Tarō's nurse warned.

Tarō quickly complied, checking to see if he was missing any part of himself.

Tarō's gaze wandered from those grotesque guardians to take in the elaborate decorations on the gate. Overhead, colorful carvings of running, jumping, growling and leering sculptures of powerful *kami,* flora and fauna of all kind—*komainu* or lion-dogs, tigers, bears, monkeys, pheasants, antlered dragons, foxes, and unicorns, twisted pine trees, sprouting bamboo, and flowering plum—adorned every side of the fabulous, towering gate. Tarō gazed spellbound, and would have done so until the proverbial twilight had his father not called gruffly for him to follow.

Equally dazzling architectural opulence decorated the inside of the shrine, but the family moved with purpose across the courtyard toward another flight of steps that led to the elaborate façade of the main prayer hall with its lilting arched roof. Surrounding the square, a dozen or so other buildings sheltered and serviced the shrine's priestly inhabitants. A hint of sandalwood incense hung in the air, but the quadrangle was quiet.

A covered wooden rack stood at one side of the courtyard, hung with numerous, brightly painted, wooden votive plaques that drew Tarō's attention. He walked closer to the display, running his hand across the stacked and jumbled plaques, each competing for space on the rack. Nearly all of them had been painted with three monkeys, their paws covering either eyes, ears, or mouth.

"Where is the priest?" Lord Takeda looked around and grunted. "He should be here to meet us."

Tarō wandered toward the short flight of steps that led to the main prayer hall. Lady Takeda and his nurse followed to restrain him, but he outpaced them both and reached the foot of the stairs to peek into the shadowy oratory. Somewhere within the vast serene complex, but nearer now, the bamboo water hammer plunked again.

Lady Takeda paused to take a tighter grip of her *kimono* and free her feet but stopped when she saw Tarō looking up at the oratory. She halted his nurse with a hand. The sight of her son in his finery, so small and full of wonderment as he gazed up at the shrine, filled Lady Takeda with profound love that made her shiver. She smiled, but her heart sank as she thought again how quickly her boy had grown, how he would soon outgrow her. She longed to hold him to her breast.

*How silly*, she thought, but she could not help it. She shivered, casting off the moment, quietly chiding herself for her wistfulness.

Tarō raised his hands in salute to the shrine. He bowed twice, clapped twice, and bowed again, as dutifully as he had been taught, and another maternal pang surprised Lady Takeda. She exchanged a smile with his nurse, both doting on the boy, but the hollow knock of the water hammer disturbed the moment, as it echoed off the buildings and across the courtyard, followed by utter, snow-laden silence waiting for the next hollow plunk.

As Lady Takeda moved closer to Tarō, followed by his nurse and her ladies-in-waiting, General Toramasa called out. He and his squire appeared from inside the abbot's residence.

"I called," he said, shaking his head. "No answer."

"Strange," Lord Takeda mused.

Suddenly, the air hissed around them. Arrows struck down two of their four escorts. They fell to the ground dead. Lady Takeda's maids cried out as another arrow struck Tarō's nurse.

"My Lord!" the General exclaimed, racing to place himself between his Lord and the attack. Drawing his sword, the General shouted, "Ambush!"

More arrows whistled into their midst, throwing the other retainers into confusion. Lady Takeda cried in fright as her maids were struck down as well. Rushing to Tarō, she pulled him close to her, looking to her husband for protection.

"Defend my Lady!" Lord Takeda yelled to the General.

Lord Takeda drew his sword and rushed back to the Twilight Gate to rally the rest of his *samurai*, but gaining the threshold, he gasped at the spectacle.

Below the shrine Lord Takeda's men had already been set upon and overrun by rival *samurai* in pitch-black armor, their iron corsets and *sashimono* banners emblazoned with their warlord's trademark golden gourd on a black field. At the head of these assassins charged a fearsome warlord wearing the mask of a black devil and a helmet adorned with a fan of iron spikes for plumage.

"Hashiba!" Lord Takeda yelled to his General, instantly recognizing his rival, as the devil cut down two Takeda *samurai* that stood in his way at the foot of the stairs to the Twilight Gate.

The clash of steel and the death-cries of the men in the forecourt filled the wintry air. Turning his attention to his family again, Lord Takeda saw the General take an arrow in his neck. The General gasped and tore at the shaft, blood gushing from his wound as he fell to his knees. All of Lord Takeda's escorts within the shrine lay dead now except for the General. Arrows whistled toward Lord Takeda from somewhere above him but missed their mark or bounced off his armor.

"Run!" Lord Takeda yelled sharply to his wife as more arrows hissed at him. "Hide!"

Lady Takeda only stared in desperation at her Lord and clutched Tarō tighter. Tarō stood paralyzed by the sight of the stricken General, his mentor, a man he feared almost as much as his father, now spouting blood from his wound and staring back in disbelief at Tarō. The General gasped, trying to speak, his eyes calling to Tarō as he fell to the ground.

"Run!" Lord Takeda yelled once more, before turning to face the first assassins mounting the stairs to the Twilight Gate.

Suddenly alert and taut with fear at her husband's command, with only a backward glance, Lady Takeda grabbed Tarō by the arm and started up the steps to the oratory. Losing a sandal on the first step she fell and hit the stone stairs with a force that tore her *kimono* and made her cry out, but she quickly righted herself, kicking off her other sandal so she wore only her white *tabi* socks. Her fingernails dug into Tarō's flesh as she tightened her grip on his arm and nearly dragged him up the stairs with her. At the top of the stairs, she turned to look for her husband, who stood just inside the Twilight Gate, arrows still hissing around him.

The first of his enemies to gain the top of the stairs paused when they perceived Lord Takeda standing before them. Then, with terrifying yells, they fell upon him.

Lord Takeda sank into his stance and deftly parried the first of five foes, before slicing one man's trunk. Two more men slashed at him but failed. He slipped between them and spun to deliver equally fatal strikes. One man dropped, clutching his bleeding head, and the other received a stroke that took his leg from beneath him, blood spraying across the snow-covered flagstones. As Lord Takeda braced for the next assassin, an arrow found its mark behind his knee. He groaned, and his leg buckled.

"Hold!" a fearsome voice boomed.

The two remaining foes froze in ready stances, as the owner of the fearsome voice appeared, mounting the stairs to the Twilight Gate, his spiked helmet rising into view, followed by the black devil mask, and finally the armored devil himself.

"Monkey!" Lord Takeda spat as he faced his enemy.

The devil mask grunted defiantly at the insult, and the two men took each other's measure. Light snow began to fall. The silence built, punctuated only by the hollow plunk of the bamboo water hammer hidden within the shrine.

Lord Takeda knew his life was forfeit, but he did not intend to go quietly. Precious time was needed for his wife and son to escape to safety.

With unexpected ferocity, he leaped to his feet and cut down one of the two assassins with a single sword stroke. As he turned to dispatch the last assassin, Lord Monkey pounced, stabbing his back.

The sword pierced deeply. Lord Takeda groaned and fell to his knees. Seeing this from their vantage on the threshold of the oratory, both Lady Takeda and Tarō cried out. From where he stood he could not see them but, hearing their cries, Lord Monkey shouted to his men.

"Find Takeda's wife and son!" he yelled, waving them toward the oratory. "Kill them!"

Horrified, Lady Takeda pulled Tarō from the entrance and hurried into the oratory, still nearly dragging him by his arm so he lost his sandals.

Returning his attention to his prey kneeling before him, Lord Monkey laid a hand on Lord Takeda's shoulder for leverage and pulled hard to extricate his sword from the armor. Lord Takeda gasped. He raised his eyes toward the oratory, searching for his wife and son, but he could not see them.

*Perhaps they have already escaped to the woods*, Lord Takeda thought. He smiled sadly, his final thought a prayer for his family's safety, as Lord Monkey separated his head from his neck.

Lord Takeda's headless trunk toppled to one side, spilling blood onto a patch of snow-covered ground, and Lord Monkey reached for the fallen prize. Grasping the head by its topknot, he held the drooping visage high for his men to behold, raising a blood-chilling cheer from his *samurai.*

Lady Takeda heard the shouting behind them and knew the terrible news it bore. Her face contorted in terror, but she did not falter. She ran blindly, desperately. Not knowing the inside of the shrine, she stumbled through one corridor after another searching for any place to hide.

"Mother?" Tarō asked feebly, still reeling from the terrible sight of his father, the Tiger, cut down before his eyes.

"Tarō, we must hide—" she said, shushing him.

She saw the look in her boy's eyes and panicked. She scooped him up in her arms. He was heavy. She had not held him long since she could remember refusing his earnest appeals. Now all she wanted to do was hold him in peace.

The world whirled around Tarō—slatted windows, paneled doors, the thumping of his mother's hurried footsteps on the cedar planks of the shrine corridors. Somewhere in the distance, but inescapably drawing nearer, the bamboo water hammer knocked tirelessly without answer.

At last, his mother discovered an exit at the rear of the shrine and bolted for the tree line. As she clambered up the snowy slope toward the dense wood, she slipped again, this time on a sinewy tree root, and once more she cried out as she took the brunt of the fall on her side to save her boy from harm. They heard shouts growing nearer from within the shrine building.

"Over here!" a voice called and another said, "This way!"

Lady Takeda raised herself, collecting Tarō in her arms. She stumbled over the crest of the cedar-lined hill but lost her footing again and tumbled down the other side. Halfway down the hill she let go of Tarō, and he fell on top of her in the midst of a snow-covered tangle of roots.

"Mother!" Tarō said, gently shaking her where she lay.

She moaned and slowly opened her eyes. "Tarō?" she said, half-conscious, then quickly raised herself and looked around, adrenaline coursing through her body. "Tarō, we—"

She stopped, panic in her eyes. So small and frail he seemed to her. She looked around again in desperation. The lofty cryptomeria trees stood silent, oblivious to their plight. She listened. The lonely plunk of the bamboo water hammer came again, unperturbed by the yells of the men drawing nearer to them. Then she heard the faint sound of rushing water.

Once again, with even greater effort, she picked herself up and scooped Tarō in her arms to stumble toward the sound of the water, sobbing softly, desperately. *He's so heavy*, she thought, *but he's just a boy.* An even more terrible thought drove her forward until, at length, she staggered onto a small, snow-laden glade, skirted by the unmistakable sound of the rushing river at the far side. In a corner of the glade, the water hammer plunked before pausing to fill itself once more from a chute fed by the river. She hesitated, looking around. Then she bolted for the river. Halfway across the glade, the water hammer plunked again and spilled its contents. At the far side of the glade, Tarō was just too heavy for her. She fell to the snowy ground, sobbing.

Tarō raised himself and knelt beside his mother, smoothing the tresses of her hair.

"Don't cry, mother," he said.

Her boy's words shook her. "Run," she said, and the wild look in her eyes frightened Tarō. "Hide!"

When Tarō did not budge, she panicked. She stood and pulled hard on his arm again. He tried to keep up with her, as she made her way through snow and brush toward the rushing river, not caring for her frozen feet sinking into the snow or the branches that scratched and tore at both of them.

Close by the river, she stumbled on a washing area where priestly vestments had been hung to dry. She set Tarō down. While she looked around for the next avenue of escape, Tarō stared at the icy, rushing river.

His mother ran back and forth. Then, spying a large wooden washtub beside the river, she knew what she must do.

"Tarō!" she snapped. "Come here!"

Tarō obeyed as if in a trance, and she snatched his wrist. She flipped the washtub on its side and rolled it to the river's edge, awkwardly pulling Tarō behind her. The washtub rolled and toppled to a stop, and she tried to force Tarō inside.

"Get in," she yelled when he did not immediately comply.

"Mother, no—why?"

She paid no heed, as she shoved against the washtub to push it into the river. Behind her, men shouted again, sending her into another panic.

"Tarō, do as I say!" she said, pleading with him.

She tried to speak, then clapped her hand to her mouth in fear and sadness, tears pouring from her eyes. She surrendered to sobbing that wracked her body. Behind her the water hammer plunked again and spurred her once more to action.

"Courage, Tarō!" she said, forcing him into the washtub.

Tarō barely fit, but once inside, she leaned against the washtub and shoved to free it from the snowy riverbank. As she did so, a terrible grip seized her, and she cried out in pain and fear.

"Don't run away, little bird!" Lord Monkey growled, tightening his iron grip on her arm.

"Hashiba!" she gasped, recognizing him immediately now that he had removed his spiked helmet and devil mask, revealing his infamously ugly, apish face.

"Lady Takeda," Lord Monkey said with an evil grin.

She reached for the *tantō* hidden in her *kimono*, but he struck her with his free hand so hard she hit the cold ground in a clump, and her dagger skipped into the river. The skirt of her *kimono* splayed, revealing her bare leg. Lord Monkey leered and smacked his lips. He leaned menacingly toward her but cried out in sudden surprise and pain as Tarō's new sword slashed his cheek.

Lord Monkey fell backward, clutching his bleeding jowl. Filled with rage at the attack on his mother, Tarō stepped from the washtub to stand over him. For an instant, both hesitated, then Lord Monkey took Tarō off his feet with a swift kick. Tarō hit the ground, the wind knocked out of him, but he quickly recovered, desperately searching on all fours for his fallen sword.

Lord Monkey's men approached, their shouts carrying across the glade, as the bamboo hammer plunked once more. Tarō found his sword and snatched it up but turned to see Lord Monkey looming over him, sword drawn and held high to cut the boy down. His mother intervened, throwing herself between them, thrusting Tarō backward into the washtub and giving it a push with all her might.

Before Lord Monkey could react, the washtub bobbed and splashed out into the icy river.

"No!" Lord Monkey howled, as he lunged for the washtub.

He charged into the water to reach for one of Tarō's legs hanging over the tub, but Tarō quickly pulled his leg inside his little boat. The river wasted no time carrying him from the shore, while Tarō stared back, still clutching his sword but powerless to use it.

With no more than a hairpin to defend her boy, Lady Takeda fell upon Lord Monkey, stabbing at his neck above his armor. Lord Monkey yelled in pain, and quickly shrugged her off, but lost his footing, splashing into the icy water beside her.

"Mother!" Tarō cried out, helplessly clutching his sword in one hand and the lip of the washtub with the other, as the little boat rocked and splashed downriver.

Lord Monkey stood, paying Lady Takeda no heed, as he watched the little washtub quickly carry his quarry away.

"Mother!" Tarō cried out once more before he disappeared from sight.

Lord Monkey grunted angrily. He turned on Lady Takeda as she raised herself from the icy river. Soaked and disheveled, her face pale blue from the cold, she was nonetheless a striking woman of noble blood. Now that her son was safe, she smiled with cold resolve, and Lord Monkey hesitated.

"Hashiba Hideyoshi," she said, her blue lips curling with contempt, "the gods will surely punish you—"

Lord Monkey's sword cut short her curse.

"That is what the priests said," he snarled at her lifeless body, her blood staining the snowy river's edge and leaking into the icy river as it licked the skirt of her *kimono*.

Looking downstream, Lord Monkey grunted disgust. He wiped his bloodied cheek and briefly regarded the red staining his fingers, which only stoked his anger. Then he yelled for his soldiers as he plunged headlong into the wood along the river bank, crashing through the brush to chase after his prey, sinking in the heavy snowdrift.

The river ran apace, and Tarō's little washtub rushed inexorably downstream until the sacred, scarlet bridge appeared above him. It seemed an eternity since he had seen it last.

The washtub passed quickly under the bridge, racing toward the muffled thunder of the waterfall somewhere below the shrine. Still clutching his sword, fighting back tears, Tarō stared in disbelief at the trace of blood on its edge.

The sound of the thundering cascade grew louder as the river hurried forward. Tarō panicked when he saw the river's end ahead. He dove his free hand into the icy water, paddling frantically but to no avail. Quickly sheathing his sword, he dove both hands into the icy water, but it was too late. The washtub slipped suddenly into the waterfall and plummeted. Tarō gasped, feeling his stomach in his chest as he fell. He clung desperately to the tub, waves of icy water buffeting him. His little boat plunged into the frozen pool below, hitting the water with a tremendous splash, and his face struck the edge of the washtub, splitting his lip. As the boat capsized under the weight of the cascade, Tarō's sword slipped from his sash to dart through the churning pool, lost in darkness.

Had he not clung to the washbasin, Tarō surely would have drowned. Lord Monkey peered over the edge of the cliff beside the precipitous falls, one hand on his bloodied cheek, as he watched the washtub bob to the surface, Tarō clinging to it like a half-drowned rat while the little boat carried him further downstream.

"*Kuso!*" Lord Monkey cursed, thrusting his chin in the air to survey the frozen landscape. "Well," he snarled, "at least the cold will surely kill the brat!"

太

The little washtub carried the half-conscious, half-drowned, half-frozen Tarō downriver, swirling through eddies, rocking over rapids, and bouncing off rocks with a force that nearly split the tub more than once but, at last, it came safely to rest on a riverbank in a secluded part of the forest at the foot of Mount Fuji. Deep snow covered the forest of cryptomeria there. A frosty fog swirled overhead, weaving in and out of the cedar trees that lined the river's edge. Tarō lay across the washtub as it rocked against the shore. He spluttered frosty breaths to cough up the last of the water he had drunk from the waterfall.

Revived for a moment by the river lapping at the washtub, Tarō raised his dripping head. He blinked in disbelief as a woman, tall and beautiful, with long black hair and blue lips, her *kimono* shining pale white, glided toward him, almost invisible against the snowy landscape. Her cold, black eyes held his gaze.

*Mother?* Tarō thought, as the white woman approached.

"There, there," the white woman whispered in a soft, reassuring tone, though her blue lips did not move. "You have traveled so far, why not take your rest with me?"

"Mother?" Tarō called weakly.

He reached toward the apparition but suddenly swooned and fell unconscious.

"Mother?" the voice echoed softly.

As she drew near to Tarō, the woman gasped in surprise.

"A child!" she cried, a chilling grin of delight wrinkling her nose, and she smacked her lips with expectant pleasure. Then, upon a second look at the sodden boy, she said, "Ah, but he will need some fattening up first!"

Hovering over Tarō, the woman reached down. Grasping his ponytail, she held the limp, dripping boy aloft and turned in the direction she had come, holding him before her, floating across the snow, up the river bank, and through the fog, leaving no footprints.

Tarō started awake, still hanging by his ponytail, feeling as though his scalp would soon be torn from his head as he floated through darkness all around him save a faint bluish glow that grew until he came to an icy cavern gleaming with glacial luminescence, its floor and ceiling pierced by icicles like the jagged teeth of some monstrous cave-creature. Nothing disturbed the deathly quiet there but the faint sound of water dripping into a shallow pool somewhere deep inside the cavern.

The white woman released her trophy, and Tarō hit the frozen cavern floor with a groan. Not meaning to injure her prize, the woman flinched in dismay.

"There, there, boy," she whispered.

"Tarō—my name is Tarō," he groaned, trying to move, but he was too weak.

"You have traveled so far, Tarō, why not take your rest with me a while?"

She stretched out her pale arms to cradle him, pulling him to her bosom. Then she opened her *kimono* to bare her pale, withered breast.

"You must be hungry!" she said, pushing her cold teat into his mouth.

Tarō recoiled instinctively, his nose wrinkling in disgust, as an earthy, rotten smell assaulted him, but the woman held him fast.

"Now, now, do not fear, I am going to take care of you," she whispered, pressing him close to her bosom. "Drink your fill!"

The liquid had an iron taste, like blood. Tarō felt as if he were drowning again. Then, as though rising to the surface of some bottomless pool, he felt a familiar, longed-for touch, a warm embrace, sweet and nourishing.

"Mother?" Tarō mumbled.

"Yes," the white woman murmured, "I am here. I am going to take care of you now."

A warmth filled Tarō's belly, swelling through his limbs, his heart racing. Then he swooned, and the world went black.

太

The encampment sat on a high mountain plateau beside Lake Tanuki, which lay dark and quiet but for the faint sound of water lapping at its shore and the distant sound of the waterfall from somewhere in the darkness above it. A bitterly cold, gusting wind blew across the highland. Flickering oil torches lit the encampment and cast shadows over the rippling tent curtains as Lord Monkey strutted past, carrying an extra sword in hand, followed by his squire, a dog of a man in stature and demeanor, both men bracing against the wind, their frosty breaths trailing behind them. Seeing the tent curtains, Lord Monkey's eyes narrowed keenly at the panels bearing the chrysanthemum crest of the imperial family.

Sentries saluted Lord Monkey at the entrance to the tent. He made an ugly face and drew a deep breath to compose himself for the meeting. Pushing aside the tent flap, he quickly knelt, bowing low, fists touching the ground. His squire did likewise, after placing his charge, a netted bag filled with some dark gift, on the floor beside him.

"It is done," Lord Monkey said obsequiously.

He offered up the *katana*, a fine sword with gilt and black lacquered fittings, the diamond crest of the Takeda clan in gold inlay on the scabbard—the blade of the vanquished Lord Takeda.

"Ah, Lord Monkey!" Lord Oda replied, using his cruel nickname for his vassal. "What took you so long?"

"My Lord?" Lord Monkey asked, raising his eyes scornfully though careful not to show it.

"I was just inquiring of Lord Tokugawa as to what had become of you?" Lord Oda said disdainfully over his shoulder.

Lord Oda's squire came forward to receive the trophy, a young man in his prime, chosen to complement his Lord who was a tall, handsome man, taller than Lord Monkey by two heads, scantily bearded, with a clear voice and a regal, hawk-like appearance, from his black eyebrows and sharp, piercing eyes to his high cheekbones, mustache and goatee. His squire gave the sword to his Lord, who laid it across his lap, and the young man returned to his place in attendance.

Lord Oda sat on the edge of his campaign chair as if he were about to spring into action, back straight, legs spread wide, fists on his knees, scowling as someone accustomed to having his orders obeyed without question. Tall candles stood on either side of him. On a rack at his left stood his sword at the ready, a handsome helmet adorned with pheasant feathers beside it.

At some distance opposite Lord Oda sat Lord Tokugawa, stockier and not as tall, but taller still than Lord Monkey, with the look of a Shiba hound with his narrow eyes and a jowl skirted by a thin scruffy beard and mustache. Lord Tokugawa's squire, a sober but capable-looking young man, stood in attendance behind him.

"Are you much hurt?" Lord Oda asked when he saw the fresh wound on Lord Monkey's cheek, an ugly scar that further marred his ugly face.

"It is but a scratch," Lord Monkey replied, but the mark shamed him deeply as he thought of the mere boy who made it.

Lord Monkey grunted at his squire, who reached into the netted *kubibukuro* to present his other trophy, Lord Takeda's head. The bloodstained, livid face hung sadly in its frozen expression, as the squire proudly held it aloft for Lord Oda to inspect. The warlord sighed and grunted.

"So, this is the end of my most worthy opponent, the Tiger of Kai," he said. "I owe my appointment as Imperial Minister to him. How time changes allegiances," he huffed ironically, then frowned. "He deserved better. He deserved to die by his own noble hand—a warrior's ode, as is the warrior's code."

Lord Monkey's squire blanched and retreated, and his master's brow furrowed in self-conscious confusion, as they perceived Lord

Oda's displeasure. Lord Tokugawa smiled diplomatically, but Lord Monkey took it as condescending.

"While you were sparring with Takeda, Lord Tokugawa laid siege to Yōgaiyama Castle and razed it to the ground. Every man, woman, and child that carried the Takeda seed burned alive. The Takeda clan is ashes. Not a soul survives."

Lord Oda smiled in cold satisfaction, but Lord Monkey flinched as he recalled Tarō's escape.

*The brat looked drowned, but what if he lived? Impossible. Even if he survived the falls, the boy could not survive the cold.*

"You have our gratitude," Lord Oda said.

"Thanks to your support," Lord Tokugawa replied.

Lord Monkey flinched again at how easily he had slipped from his Lord's grace, but he quickly recovered.

"Such loyalty," he said, smiling at Lord Tokugawa, who nodded as Lord Monkey slyly added, "How difficult it must have been for you—" Seeing he had his rival's attention, he pressed his advantage, "to accept the order to execute your wife and only son, when their plot against Lord Oda was discovered."

Lord Tokugawa did not react, but his eyes held Lord Monkey's gaze. The two men regarded each other for a tense moment. Lord Oda studied their interaction with amusement.

"At least," Lord Monkey added, "I understand you still have a lovely daughter—"

"Lord Tokugawa has proven himself a faithful ally," Lord Oda intervened. "I am satisfied he had no part in Lady Tsukiyama's communications with Takeda. We can ask no more of him."

Lord Tokugawa bowed graciously.

"Together we will protect the Emperor from the remaining rebellious clans," Lord Oda continued, casting an unflinching eye on the severed head staring back at him. "My esteemed enemy is dead, his plot exposed. Lord Tokugawa proved his fidelity when he punished his wife and son for their treachery," he added, giving Lord Monkey a reproachful look. "Only a handful of clans still oppose us. Soon, the whole country will fall under one sword."

"The *Ikkō-ikki*—"[4] Lord Monkey interrupted, but his Lord's look of displeasure immediately silenced him.

"I will deal with the *sōhei* of Kyōto, those fanatical warrior monks," Lord Oda finished Lord Monkey's thought without a care for his vassal's opinion, and added, "The Jesuits offer much in trade. I will build them churches." He huffed amusement. "Let the monks trouble themselves with religion."

"What of their fabled spell-craft?" Lord Tokugawa asked.

"If they defy the Emperor, then they face the Demon King of the Sixth Sky! I burned Mount Hiei to the ground once, and I will do it once again if those charlatans dare show their cowardly cowled faces in Kyōto!"

Lord Monkey held his tongue. His squire shifted uneasily, but Lord Monkey rebuked him with a look.

"Lord Tokugawa will deal with Uesugi and the northern clans that support him," Lord Oda continued.

"Even in victory, we shall tighten our helmet cords," Lord Tokugawa said, nodding graciously.

"You, Monkey, you will go to Mōri Province and crush it," Lord Oda ordered. "This time, bring me a castle instead of a head."

"It will be done, my Lord," Lord Monkey said without hesitation, bowing obediently and standing abruptly, but when he turned his eyes narrowed, smoldering with jealous rage at the respect Lord Oda accorded Lord Tokugawa.

---

[4] [一向一揆], "single-minded rebellion," an uprising against feudal rule led by a zealous sect of Buddhist monks.

As he exited Lord Oda's tent, Lord Monkey observed the imperial crest once more and halted so abruptly that his squire bumped him from behind.

"Damned fool!" Lord Monkey snapped and reached for his sword.

His squire immediately fell to the ground, prostrating himself. Lord Monkey stared contemptuously at Lord Oda's sentries, but they gave him no quarrel.

"Get up!" Lord Monkey snapped, giving his man a merciless boot in the ribs before striding away across the camp, his squire following like a kicked dog.

"I can smell their contempt for my humble birth," Lord Monkey muttered when he was out of earshot of the sentries. "Does he think to cast me aside and raise Lord Tokugawa in my stead? That Mikawa ruffian,[5] he pretends to be unassuming, but he made certain everyone knew his lineage to the Minamoto *Shōgun*."

Lord Monkey turned to his squire, who struggled to keep up while maintaining a safe distance so as not to risk his neck by bumping his master again.

"Send to the monks," Lord Monkey ordered. "There is work to be done! We will have need of their arms—" then, recalling his meeting with Lords Oda and Tokugawa, he added contemptuously, "and their spell-craft!"

[5] Mikawa Province was famous for its *bushi* [武士], "warriors."

# 3

## GOLDEN BOY

*Kai Province*

*Spring, Year of the Rat*

Four years passed in the world of men from the fateful day that orphaned Tarō, but the animal denizens of Mount Fuji took little notice of human affairs. The natural world counted the passage of time by the changing seasons and the moon, and the fourth full moon of the new year had just crested Mount Fuji, bathing Hachiman Shrine in a silver light that made the gossamer pink blossoms of the cherry trees shine in the forecourt below the shrine. On the opposite side of the court, the mossy stone lanterns beside the sacred reservoir glowed with a greenish torchlight that danced across the ornate facades of the shrine buildings and the dark, fragrant, bushy forest of cypress trees encircling them. Beneath this ethereal spell the shrine itself was peaceful, its priestly residents fast asleep, crickets chirping serenely in the dark, but below the shrine, chattering voices filled the forecourt with no regard for the quiet.

Taro Wins!

The grassy park beside the flagstone court had been marked off as a wrestling ring in the sacred *sumō* tradition. All manner of beasts jostled each other on the sidelines beneath the evanescent cherry blossoms scattering in the gentle spring breeze—bear, fox, badger, deer, dormouse, rabbit, fish owl, pheasant, crane, frog and toad, red-faced monkey, and raccoon-dog—each vying for a better view, their hubbub rising and falling, punctuated by grunts, growls, squeaks, squawks and howls, as they watched two massive silhouettes strain against each other in the torchlight. Circling the wrestlers, a red fox with a bushy tail served as referee, waving a pine frond to punctuate his remarks.

"Not yet! Not yet!" the fox barked.

"Go on, Tarō, you can take him!" a voice shouted at the smaller of the two wrestlers.

Although slighter than his beastly opponent, the hulking boy had indeed grown. Tarō looked exceptionally large and muscular for his age. His opponent seemed to be having real difficulty using size and weight to advantage, while the boy had the lower center of gravity and an uncanny sense of balance.

The witch's teat had magically transformed Tarō. In just four years, he had grown into a brawny adolescent—tall, much taller than the average boy his age, and every inch of him swollen with muscle, although his face had hardly changed, except it was quite a bit larger, his cheeks even pudgier.

The remnant of his golden *kimono* was little more than a frayed, sleeveless tunic to accommodate his tanned, powerful biceps and even more massive reddish-brown legs, his whole body rippling as he locked his hold on an enormous black bear twice his size in height and girth, each of them vying for advantage. The bear looked as though he could swallow Tarō in one bite, but still it grunted from exertion, and Tarō growled back, as the two wrestlers strained against each other, haunches shivering from the conflict.

Tarō moved to sweep the bear's hind leg, but it sensed the attack and retreated, baring its teeth with a snarling growl and swiping at the air. They both rushed each other and clashed, flesh and muscles shivering again, but Tarō shifted his weight, and all at once the bear toppled. Tarō gave his opponent a swift nudge with his body, and a swaggering wave of his own paw-sized hand, and the bear fell, rolling into the sideline, knocking over several furry spectators.

"Tarō wins!" the fox barked, waving his pine frond from center court.

Tarō smiled as he left the ring to raucous cheers. He took a seat away from the crowd, beneath the ethereal pink clouds of cherry blossoms that bordered the arena. Still sweating from exertion, he lay back with his hands crossed behind his head, thoughtful. Drawing a deep breath of the fragrant forest air, he closed his eyes.

*"Tarō, we must hide—"* a voice whispered in his head.

Troubled by his thoughts, Tarō opened his eyes as Tanuki the raccoon-dog shuffled up to him, a jug of rice wine under one arm, rubbing his oversized belly in satisfaction, and wagging his fluffy brown tail. He stood about half as tall as Tarō, with a jovial face of light brown fur, a double chin, and black markings around his eyes just like a mask, but he smiled his toothy grin with ease. Tarō sat up, still looking a little shaken from his dream. Tanuki frowned like a worried coach and moved to knead Tarō's shoulders with his little paws.

"Just one more round for the champ—" Tanuki whispered excitedly in Tarō's ear, "and this one should be something!"

As if on cue the sound of beating wings filled the forecourt as a gaggle of goblin *tengu* descended in their midst to strut toward the wrestling ring, shape-shifting from large kites to tall, gangly, red-skinned men wrapped in loincloths, their long noses arrogantly poking the air, which annoyed the other forest animals.

Tarō watched as Tanuki and the *Tengu* Chief exchanged greetings. The Chief held a single feather in his hand, as did all of his *tengu* subjects, and he used his feather to punctuate his conversation as if conducting an orchestra. Tanuki magically produced a large bag from thin air. Then, diving his paw into his trove, he held up a paw full of gold coins whereupon the Chief and his retainers' eyes grew large with gold lust. The Chief put up his feather as his stake in the match. Both nodding their agreement, they parted, and Tanuki rejoined Tarō.

"You can take him," Tanuki encouraged Tarō once more before grabbing his jug of rice wine to take a seat on the sideline with the other forest spectators.

Tarō shook himself and slapped his muscles, working himself up for the fight. Then he stepped into the ring, facing off with the *Tengu* Chief, each staring down the other as they stamped and clapped their hands in ritual dance to begin the fight.

Tanuki looked down the sideline to where the other *tengu* sat cheering their Chief, watching them nervously jabber among themselves. First looking around to make certain no one was watching, Tanuki instantly transformed himself into the likeness of a *tengu*. A bouquet of pheasants, startled and upset by the sudden appearance of a *tengu* in their midst, took flight to settle in a different spot, while Tanuki crept down the sideline to where the real but oblivious *tengu* flocked.

The match began, but the wrestlers did not immediately rush each other, each taking measure with feints and dodges. The red fox circled them, barking and waving his palm frond.

Kicking, gesticulating, jabbering loudly to their Chief and waving their noses in the air in exasperation, the *tengu* watched Tarō smartly evade their Chief's every move to attack. Tanuki moved closer to listen to two *tengu* in conversation.

"This boy is no ordinary human," one said.

"Perhaps, but the Chief will take him, just wait and see," the other said. "Our Chief's front kicks are unbeatable."

Tanuki crouched, his *tengu* nose poking in the air, trying to look inconspicuous, but soaking up the dialogue. Meanwhile, Tarō and the *Tengu* Chief broke and faced off again.

Magically throwing his voice so it seemed to come from some other side of the arena, Tanuki's *tengu* likeness shouted to Tarō, "Watch out for his front kick!"

The *tengu* exchanged looks of dismay and anger, searching the area to see who might be the meddler. Tanuki feigned innocence as he pretended to join them in their search for the culprit. Then he turned to his look-alikes and shrugged his shoulders. One *tengu* eyed him for a tense moment, but Tanuki brushed it off with a poke of his nose in the air, which seemed to satisfy his skeptic, who soon returned his attention to the match. Undiscovered, Tanuki bounded off to the other side of the ring, popping back to his old self with the *tengu* not any the wiser.

The *Tengu* Chief proved a worthy adversary with his vicious powerful kicks, but Tarō ducked and weaved, nimbly evading most of his opponent's strikes. Despite Tanuki's warning, one front kick landed under Tarō's chin and sent him reeling.

"Look out!" Tanuki yelled, leaning forward, his mouth hanging open.

Tarō quickly regained his wits, winking to reassure his worried coach. Just as the *tengu* kicked again, Tarō grabbed the Chief's leg by the foot. As the confounded Chief hopped on one free leg, Tarō kicked and swept his other leg, and the Chief fell to the ground to the great and vocal dismay of the other *tengu*, while the rest of the forest audience cheered Tarō once again.

"Oh! My back!" the *Tengu* Chief cried out with a long face.

Tarō extended a hand to his beaten adversary, and the *Tengu* Chief stood, his nose hanging in defeat. When the Chief conceded with a less-than-gracious bow, Tarō wheeled and kicked his feet, imitating the *tengu*, poking his nose in the air for effect. The audience howled and barked and chirruped in delight.

On the sidelines, Tanuki shuffled up to the defeated Chief to collect his bet. The Chief's annoyed *yōjimbō,* his bodyguards, crowded round, but Tanuki gave a sudden, shrill bark, much louder than might be expected from one so small except for his great belly and an enormous pair of testicles, usually hidden by his rotund belly, until now, when he intended to collect his bet. Indeed, his bark and balls had their intended effect, for the other *tengu* immediately backed away. Tanuki looked around with a smug wave of his chin, which the *tengu* understood well, judging by the way they shook their heads and spat.

With a flourish of his foreleg, Tanuki extended his open paw. Reluctantly, the *Tengu* Chief called to a squire, who stumped forward to give his Chief the feather he held for safekeeping. Eyes averted in distaste, the Chief dropped his magical feather in Tanuki's paw, which immediately clapped shut on the prize. Tanuki grinned, not too diplomatically, and sauntered off, leaving the *tengu* to fume in their defeat, before the wake of them transformed into kites again and flew off in a rush of beating wings.

Tanuki rejoined Tarō, waving their trophy. As they embraced victoriously over the final match, the boisterous audience drifted away into the dark forest, and the luminescence of the festival faded with the setting moon.

In the darkest hour of the morning when the moon had disappeared, the forecourt lay quiet but for the constant chirping of crickets in the forest and the hollow plunk of the bamboo water hammer from the shrine compound above. Tarō and Tanuki lingered, sitting quietly on the stone stairs beneath the Twilight Gate. Tanuki took a swig from his bottomless jug of *sake* before offering it to Tarō who shook his head.

"Oh, right," Tanuki nodded, rolling his eyes, "training."

Tanuki snapped his fingers, and his large, magical bag appeared in his lap. He reached inside it and groped around, his face twisting determinedly until, at last, he produced the *Tengu* Chief's feather.

"This might come in handy," Tanuki said.

"Oh, the *tengu*," Tarō said upon seeing the feather.

He jumped up to imitate the *Tengu* Chief's poking nose and powerful kicks. Tanuki grinned and nodded, regarding the feather once more before tucking it away. He rummaged in the bag again and pulled out an impressive, whole salmon nearly as big as himself.

"The bear!" Tarō said quickly.

Tanuki smacked his lips and nodded eagerly. Tarō grinned and reared up just like a bear, giving the air a great big swat with his "bear paw," as he turned and started clambering up the stone stairs on all fours. Tanuki chuckled. He eyed the salmon hungrily, smacking his lips once more, then he hurriedly shoved it back in his magical bag and bounded up the steps to catch up with Tarō who had already climbed to the Twilight Gate, its white and gold arches pale against the night. Tarō stood musing upon the guardian Gods of Wind and Thunder, their crystal eyes still glinting faintly. A hint of incense hung in the air.

"What is it?" Tanuki asked, looking around.

"Nothing," Tarō said, shaking his head as the bamboo water hammer plunked in the distance.

"I'll say," Tanuki huffed, looking the guardians up and down and nodding at Raijin. "That guy still owes me."

Tarō gave Tanuki a doubtful look.

"What?" Tanuki said defensively. "Did you ever try to collect from a god?"

Tanuki hugged his bag of winnings, eyeing the watchful guardians. Tarō sighed deeply.

"What's with you?" Tanuki asked.

"I don't know," Tarō said, "Somehow they make me think of my father. I wish I could remember him. It's just, sometimes I feel I don't belong here."

Tanuki eyed Tarō for a moment. He knew what the boy meant, but he laughed it off.

"What, here?" Tanuki said. "Wherever you go, you're here! You need to let go!" he puffed. "You sound like your mother—"

Tanuki stopped, realizing he might have overstepped. He shot a look to check Tarō who stared him down for a tense moment. Tarō broke into a laugh, and Tanuki relaxed.

"I'm glad Yama Uba prefers humans!" Tanuki said with a nervous gulp that belied his genuine apprehension. "Oh, sorry," he quickly added. "Well, she hasn't eaten you yet." He shrugged and plied, "All I'm saying is, you have to live for the day! Here today, gone tomorrow!" He drank a toast from his jug of *sake.*

The bamboo hammer plunked again. Tanuki looked around, suddenly self-conscious.

"We should not tarry," he whispered hoarsely. "The moon-spell has nearly faded. The priests will be about their business soon." Tanuki scanned the dark buildings to reassure himself that the shrine's occupants still lay asleep. Shaking his head, he added, "Some of those shamans scare me more than Yama Uba!"

Looking this way and that for any sign of humans, they bolted across the quadrangle and bounded into the forest beyond. Crickets chirped loudly all around them as they made their way through the forest.

"Still, lucky for us, your mother is a witch," Tanuki said, grinning. When he saw Tarō's dubious look he insisted, "No, really, we're raking in the winnings! The buzz is getting around. That bear came all the way from Hokkaido to fight you!"

"Hokkaido? Where is that?" Tarō asked.

"It's—" Tanuki racked his brain. "Well, it's up north. Pretty far, I think. Never mind. The point is, stick with me, I'll make you famous!"

By this time, they had arrived at Yama Uba's cave, a black hole in the black of night. Tarō entered, but Tanuki paused at the mouth of the cave.

"See you tomorrow," he whispered warily.

Tarō nodded and waved, disappearing into the dark hole. Tanuki peered after him for a moment, then with a shudder he bounded off into the woods.

Tarō crept along the rocky cave wall, feeling his way in the darkness. The air was cool and moist, the cave quiet except for the tread of his feet and a faint squeaking overhead. Although too dark for the eyes of an ordinary human, Tarō saw keenly in the cave. He knew the many bats that made their homes on the cavern ceiling. Tarō blinked, and the darkness flashed.

*"Tarō, we must hide—"* a voice whispered.

Tarō looked around. He was alone in the darkness except for the colony of bats. He sighed.

Squeaking a polite reply and goodnight to his neighbors, he moved deeper into the cavern. The darkness lightened as he came to the blue luminescent chamber where Yama Uba dwelled. Nothing disturbed the silence there but the faint sound of water dripping into a shallow pool somewhere deep inside the cavern.

The white witch did not see him. She hovered at the far side of the cavern, holding a small mirror close to her face.

Tarō crept forward, making for the opposite side of the chamber, but he slipped and sent a rock skittering across the cavern floor. Yama Uba quickly hid the mirror in her pale *kimono* and turned on him.

"Where have you been?" she scolded, although her blue lips did not move when she spoke.

"Around," he said bashfully, then confessed, "with Tanuki."

"Oh!" she scoffed in a harsh, raspy voice, "that beast! He's a terrible influence!"

"He's my friend!" Tarō growled.

"Now you listen to me, Tarō!" she said, hovering menacingly toward him. "I am your mother. I made you—and if you don't behave," she warned, assuming an ugly, scorned appearance, "well, I might just eat you after all."

"Then go on and eat me!" Tarō growled.

Yama Uba flinched, taken aback by the fearsome brat she created, but Tarō only stumped off to a corner of the cave to pout. She shook her head, fuming so wisps of her ethereal ire trailed upward from her nostrils.

Yama Uba turned, looking about for some object to exact relief from her frustration. Then, remembering her *kagami*, she pulled it from inside her *kimono*.

Holding it up to her face, she stared into the little looking glass until her pale reflection faded. Another visage materialized in its place, the face of a monstrous old crone with unkempt white hair and piercing black eyes that stared back with tormented, bloodthirsty, murderous rage.

Tarō saw none of this. He lay in his corner of the cave, staring at the luminescent cavern wall, thoughtful, troubled. Although he fought against it, at length his eyelids grew heavy until, at last, he fell asleep, and dreamed—

*"Tarō!"* the voice echoed in his head again from deep within his memory. *"We must hide!"*

Haunted by the voices in his head, Tarō wandered the wood alone the next day, but eventually his thoughts drove him back to the shrine. He had always avoided the shrine in daylight. In his time in the forest, he had seen and been seen by the humans who lived there, but never up close, and he had always run off. Yama Uba had warned him about men, and his animal friends naturally avoided human interaction whenever possible. Tarō had not forgotten Tanuki's trepidation of the shrine's mysterious shamans, the *Shintō* priests, but curiosity and his troubled mind drove him back to the shrine, even in daylight.

Tarō entered the shrine from the rear, sneaking behind the buildings, taking care not to be discovered, for he knew the human inhabitants would be awake, and he no longer had the protection of the night's enchantment when the forest's denizens reveled in their festivities. Indeed, Tarō found one bald priest sweeping the grounds before the main hall, and he watched him for a time, thinking it curious that this man should spend so much effort sweeping. It seemed an impossible task since there would always be more dirt, and the priest did eventually tire of his chore, disappearing into one of the shrine buildings.

Tarō waited to make certain the man did not immediately return, then crept into the square, as quiet as the forest, darting along the walls of the buildings in an effort to remain undiscovered. The air smelled of sandalwood incense burning in the main hall, and Tarō heard the faint murmuring of human voices chanting.

Many brightly painted wooden votive plaques hung from the covered wooden rack that stood on one side of the courtyard. Tarō crept closer to the display, running his hand across the stacked and jumbled tiles, each competing for space on the rack.

*There are so many of them—hundreds of them—what could be their purpose?* he wondered.

Nearly all of the plaques had been painted with the image of a white rat and branches covered with pink plum blossoms. Humans had written on the backs of these wooden tablets in their inky markings. One plaque caught Tarō's eye, and he surprised himself when he found he could read it.

"I want to be a great *samurai*," Tarō read aloud the characters written on the back of the prayer plaque.

"Ah, you can read," a voice said behind him.

The priest had returned so quietly that Tarō had not heard him approach. Tarō immediately darted behind the covered rack to hide, peeking out between the many stacks of plaques, tensed to bolt if the priest came any closer.

"Don't be afraid," the priest coaxed. "Where are you from?"

Tarō did not respond. The priest had kind, insightful eyes. He looked around, then spurred by a thought, he disappeared into one of the shrine buildings again.

Tarō watched cautiously for a time, expecting the priest to reappear at any moment. Just when Tarō thought it might be safe to retreat, the priest returned, holding a small earthenware plate with two rice balls.

Tarō immediately recognized the offering as food, and his mouth watered at the sight of it, but he did not come out of his hiding place behind the covered rack. He watched and waited, while the priest approached as close as he dared without alarming his guest. The priest placed the plate of rice balls on the ground and stepped back to the porch of the nearest building to see if the wild boy would be enticed.

Somewhere in the recesses of his memory, Tarō knew this offering was a delicacy that could not be ignored. Slowly, cautiously, he emerged from his hiding place to squat before the plate. He lowered his head to smell the food. One whiff satisfied him. He grabbed up one rice ball and shoved it in his mouth, chewing it noisily, happily, but with one eye on the priest where he sat on the veranda of the shrine building.

"Where are you from?" the priest asked again, studying the ruddy, burly boy.

Tarō did not respond.

"You cannot be a mere mountain wildling," the priest said, answering his own question. "Were you abandoned? Lost?"

Tarō quietly finished the first rice ball and shoved the second in his mouth, then he looked sadly at the empty plate. The priest shrugged.

"A wise man's belly is never full."

Tarō cocked his head. The words sounded oddly familiar, although he knew not why.

"Where did you learn to read?"

Tarō did not respond. An awkward silence passed.

"When I'm lost," the priest said, still trying to engage the strange boy, "I often find myself in books."

Tarō looked as if he understood, but again he did not respond. Spurred by another thought, the priest stood. Tarō tensed to bolt, but the priest held up his hand.

"No, wait—don't go," the priest said, slowly backing away until he disappeared again into the shrine building.

As he finished the second rice ball, Tarō watched the doorway where the priest had gone. Soon the priest emerged again, cautiously, so as not to scare off his guest.

"Look," he said, holding up a book. "You can read this—"

The priest held out his gift. He started to descend the steps, but Tarō took flight, bolting for the woods, leaving the priest to puzzle over his mysterious visitor, for he knew providence must have had a hand in the boy's appearance.

太

A hawk's cry pierced the heavens as it soared over the verdant shoulders of Mount Fuji, now climbing, now diving, surveying the land. The hawk wheeled, its shrill, lonely cry carrying across the mountainside. Diving over a high mountain meadow resplendent with magenta wild flowers in full bloom, the hawk returned to alight on Lord Tokugawa's outstretched glove.

Wearing splendid hunting attire of rich green and brown silk, the warlord sat on his steed, admiring the silver crown of *Fujisan* rising toward heaven, subordinate only to the sun. The passage of years did not show in his face, although he had been perpetually at war with the northern provinces since his alliance with Lord Oda against the Takeda clan. His squire sat beside him on another horse, and the rest of his Lordship's entourage rode in attendance behind them, forty *samurai* in all, some dressed in hunting attire with *kimono* sleeves tied back, others in light armor. On horseback beside Lord Tokugawa, dressed in handsome hunting attire of light blue and brown silk, a fine-looking young *samurai* of fourteen or fifteen, with black hair tied in a ponytail, stared dreamily at the magnificent meadow.

"If you suspect Lord Monkey," the young *samurai* inquired, "why not inform Lord Oda?"

"The wise hawk hides its talons."

The young *samurai* nodded, grateful for the wisdom.

"Shall we return to camp?" his young ward asked.

Lord Tokugawa dismissed the question with a wave of his hand. He called on his squire to take charge of the hawk. Then he spurred his horse, and his entourage followed, leaving the high meadow to descend through the cedar forest.

"Ah, here it is!" Lord Tokugawa said, as he emerged from the woods just below the sacred vermillion bridge.

The sound of the rushing river and the muffled thunder of the distant waterfall filled the air. Lord Tokugawa prompted his steed to cross the bridge, and his young ward and squire followed.

At the top of the arch, Lord Tokugawa's horse balked at the haunting, breathy whistle of a lone bamboo flute. A monk approached from the other side, clothed in his simple habit, his bowed head hidden by a conical hat of woven sedge grass. He blew another long, low note upon his *shakuhachi* as he stepped onto the bridge. Lord Tokugawa's steed whinnied and stamped nervously.

"Monk!" Lord Tokugawa shouted. "Move aside!"

The monk took two steps nearer and stopped, stretching forward as if to bow, then leaped like a frog, over the horse's head and onto Lord Tokugawa. The steed reared in surprise and fright, spilling its Lord and the monk onto the bridge and bolting back into the other horses, which took fright as well. The entourage was thrown into great confusion, with the young *samurai* and the squire clinging desperately to their horses so as not to fall off.

Lord Tokugawa stood and gasped, recognizing his attacker, who no longer wore the straw hat that had concealed his wan, pinched face, framed by a ring of bushy black hair and a deeply dimpled crown on his head that sloshed with a halo of water.

"*Kappa*!" Lord Tokugawa cried, grabbing the hilt of his sword. "Monkish sorcery!" he yelled back over his shoulder, then realized he was alone on the bridge.

The *kappa* threw off his habit, revealing his tortoise carapace armor on his back. With a grim face, Lord Tokugawa faced the shape-shifter, hands ready on his sheathed sword.

His assassin grinned with wide, ugly greenish lips, then leaped suddenly onto his target again, one slimy, webbed foot stopping Lord Tokugawa's sword hand with an iron grasp. Lord Tokugawa cried out. He tried to shake his attacker, but the *kappa* clambered onto his back, restraining his arms, while reaching with one of its gangly legs to grasp the railing of the bridge. Both strained against each other, but at last the *kappa* grabbed hold of the railing and gave a mighty tug, pulling Lord Tokugawa with it, over the bridge, to splash into the river below.

Sounds of this commotion reached Tarō and Tanuki in the midst of their relaxing soak in a nearby steaming, sulfurous green hot spring. The uproar grew until they felt compelled to investigate.

"*Kappa!* Nasty creatures," Tanuki said, as they watched from a ridge overlooking the bridge. "Looks like that human is in some serious trouble. I wouldn't bet on him."

As they watched the splashing fight, Tanuki perked up.

"What do you think? You've never fought a *kappa*."

"So—"

"Well, if you're not up to it," Tanuki goaded.

"Okay," Tarō said, rising to the bait, "but if I win, I get all your winnings for the next moon!"

Tanuki's face twisted in distaste. He looked at the *kappa* still intent on drowning its victim as they thrashed and splashed downriver, then at his naked, brawny buddy still steaming from his soak in the hot spring. He cocked his head, considering the wager.

"*Kappa* are tough, you know," he said with a wink. "Agreed!"

"Agreed!" Tarō shouted over his shoulder, already bounding naked down the hill toward the river, swift as the wind.

He dived into the rushing water and quickly grabbed hold of the *kappa*, who released its quarry in surprise. Lord Tokugawa spluttered, trying to swim toward the shore, but the current was too strong and carried him toward the waterfall.

Dismayed by Tarō's interference, the *kappa* twisted and wrestled, but it was no match for Tarō's brawny arms. As they grappled with each other, the current swept them toward the falls.

Meanwhile, Lord Tokugawa's ward and squire drove their horses into the bramble along the riverbank, the rest of the entourage trying to keep pace. Tanuki bounded along the rocky shore ahead of them and reached the cliff's edge just as Lord Tokugawa, the *kappa*, and Tarō spilled over the misty falls.

They all splashed into the pool below. The thundering cascade beat Lord Tokugawa down so he sank like a stone. Desperate bubbles of air burst from him as he struggled toward the surface.

Tarō and the *kappa* hit the pool fighting, but Tarō found his rival to be more than he reckoned, as they twisted and turned beneath the falls. The *kappa* tried to leap out of the water, only to splash in again as Tarō pulled it down.

When their horses reached the cliff's edge, Lord Tokugawa's men looked down at the thundering waterfall throwing spray into the air as it crashed into the pool below. They realized there would be no easy way down on horseback or on foot. The young *samurai* shouted to rally them on a detour through the woods, and the others followed.

No one noticed Tanuki bounding deftly down the wet, rocky cliff face into the mist below. He strained to get a glimpse of the fight, but Tarō and the *kappa* had disappeared into the pool.

Lord Tokugawa fought against the waterfall, spluttering and gasping for air. He swam for the rocky cliff face and found a shallow outcropping where he clung to the mossy rocks, trying to catch his breath while the falls crashed all around him.

Reaching the bottom of the cliff, Tanuki ran back and forth along the edge of the pool, hoping for another glimpse of the fight. At length, Tarō burst from the water into the misty, thundering air and waded toward the shore, dragging his catch by one slimy, gangly arm, while the *kappa* tried to wrench free using his other limbs to push off Tarō to no avail. Tarō's grip was too tight.

"See!" Tarō declared.

Tanuki smiled and nodded, but the *kappa* suddenly transformed into an enormous black carp, twisting and jerking until it wriggled free from Tarō's grip to leap back into the pool with a tremendous splash.

"You didn't say they could change themselves!"

"It's still a *kappa*!" Tanuki said, conceding, "more or less."

The giant *koi* leaped out of the pool, swatting Tarō with its tail so hard he lost his footing and fell backward with a splash. Tarō emerged in an instant, gritting his teeth as he dove after the fish.

Tarō swam deep into the pool. The light came dim from above, and the murky water dampened the thunder of the waterfall. When he reached bottom, he hovered there for a moment, looking around, blinking in the dark, churning water, straining to spy some sign of his quarry. Just below him, on the bottom of the pool, sticking up between two rocks, a shiny stick caught his eye. He reached for it, but the carp swam suddenly into him, driving him onto the rocky, muddy bottom.

Tarō quickly recovered, springing from the bottom to cut through the water, grabbing the *koi* as it swam past. Fierce as fire, he sunk his fingers into the carp's scaly tail. The fish yawned in surprise and pain, thrashing desperately.

On the surface, still fighting to cling to the mossy cliff against the plummeting waterfall but exhausted from his efforts, Lord Tokugawa spluttered and gasped his last breath. He sank below the surface and succumbed to the water.

On dry land, Tanuki sighed, still listlessly awaiting another glimpse of the fight until Tarō burst suddenly from the pool, wading toward shore again, dragging the thrashing *koi* by its tail with both hands. Winding himself up, he spun round to toss the carp onto the rocky ground beside the pool. The fish struck its head on a sharp rock and flopped about for a moment before lying still. Instantly, the *koi* returned to its *kappa* form, but it was dead, the last drop of its life's water spilling from its dimpled head.

Before Tanuki could say a word, Tarō dived into the pool again and, presently, he emerged, holding Lord Tokugawa by the back of his *kimono*. He tossed the waterlogged warlord onto the shore so roughly that it forced the water from his lungs.

Lord Tokugawa spluttered and coughed for a moment, then revived. Instinctively, he reached for his sword and looked around for his assailant. He saw the *kappa* lying dead nearby. Then he beheld the dripping, naked, brawny boy who had just saved his life.

Clinging stealthily to the mossy rocks in the cliff face above them, hidden in the mist, another monk, cloaked in a dark habit and cowl, spied upon the scene below. When he perceived the *kappa* was dead, the monk scaled the cliff and slunk quietly away.

Down below, Tarō shook like a dog to dry his long, raggedy hair, which burst into a bushy mane around his boyish face.

"Hey!" Tanuki said, annoyed as Tarō shook water on him.

Lord Tokugawa looked askance at the *tanuki* chattering sharply at Tarō. Then he sized up the wild, naked burly boy.

At this point, Lord Tokugawa's entourage arrived, their horses crashing through the wood to come to their master's aid. He raised his arm to halt them, and they reined their horses. Several men dismounted to inspect the *kappa* corpse.

"I owe you my life," Lord Tokugawa said, somewhat grudgingly, ignoring the chattering Tanuki.

"It was nothing," Tarō said glibly, swaggering for Tanuki.

Lord Tokugawa immediately took Tarō's statement as an insult, his eyes flashing, but he restrained himself with a forced breath as he considered Tarō's uses.

"Who is your master?" Lord Tokugawa demanded, as politely as he could ask of one so rough and obviously untutored.

"I have no master," Tarō said, throwing a glance at Tanuki.

Tarō caught Tanuki's look and shrugged, but Lord Tokugawa did not notice.

"You have some fighting skill," Lord Tokugawa remarked. "I could use your talent."

Tarō and Tanuki looked at each other quizzically, which Lord Tokugawa mistook as a negotiating tactic.

"I will pay you handsomely," he said impatiently.

At this, Tanuki chattered excitedly and began dancing around Tarō's legs.

"I can offer you lodging in my castle as well." Lord Tokugawa pressed. "What say you?"

This generous offer raised more than a few brows among his retainers. His young ward rode forward to get a better look at this tanned, naked wildling that could command such a price from their Lord. Tarō took brief measure of the young *samurai* before conferring with Tanuki.

"I will consider it," Tarō said, looking up from his chat with Tanuki.

Lord Tokugawa eyed Tarō with quiet displeasure. Reluctantly, he nodded. He had seen the boy in action and did not wish to make an enemy of him.

"Well," he said, "Do not take too long in consideration."

Lord Tokugawa called to his squire who road forward and, speaking aside to him, the squire produced a palm-sized wooden disc painted in gold lacquer, which bore the carved seal of the Tokugawa clan, three hollyhock leaves arranged in a circle so the points of their heart-shaped leaves met in the center of the circle.

"This seal will permit your safe passage along the Tōkaidō to Edo Castle," Lord Tokugawa said, handing the disc to Tarō. "Do you know the way?"

Tarō nodded, even though he did not know the way.

"It's okay," Tanuki said eagerly, "I know the way."

"No pets," Lord Tokugawa added, looking sternly at the chattering Tanuki who stopped chattering and stood upright, a look of dismay on his striped face.

Later, undeterred by the exclusive invitation, Tanuki chatted excitedly, talking up Tarō as they made their way through the forest.

"I'm telling you, we could make a killing!"

"We can do that here," Tarō said, shaking his head.

"You said you don't belong here," Tanuki poked.

Tarō frowned.

"It'll be fun!" Tanuki pressed. "Gambling, and lots of food and wine!" Tanuki paused in thought, then grinned, "and girls!"

Tarō made a face.

"Oh, right, not much experience there!"

Tarō made another face.

"I know just the place!" Tanuki said with a lascivious grin.

Although he had already made up his mind, Tarō allowed Tanuki to chatter on until they arrived at Yama Uba's cave.

"Why don't we just sneak off," Tanuki tried. "Probably much less trouble in that."

"No, just wait here."

"Oh, yes," Tanuki quickly agreed, trying to sound considerate, "that's probably best."

With no small amount of unease, Tanuki listened to the voices echoing in the cavern as he waited for Tarō to return.

"It is a dangerous place, cruel, the world of men!" Yama Uba warned, although her blue lips did not move as she hovered over Tarō. "You cannot go. You must never go there!"

"You don't understand!" Tarō complained.

"I am your mother, and you are my son! I forbid it!" she said, hovering closer to him.

"You can't make me stay!" Tarō shouted defiantly.

His voice boomed in the cavern, disturbing the bats, who took frenzied, squeaking flight to exit the cave and dart across the moonlit sky. Tanuki dove for cover.

A tense moment passed as they sized each other up. Tarō had not forgotten how Yama Uba raised him, nursing him with her magic milk until his body swelled. She was the only mother he could remember, but now he stood nearly eye to eye with her, and his boyish tantrum was fierce to behold. Yama Uba's magical aura glowed coldly, but when she looked at Tarō, she faltered. He was a very big boy now, with a power all his own.

"I don't belong here!" he yelled. "I am human!"

"So was I—" she muttered coldly, "once upon a time."

"What happened to my father?" Tarō demanded. "Where is he? Why don't you want me to know about him?"

"He is gone. That is all that matters," she sighed. "It is better you do not know."

"Why won't you tell me?" Tarō said, stamping his foot. "What are you hiding?"

She turned her back to him, as if it might stop his questions.

"Why do you look in that silver circle all night long?" he said suddenly. "You think I don't see you, but I do."

As if compelled by the mere mention of it, Yama Uba reached in her *kimono* and drew forth her mirror. She held it up, trembling, but she resisted the urge to look into it.

"I want to go, Mother," he said as firm as Mount Fuji itself. "I want to find my father."

She sighed and turned, floating closer, and gave his cheek a quick, cold pinch.

"Ow!" Tarō said angrily, backing against the cave wall to defend himself.

"Well," she said with a spiteful grin, "if you are going to leave me, it should hurt a little!"

Tarō frowned.

"My big boy!" she said with a sad shudder, then stiffened. "If you must go, you shall not go alone!"

Tarō frowned again.

"No, silly boy," she said, when she saw the look on his face. "I cannot leave this place—but here," she said, holding up her mirror. "Take this!" She covered the mirror with both hands. "Take it!" she said, pushing it toward him.

Tarō glanced at the mirror, a small, silver disc with an elegant handle, its face hidden by her pale hands. He hesitated, then reached for it.

"This will protect you," she said. "Keep it with you always, but listen to me—"

As he took hold of her treasure, she rose forbiddingly over him, drawing his eyes to hers.

"You must never look in this mirror. Do you hear me?"

"But why not?"

"Never mind," she said. "Promise me, you will never look in the mirror."

Tarō hesitated only a moment, then he nodded.

"Say it!" she ordered in her raspy voice.

"I promise."

"Good!" she said, surrendering her talisman.

She hovered close, smoothing the hair on his head, as Tarō tucked the mirror in his tunic. Then he surprised her with a hug that warmed her cold heart even if only for a moment.

Bidding goodbye to her restless son, Yama Uba stopped at the mouth of her cave. Tanuki shuddered when he saw the witch and wasted no time bounding off into the woods as soon as Tarō joined him.

"I will miss the boy," she sighed sorrowfully.

As she watched Tarō disappear into the woods, Yama Uba transformed suddenly from the white lady into the monstrous old crone with wild, white hair who had appeared in her mirror. She lingered for a moment, her piercing black eyes surrendering to grief until, all at once, she vanished in a whirling, flurry of snow.

# PART TWO

---

## URASHIMA TARŌ

## 浦島太郎

Urashima Taro

4

# THE TEMPLE AND THE CASTLE

*Yamashiro Province*

*Spring, Year of the Rat*

A bush warbler called in the early light outside the tea house, its long whistle followed by a staccato one. Beside the narrow window, which appeared to be hung upon the wall like some sacred scroll—a design by Master Rikyū himself—Lord Oda sat contemplating the verdant, mossy garden, the landscape intended to inspire *yūgen*, that awareness of the universe that evokes an emotional response too profound and mystical for words.

Lord Oda frequented Honno Temple as a peaceful retreat on his visits to Kyōto. Each time, the garden delighted his eye, and this day was no exception with its bearded iris in full bloom, their extravagant purple blossoms and spear-shaped leaves marching in a verdant phalanx around the small placid pond fed by a babbling brook that ran beneath the stilts of the temple's tea house.

The warlord spoke of the water iris with a groan of approval, and the bush warbler called again, punctuating his observation. He sat cross-legged on the *tatami*, back straight, fists on his knees, sword at his side. His handsome young squire knelt motionless behind him in a shady corner. Opposite, a bent, slight man, with a wide face like an owl's, knelt on his heels, tending an iron brazier. He acknowledged his guest's observation with a quiet nod. His simple dress—a *kimono* of brown silk and a matching square cap—suggested he was but one of the lord's servants, and indeed he would have been pleased to hear such a pronouncement, for he strived to serve his guest with utmost sincerity and humility. The astute observer could see this in his deliberate movements, as he made his preparations for the ceremonial tea, his focus in that moment without extraneous thought or action.

Steam rose from the iron kettle on the brazier. His host's movements momentarily mesmerized Lord Oda, then he woke and drew a deep breath of the sweet, citrus fragrance of the iris. He stroked his mustache in satisfaction as he mused upon the garden once more.

"Martial spirit," he said, pleased with his wordplay, using a homophone for *shōbu,* the iris, with different Chinese characters.

"Victory or defeat," his host replied enigmatically in their poetic repartee, fencing with an even more esoteric homophone described with yet another, completely different pair of *kanji.*

Lord Oda's eyebrows furrowed but a moment, then he slapped his knee in approval.

"Of course!" he said, shaking his head, then declared, "Ah, Master Rikyū, it is indeed a pleasure to see you again!"

Whether he understood the repartee or not, Lord Oda's squire relaxed to see his Lord pleased. Lord Oda studied Master Rikyū's measured preparations for the tea, the careful arrangement of the utensils and accoutrements he had brought to serve his guest—a finely lacquered tea caddy, the *chawan*, a black *raku* tea bowl of striking simplicity, and inside it, a folded white strip of cloth, a whisk of split bamboo, and a narrow tea scoop of polished bamboo—carefully situating all of these in front of him, each piece arranged to complement the effortless economy of his ritual.

Master Rikyū moved consciously but naturally, as if in a single breath. Lord Oda watched transfixed, as his host drew a red handkerchief from his sash. At first glance, Master Rikyū might have been an actor feigning a mortal wound as he flourished his blood-red handkerchief, but he was solemn in his performance. He held the napkin before him, carefully folding and creasing it with his fingertips. Taking up the tea caddy, he reverently wiped the lid. He gave the same deliberate attention to the tea scoop. Then he arranged the tea bowl and whisk in front of him, standing the whisk upright near a brown ceramic jar to his right.

Removing the lid from the kettle, Master Rikyū ladled hot water into the *chawan*, ritually rinsing the tea whisk in it, then he dumped the used water in a large empty bowl beside him and dried the *chawan* with the white cloth. Taking up the tea scoop, he then turned and bowed to his guest, and Lord Oda bowed in return.

Master Rikyū opened the tea caddy and ladled two heaping scoops of bright green, powdered tea into the black *raku* bowl, tapping the scoop twice on its lip. Adding a ladleful of hot water from the kettle, he took up the whisk. With quick, measured effort, he prepared the tea, whisking it into a bright green froth until it had just the right consistency.

The bush warbler whistled outside the tea house, its call deepening the mystic communion between host and guest. The tea master took a breath as he raised the *chawan*. Holding it reverently with both hands, he turned the bowl twice before offering the most attractive profile to his guest, which he did by placing it on the floor near Lord Oda. Guest and host bowed once more.

"Thank you for making the tea," Lord Oda said, raising the tea bowl with both hands.

"One time, one meeting," Master Rikyū replied, intending to convey the fleeting, unrepeatable nature of the moment.

Lord Oda acknowledged his appreciation for the insight with a breath. Then he turned the bowl in his hands as his host had done and took a deliberate sip, savoring the bitter green foam.

"How is the tea?"

"It is excellent," Lord Oda replied, taking two more deliberate sips, a little green foam lingering on his mustache but he paid no heed, focused as he was on studying the exquisite simplicity of the artifact in his hands, a quintessential token of *wabisabi,* the aesthetic of imperfection and impermanence.

"The tea was delicious," Lord Oda said, observing the same ritual revolution of the *chawan* before returning it to his host.

Time stood still for host and guest, and Lord Oda relished the mystical quality of the moment. The bush warbler whistled again, but it choked suddenly on the unmistakable sound of shouts and clashing steel.

Lord Oda glanced at his squire who stood stiff with alarm. Master Rikyū met the sounds of escalating conflict in the temple courtyard with quiet aplomb, taking his cue from his guest as Lord Oda stuck his head out the narrow window. He had to crane his neck to get a glimpse of the temple gate where his small contingent of *samurai* fought against a much larger force of warrior monks wearing armor beneath their robes, white cowls covering their heads, and wielding cruel *naginata*, which they used with vicious skill, their pole-swords slashing and cleaving Lord Oda's men so that many lay dead already.

"*Sōhei*!" Lord Oda cursed. "Ran," he called to his squire, "my bow!"

Mōri Ranmaru already had his Lord's bow in hand and gave it to him. Taking up his sword as well, Lord Oda charged from the tearoom with Ran at his heels.

The tea house stood behind the temple, a variety of bushes and trees obscuring the little one-story building, its tile roof shaded by a stately cherry tree. Delicate pink petals littered the flagstone path between the house and the decorative entrance to the garden, a bridge covered by a thatched roof spanning the small stream that ran through the temple.

"Ambush, my Lord!" a *samurai* shouted as he charged across the bridge. "Warrior monks from Mount Hiei! The temple is surrounded."

As if to confirm the ill news, the great iron temple bell rang a resonant, frantic warning as Lord Oda sprang into battle with Ran at his side. The *sōhei* attack centered on the gate and main hall when they joined the *samurai* contingent in pitched battle. Lord Oda took aim with his powerful bow, slaying five monks, but on the sixth arrow, fate snapped his bowstring. Throwing down his bow, he snatched up a fallen *naginata* and attacked with unbridled ferocity, fueled not simply by life-and-death struggle but also by his intense hatred for his nemeses, the *Ikkō-ikki Sōhei.*

Perhaps he realized his private, decades-long war against these monks had come home to roost, for Lord Oda fought with an abandon that seemed to acknowledge his fate, rushing headlong to engage the enemy, parrying their pole-swords to close the distance. Ran did his best to cover his Lord with bow and arrow, as Lord Oda cut down another four monks in turn before he sustained a wound from a *naginata* slash to his thigh.

His assailant was taller than the other monks, with a sallow face, and long, almost beastly teeth and fingernails. When he wounded Lord Oda, the *sōhei* grinned fiendishly, raising his *naginata* overhead to deal a mortal blow, but Ran quickly dispatched the evil monk, putting an arrow through his eye.

Several of Lord Oda's steadfast *samurai* rallied to defend their Lord's retreat to the tea house with Ran helping him. Standing on the little covered bridge, Lord Oda and his faithful ward could see their small *samurai* contingent was hopelessly outnumbered as it fought to hold back the crush of the enemy, but neither dwelled on the warlord's complacent but imprudent election to visit Honno-ji with only some fifty *samurai* and servants. Lord Oda glanced back at the tea house, pausing only a moment in thought, and Ran saw the gravity of their circumstances in his Lord's face.

"So be it!" Lord Oda said, his eyes narrowing with cold resolve. "Go!" he shouted. "Set the temple alight!"

His bodyguards hesitated, then quickly bowed and raced away with noble resignation to carry out their Lord's final order.

Master Rikyū did not speak or inquire when Lord Oda rejoined him. The two men sat in silence for a moment, each cognizant of his fate, as Ran bound his master's wound and the clamor of battle filled the courtyard.

"Your life has not been wasted," Master Rikyū said at last. "In the history of this land, no one has accomplished more."

Touched by his words, Lord Oda exhaled sharply, bowing so his fists touched the floor.

"It is rude of me, but I humbly take your leave," Master Rikyū said.

Lord Oda glanced at Ran, then nodded stiffly to his host, adding simply, "Thank you for the tea."

Master Rikyū smiled and nodded. Then he bowed low and quietly withdrew from the room, closing the door behind him.

Lord Oda looked at Ran, smiling grimly. As the sounds of the melee continued outside the quiet tea house, he moved to admire the scroll hanging in the decorative alcove, taking a deep breath, soaking up the moment.

*One moment, one meeting,* Lord Oda thought, as he prepared himself for *seppuku.*

The warlord stripped his *kimono* to his torso and removed his *tantō* from his sash. Unsheathing the knife, he lay the scabbard on the floor and composed himself. Then slowly, gutturally, with thickly resonant words that filled the room, Lord Oda sang his death poem.

"Compared to the vast expanse of the heavens, human life is but a dream and illusion," he chanted. "Once life is given by the gods, it is destined to perish!"

Moved to tears as he stood behind his lord, Ran raised his sword to assist.

"So it goes," Lord Oda said, placing the tip of the *tantō* to his belly. He did not blink. Teeth clenched, he pierced himself with his knife, opening his belly in the warrior way.

"Ran?" he grunted. "Don't let them get my head."

Lord Oda stared but a moment in stoic agony. Then Ran deftly separated his head from his body with a merciful stroke, followed by a quick snap of the blade that severed the remaining strip of flesh and dropped his Lord's head onto the floor with a muffled thud.

Ran regarded his fallen Lord for a moment, then cried out and thrust his *katana* deep into the decorative pillar that stood beside the sacred alcove. Leaning hard against his sword, he snapped the end off and threw the headless blade on the floor in anger, disgust, and shame. He fell to his knees, bowing to his Lord's lifeless body, sobbing softly.

Blind with grief and rage, Ran recovered himself as the sounds of raging battle pricked his ears. He quickly removed his vest and carefully placed his Lord's head in its folds, wrapping his treasure with care before setting it in the sacred alcove. Then he quickly exited the tea house, running for the main hall of the temple, which had begun to throw flame and black smoke into the morning sky.

Prying loose a burning timber, Ran raced back to the tea house with his torch, using it to light two corners of the building. Watching for a moment, then satisfied the fire would take, Ran stepped back inside the burning hut. Reverently, he knelt in front of the sacred alcove where he had placed his master's head.

Mōri Ran did not sing his last words. He simply bowed to his master's head swaddled in his vest. Then, composing himself, he knelt, opened his *kimono* to his belly, and honored his master with his Lord's own sword, giving his life's blood in expiation of his shame that he had not better served his beloved patron.

Outside the tea house, shouts and screams of the men caught in battle and conflagration filled the temple courtyard. The temple bell rang frantically, then ceased.

Inside the main hall, Master Rikyū knelt on a cushion on the dais, contemplating the placid face of the Daibutsu, the great bronze statue of the Buddha of the Void. The bronze glowed from the orange flames consuming the hall, but the effigy of the great teacher stared unperturbed, holding up a reassuring hand, palm outward as if to signal imminent revelation of the ultimate *kōan*.

"Welcome to thee, sword of eternity!" Master Rikyū said, as the temple blazed around him, "Through Buddha and Daruma alike, thou hast cleft thy way!"

Master Rikyū closed his eyes, embracing the great mystery with profound calm, as the temple collapsed in flame.

Meanwhile, Lord Monkey watched Honno-ji burn from his verdant vantage at Enryaku Temple on the summit of Mount Hiei, the scar from Tarō's blade long-healed but still noticeable on his jowl. His squire crouched behind him like a dog that knows its master's displeasure, keeping his head down lest he become the target of his owner's rising ire.

Mount Hiei afforded a strategic vista of Kyōto. Since ancient times, the Mount was known to be the home of gods and demons of *Shintō* lore, so shamanic geomancy ordained the foundation of the temple on its summit to "protect" the heavenly Capital of Peace and Tranquility. The irony amused Lord Monkey. The centuries-old Tendai sect of Buddhist monks had become the most powerful in all Nihon, terrorizing the imperial court whenever they intended to enforce monastic demands. Marching on Kyōto from Enryaku-ji, an army of warrior monks thousands strong, carrying their large *o-mikoshi*, the portable shrine housing their deity, the Mountain King, the crooked *sōhei* chanted a sutra curse that was said to rumble through the city streets like a thunderstorm descending from the mountain. Small wonder they had been dubbed evil monks. Lord Oda despised them, not least for their mercenary alliance with the rival Asai and Asakura clans whose domains surrounded Lake Biwa and who vigorously opposed Lord Oda's dominance in the name of the child Emperor.

Lord Oda was not religious, and yet he regarded these monks as an abomination to *samurai* and Buddhist principle alike and wholeheartedly embraced Lord Monkey's plan to obliterate their enclave only twenty years before. This irony amused Lord Monkey even more since, owing to his humble birth, the plan he alone conceived, to raze the temple and annihilate Lord Oda's rivals, had been credited to another, Akechi Mitsuhide, a *samurai*, which deeply offended Lord Monkey since it seemed he could never rise above his birth—and yet it immunized him from suspicion. The *sōhei* never suspected, even though he had devised a "siege" more properly described as an unspeakable massacre, the horrific slaughter of some twenty thousand men, women, and children inhabiting the monastic commune, many of them burned alive, barricaded in the temple buildings against Akechi, who led the onslaught as coveted "first spear" in the vanguard.

So it was that Lord Monkey stood upon the brink of his precipitous but long-sought advantage, and the monks, although unwitting stones in the game, threatened his prize with their incompetence. Honno Temple kicked orange flame and cinder and thick smoke into the sky just a few thousand steps from the imperial palace. If the palace caught fire, it could seriously jeopardize his grand design.

As Lord Monkey fumed silently over the conflagration, a white-cowled figure approached, armed with his cruel *naginata*, followed by a cabal of monks in similar dress, their cowls shadowing their faces. Lord Monkey's squire shrank at the sight of these *Ikkō-ikki Sōhei*, for he knew them to be deadly warriors with the power of spell-craft. Some of those shamans were said to have delved ever deeper into spirit lore until they themselves became possessed by *yōkai*, the evil spirits with which they communed.

"The temple burns, Lord Hashiba," the monk said.

"I can see it!" Lord Monkey spat, looking as if he himself would spontaneously erupt in flame. "Did I tell you to burn it?"

"Oda's men barricaded themselves inside and set fire to it."

"You had the temple surrounded," Lord Monkey ranted. "Oda had only some forty servants and retainers."

He crowded the much taller monk who did not move, but Lord Monkey recoiled when he glimpsed the dreadful visage beneath the cowl. The man had cold eyes and a sallow face that sat upon an unnaturally long neck. Lord Monkey turned aside.

"I suppose another naked brute appeared to champion Oda as well?" Lord Monkey blurted.

The monk did not respond.

"A lord for a lord. I alerted you to Oda's clandestine visit to the temple. I delivered as promised," Lord Monkey smoldered. "I have no use for your excuses. Your brethren have yet to deliver Tokugawa. May I remind you, he is no better than Oda? I am all that stands between the Emperor and the barbarian Christians. I trust you will fulfill our accord."

"We shall honor our agreement," the monk hissed.

Lord Monkey gave the monk a final, sideways glance intended to underscore his displeasure. Bowing, the monk quietly withdrew, and his disciples followed, leaving Lord Monkey to watch the smoke from the burning temple foul the naked sky.

*Kai Province*

*Spring, Year of the Rat*

A waning full moon lit the forest on the night of their departure, so Tarō and Tanuki had no trouble finding their way as they set out toward Edo to take up lodging and service to Lord Tokugawa, a man they barely knew. Even so, they talked excitedly about the adventure ahead of them, while bounding through the thick, pungent forest of cypress and underbrush, or weaving through enormous stands of bamboo, crickets chirping all around them.

Their hike brought them at last to the Eastern Sea Road as men referred to the great path they had made to traverse their domains from the West, where the Emperor of Nihon presided over the affairs of a country at war with itself, to the East where Lord Tokugawa awaited in Edo City, the capital of his domain.

"Ah," Tanuki said, when they came through the last dense thicket of bamboo and discovered the road. "It's down this way. We could be there by tomorrow morning if we trot—"

Tarō looked back in the direction they had come. While he had ranged all through the forests of Mount Fuji, he had never come this far from the only home he could remember. He felt for the mirror inside his tunic, but remembering his promise to Yama Uba, he did not take it out.

*Did he even need its protection*, he wondered. He felt strong and ready for adventure. And yet, he was anxious about what lay ahead, especially since he remembered nothing of his past.

*Could he find his father? Would he even recognize him if he found him? And what would he say if they were reunited?*

These and other thoughts troubled Tarō as he stood on the border between the natural and human worlds. Tanuki started to leave the forest, nodding for Tarō to follow, then darted back to crouch beside the road, looking from side to side.

"I nearly forgot myself!" he declared, instantly assuming the likeness of a jolly-looking, fat man of middle age, with graying whiskers and a bald spot, ruddy cheeks, a jovial smile, and a truly enormous, rotund belly bulging beneath his brown *kimono*. Tarō doubled over laughing to see his companion so transformed.

"Just call me 'Uncle'—" Tanuki said, frowning. "And let me do all the talking! You may be human, but trust your Uncle Tanuki, you're just a cub when it comes to the world of men!"

Uncle Tanuki strode boldly into the road and led the way, sparing no breath on how often he had visited the cities of men and how much he knew and loved their culture, not least the eating and drinking, although he also talked glibly of women in a way that Tarō little understood.

"You see?" Tanuki tried to explain, looking back at Mount Fuji, blue and silver in the moonlight as it receded behind them. He held up his hands, framing its majestic bosom to underscore his point. "Perfect, right?" he posed. "Now imagine two of them!"

Tarō laughed boyishly, naively, which only encouraged Tanuki, who proceeded to regale Tarō most of the way, until his head rattled with tall tales of how Tanuki had infiltrated the world of men—and women—on countless occasions. As they made their way along the Eastern Sea Road, Tanuki laughed to see Tarō react to the villages teeming with people, and the monolithic fortress of Odawarajo, but none of Tanuki's embellishments could have prepared Tarō for his first glimpse of Edo.

They stopped only at several fortified post stations along the road, guarded by formidable *samurai* loyal to the Tokugawa clan. Travelers had to present permits at each station in order to cross into the next territory, but not once did anyone suspect Uncle Tanuki, and they passed easily each time they displayed the official seal that Lord Tokugawa had given them to permit their passage. Even when they stopped at an inn in a sizable farming and fishing settlement near the seaside, and Tanuki ate and drank and gabbed and gambled with abandon, no one imagined he was anyone other than Tarō's boisterous uncle with a lust for life and a penchant for excess—so much so that Tarō had to remind Tanuki they should be going before he gambled the night away.

Hours later, although some fishermen and merchants had begun to stir and move along their route, carrying baskets on poles or on their backs or heads, Edo lay mostly sleeping when Tarō and Uncle Tanuki crossed the Tama River by barge, arriving at Shinagawa Station in the Hour of the Tiger. The sea was much closer to the road, and the salty humidity clung to their bodies and made Tarō miss the crisp mountain air they had left behind.

Nearby, the silhouettes of ships and boats rocked and creaked quietly against their moorings from the lapping ocean, the port quays filled with a great multitude of vessels of all size and origin—fishing boats and junks and a monstrous tall Jesuit ship, a "floating castle," Tanuki called it, its sails rippling in the wind that rolled off Edo Bay. The streets began to fill with hawkers opening their stalls, and the occasional *kago,* carried by men jogging past, bearing customers to early appointments.

Tarō took a deep breath, feeling suddenly very small and out of place in this great cityscape. Even at a distance, Edo appeared immeasurably vast, a sprawling capital encircling a flatland castle of walls and towers surrounded by timber mansions and residences to the west, and the various shops and buildings of the townsfolk to the east.

In his life, Tarō had never seen so many buildings, and Tanuki assured him tens of thousands of humans lived in this one city nestled in the confluence of three great rivers glittering in the moonlight. Here and there, lanterns twinkled, whether lit through the night or more recently as their owners stirred in the twilight.

As Tarō and Uncle Tanuki made their way through the labyrinthine city, the sights and sounds and smells—of sea and fish and wood fires and cooking food, but also the acrid odor of human sweat and urine and excrement—overwhelmed Tarō. Even Tanuki looked a tourist, pointing at a group of pale-faced Jesuit priests in black robes and gesticulating excitedly as he explained those strange men came from the "floating castle" they had just seen.

Taro and Tanuki on the Tokaido

They passed through the city slowly waking around them until they arrived at Nihon Bridge, the last station on the Tōkaidō, where the city's fisherman, craftsmen and merchants had built their storehouses to ply their trades, and shippers managed their barges on the sea and river routes to and from other cities to the north and south of Edo, and customers came to market.

Tarō watched curiously as citizens bartered or paid for goods, while Tanuki grew restless and talked eagerly of visiting the nearby "pleasure quarter," which he abandoned only because it was nearly sunrise, by which he meant breakfast. With a sigh, he turned away, leading Tarō toward the stately silhouette of Edo Castle looming ever larger, much larger even than Odawara Castle.

Arriving at Big Hand Gate under heavy guard as it was the main castle ingress, they presented Lord Tokugawa's seal again, but here they fell under more circumspection than before. Even after their invitation had been confirmed, the guards continued to look on this overgrown, brawny boy and his rotund "uncle" with suspicious curiosity.

They waited for a time until a squad of *samurai* appeared to usher them into the castle. Armed with spear or musket and swords, twenty men in armor led the way, weaving through a vast, elaborate complex of deep trenches, and massive, dry stone walls and ramparts of granite taller than ten men, with stones as big as Tarō. Gates and courts were staggered so as to confuse and confound navigation by any outsider. Venturing deeper into the fortified city, they passed through different wards, each with citadels guarded by their own moats and walls and defensive towers, each ward accessed by wooden drawbridges buffeted by gates on either side, though none as heavily guarded as the Big Hand Gate.

The castle was still waking, but Tarō marveled at the number of garrisons they passed from the main gate to the inmost keep, ranks of soldiers too numerous to count, already drilling with spear and musket, their shouts and cries and the clash of their weapons harsh in the early morning as first light slipped over the castle walls. The thundering reports of *tanegashima* matchlocks made Tarō and Tanuki jump, and the air smelled sharply of gunpowder and torch oil and human exertion, all of which twisted Tarō's nose and stung his eyes.

At last, their escort brought them to the *honmaru,* the first enceinte surrounding the main citadel and castle donjon and the residences of Lord Tokugawa and his family and closest retainers. They crossed the drawbridge over the lotus-filled moat into the citadel where the stately main buildings within the first enceinte occupied an enormous area.

Just as the other wards had their share of residences and buildings to serve the castle residents, there were even more buildings within the *honmaru*—residences, storehouses, and stables for retainers and servants, too many for Tarō to guess at the number. On top of the walls surrounding the citadel, double and triple keeps stood watch at strategic points. The five-story donjon, thirty men tall, the tallest castle keep in all Nihon, stood in one corner of the *honmaru,* its upturned roofs ornamented with gold glinting in the twilight.

For a time, Tarō and Uncle Tanuki waited outside the low-level residential buildings congregated around the castle keep. Tarō thought nothing of sitting on the ground in the midst of their armed escort, and Tanuki joined him, which set the guards to murmuring, eyeing their charges with quiet disdain until the Karō*,* Lord Tokugawa's Chief Retainer and Steward of the Castle, came to greet them. Had it not been for Lord Tokugawa's patronage, such an affront from "peasants" would have been met with drastic retribution pursuant to the entitlement of *kirisute*, the right to strike down anyone of lower class who compromised their honor, but these *samurai* did not know what to make of this ruddy, brawny boy and the corpulent old man with him, so they settled for disapproving whispers among themselves. Tarō paid little heed to their muttering and passed the time in observation, remarking how different his home was from this place where these humans sought to contain and control the spirits of nature within their many buildings, while the shrine below Mount

Fuji embraced its surroundings in homage to the powerful *kami* of the forest world.

"Your quarters are located in the exterior building," the Karō explained after greeting them.

A somber man, no doubt burdened by his years and his many responsibilities, the Karō led them into the exterior building and down a series of corridors. They passed many reception rooms and apartments for castle guards and officials before arriving at their quarters, a modest room with a view of the castle gardens when they opened the translucent, latticed *shoji* doors onto the veranda that skirted the building.

"You will dine with our Lord tonight. A servant will come to collect you. Access to the interior building, where his Lordship resides, is otherwise strictly prohibited," he warned. "But first," the Karō said with a quiet look of contempt, "I am sure you want a bath to wash off the dust from your travel."

Tarō and Uncle Tanuki exchanged quizzical looks, especially when the bath smelled of wood smoke from the fires burning beneath iron cauldrons prepared for them. Although skeptical at first, and particularly when their appointed servants insisted on scrubbing them head to toe, they soon embraced bath time. They stood on wooden grates to soak in the steaming cauldrons, Uncle Tanuki nearly flooding the room so the servants danced when his enormous belly displaced most of his bath water.

Still steaming from their soak, their attendants dressed them in lightweight robes, which they wore to breakfast. Tarō had been extremely careful and secretive with Yama Uba's mirror ever since he left his wilderness home so no one had discovered his talisman, which he hid again in the sleeve of his *yukata* before leaving their room.

Uncle Tanuki welcomed breakfast—steaming *miso* soup with seaweed and an egg, *tofu* bean curd with grated radish and soy sauce, grilled sea bream, a delicacy and Tanuki's favorite, and steamed brown rice with various crunchy, pickled vegetables on the side. Tanuki wiggled with anticipation, but Tarō immediately dove into his rice bowl. He shook his hand in dismay when the steaming rice stuck to it, which amused the servants.

Tanuki wagged his head with a reproachful "tsk tsk." He picked up his chopsticks and nodded deliberately at Tarō's pair.

Tarō took up his chopsticks with a quizzical look. Tanuki rolled his eyes and demonstrated.

"I will partake," he announced, expertly dipping his chopsticks in the *miso* soup to procure a piece of *tofu*, delicately pinching his selection and popping it in his mouth, then smacking his lips in satisfaction.

"I will partake," Tarō parroted and fed himself a pinch of rice with such aplomb that he surprised himself and Tanuki.

They zealously dispatched every morsel before retiring for a nap on *futon* their servants had prepared for them.

"Ah," Tanuki sighed, snuggling into his mattress, "This will do nicely!"

His "uncle" was soon snoring. Tarō, on the other hand, lay staring uncomfortably at the ceiling for some time, uncertain as to why he should feel uneasy but troubled nonetheless by his impression that his surroundings felt strange yet somehow familiar. The feeling haunted him until, at last, he surrendered to a fitful sleep and dreamed of wrestling a shadowy figure whose face he could not see. All the while, he felt the gaze of a fearsome audience, their crystal eyes flashing, the Gods of Wind and Thunder.

Tarō and Uncle Tanuki could scarcely believe they had slept through the day when servants awakened them shortly before dinner time to dress in fine *kimono*. The servants brought tea, but neither Tarō nor Tanuki wanted to drink bitter water, let alone hot, and yet the smell of it hit Tarō again, strange yet familiar. He did not have long to puzzle on it. Their servants led them to a large room, two hundred *tatami* mats in size, cordoned by *fusuma* doors painted with gilt designs proclaiming the wealth and noble lineage of the

Tokugawa clan—venerable twisted pine trees and fabled lion-dogs. Tall candles lit the room, their light playing upon the gilded screen paintings.

At the far end of the great hall, Lord Tokugawa sat upon a purple cushion on the raised dais of the room, his sword on a rack beside him, and his squire in attendance behind. A Chinese scroll with a pen and ink drawing of some sacred landscape hung in the decorative alcove behind them. *Samurai* guards knelt on either side of the dais, and between the platform and the door, numerous cushions of red silk had been set out for the guests, most of whom were already seated, among them Lord Tokugawa's closest retainers and lords of the major provinces and their fiefdoms over which he held sway by blood and oath and allegiances made.

Servants moved quietly through the room, but everyone stopped to look at Tarō and his "uncle" as the Karō announced their entrance, directing them to bow. Tanuki managed easily and nudged Tarō. Tarō knelt beside him, looking around at everyone, and a tense moment followed before he managed his bow.

Lord Tokugawa nodded from his seat upon the dais, and the Karō led the way, directing a servant to guide Tarō and his uncle to their places just below the dais and opposite the Karō. Each place had been set with a large footed tray of several dishes. Hanging on the delicious aromas floating through the room, Tanuki nearly fell over on the way to his seat.

Although a place beside the Karō was vacant, the other seats had all been filled, and the room buzzed with conversation, which Tarō and Tanuki rightly guessed to be mostly about them. Lord Tokugawa's bodyguards eyed Tarō suspiciously from their posts. Tarō sat closest to the dais, Uncle Tanuki on the cushion next to him, while next to Tanuki sat two imposing warlords, and two equally formidable-looking lords sat opposite. The lord seated nearest to them, a very capable-looking, stocky man with a refined mustache and thin wavy eyebrows, eyed

Uncle Tanuki, sizing him up. Tanuki put on his best sociable smile, but failing to charm his sour neighbor, he hung his head sheepishly.

Tanuki's eyes widened when he caught sight of an appetizer of fermented, salted squid viscera waiting on the tray before him. He was about to help himself when he saw the Karō frowning as Tarō impetuously lifted the very same appetizer from his own tray to hold it to his nose.

"Tarō," Tanuki said with a pained gulp, "we should wait."

One sniff, and Tarō decided the dish was not for him. He quickly replaced it, but this did not deter Tanuki who looked at his appetizer longingly and might have expired on the spot if not for the servants who brought *sake* around. Tanuki licked his lips and wiggled expectantly, which drew another glance from his neighbor.

The Karō looked to his Lord who stared in annoyance at the empty cushion beside his steward and gave a curt nod.

"My Lords," his steward began, speaking to the imposing *samurai* around the room, while Lord Tokugawa surveyed the audience, watching Tarō and Uncle Tanuki with particular curiosity.

Tanuki shifted impatiently on his cushion, eyeing his *sake*, doing his best not to drool in anticipation as he waited for the toast.

"Honorable guests," the Karō said, working his way from lord to lord, "the Four Guardians, Lord Tokugawa's most trusted generals. Lord Honda, *samurai* among *samurai*; Lord Ii, the hawkeyed musketeer; Lord Sakakibara, the horse master; Lord Sakai, the Boar Slayer."

The four lords nodded in turn, all of them regarding Tarō and Uncle Tanuki suspiciously.

"My Lords, may I present Tarō and—" the Karō paused, uncertain, "his uncle." The Karō, caught off guard for once, quickly recovered. "I apologize," he said, "but we do not know your family name."

Also caught by surprise, Tanuki stuttered, then blurted, "Tsukiyama!"

A hush fell upon the room. The Karō looked to Lord Tokugawa who stared thoughtfully. Realizing he had mis-stepped but uncertain how, Uncle Tanuki's head sunk self-consciously between his hunched shoulders.

"Lady Tsukiyama was my Lord's late wife," the Karō said, eyeing Uncle Tanuki who flushed and gulped.

"My Lord, I did not know," Tanuki apologized. "We are—we are just a family of woodcutters who took our name from the moon and the mountain a long time ago."

Four years had passed since the demise of his wife and son, but the wound seemed fresh, judging by how the room held its breath for Lord Tokugawa to speak.

"A propitious coincidence," Lord Tokugawa said at last. "Perhaps my late wife sent Tarō to be my bodyguard," he added graciously. "My Lords," he announced, taking up his *sake* cup.

Relieved, Tanuki readily raised his cup.

"To my—" Lord Tokugawa hesitated, and the suspense was a special kind of torture for Tanuki until their host added tentatively, "savior, Tsukiyama Tarō. Empty cup!"

The room roared in unison, "Empty cup!" and everyone downed their *sake*, though no one as heartily as Tanuki who quickly welcomed a refill from a servant.

"Tarō," Lord Tokugawa said, "my thanks. The Tokugawa clan welcomes you. As a token of my gratitude, I offer you my name—if you will have it."

"Ah," Uncle Tanuki quickly piped, "he would be honored, my Lord."

"Very well," Lord Tokugawa said and, after a moment's thought, he pronounced, "I offer you my name, *Toku*, and dub thee *Toku*yama Tarō, the 'virtuous' mountain!"

Tanuki pounced on the occasion, declaring "Empty cup!"

"Empty cup!" the room replied in unison.

"I've already got a name," Tarō said aside to Tanuki, downing his second cup and frowning.

"Relax, it's just a formality—and go easy on that," Tanuki said with a grin, "you're in training, remember?"

As Tarō finished his *sake*, his eyes found a young girl in *kimono* who had appeared at the entrance.

"Ah! My Lady Kamehime," the Karō said upon seeing her, exchanging a glance with Lord Tokugawa as the young girl bowed in the vestibule.

A maiden of fourteen or fifteen, with long black hair, and dressed in a *kimono* of sumptuous blue silk, she glided into the room, followed closely by her nurse, a tough-looking middle-aged woman, whose large black wig framed a perpetual scowl as if she had just eaten an unripe persimmon.

Wide-eyed Tarō watched the girl glide to her seat. Seeing Tarō's face, Uncle Tanuki shook his head knowingly. With all eyes upon Kamehime, Tanuki could wait no longer and pounced on the chance to slyly down his appetizer with no one the wiser.

"Please excuse my lateness," Kamehime said.

"My Lady," the Karō responded as she took her seat, assisted by her nurse. "May I present Tokuyama Tarō, and his Uncle—" The Karō stopped short, quite nonplused at having been caught off guard a second time.

"Ki-nu-ta, at your service!" Uncle Tanuki quickly offered as his given name.

"Tree in *miso* dressing?" Lord Tokugawa said with a laugh. "You woodcutters have strange names indeed!"

"We're just simple folk, really," Tanuki offered, chuckling self-consciously. He bowed to Kamehime. "My Lady," he said with his most charming smile, "Our meeting is a happy occasion!"

Kamehime bowed gracefully. Her nurse dourly followed her lead, her sour face robbing Tanuki of some of his smile.

"Kamehime's nurse, Nun Tokiko," the Karō said.

Tanuki nudged Tarō, and he followed with a bow, but the *sake* had gone to his head. He slipped off his cushion and bumped the tray in front of him, spilling some soup from one of the bowls.

"Clumsy boy!" Uncle Tanuki chided.

Tarō frowned, and Tanuki chuckled nervously.

"I must admit," the Karō said, trying to mend the awkward moment, "we are truly grateful for your assistance on the mountain, and My Lord is very pleased that you have reconsidered his patronage, although," the Karō paused before adding, "we did not expect your uncle."

Uncle Tanuki smiled sheepishly.

"He goes where I go," Tarō said with boyish bluntness.

The Karō exchanged a glance with his Lord who nodded, whereupon his steward declared, "Yes, of course. So long as you fulfill your end of our bargain, you will be handsomely rewarded."

On cue the servants began ferrying additional trays to the guests, a multitude of delicacies in the traditional style that made Tanuki clap his hands and rub them together, licking his lips expectantly, his eyebrows dancing as he surveyed the sumptuous fare: On the main tray, steamed brown rice, *miso* soup with turnip and chrysanthemum leaves, a dish of sea bream roe and butterbur simmered in soy sauce, a dish of fresh surf clams and scallions seasoned with vinegar and *miso*, and a bowl of *miso*-pickled radish and ginger; a second course of tender, young bamboo shoots, in a clear broth with sea algae and its steamed accompaniment dressed with *miso* and prickly-ash pepper; and a third course of steaming clear soup with sea bream and baby water lilies—Tanuki's favorite—and a side dish of pheasant meat and royal fern simmered in soy sauce; with one final dish of salt-grilled sweetfish. In his life, Tarō could not remember ever having eaten so much, and Tanuki was positively ecstatic with the variety of flavors, each and every course accompanied by its quintessential complement of rice wine.

At one point in the seemingly infinite parade of delicacies, a servant came to pour Tanuki more *sake*, which he eagerly received, downing it in a single gulp and holding out his cup for more before the servant could leave. The servant poured another cupful, but Tanuki quickly downed it with equal ease.

"Here," he said, "I know it is a bit rude but, at my age, time is precious—just leave the pitcher, thank you."

The servant bowed, perplexed, and looked for direction from the Karō who nodded and waved him away.

"Anything you require," the Karō said graciously, "all you need do is ask."

Throughout the meal, Tarō glanced furtively at Kamehime, entranced, thinking her face looked oddly familiar. When their eyes met perchance, suddenly self-conscious, he grabbed his rice bowl with both hands and hid his face in it. Nun Tokiko recoiled, repulsed by his ill manners, while Kamehime stifled a giggle.

Her nurse made an even sourer face, quietly reproaching her mistress. Tarō laughed nervously, while the Karō shook his head, muttering under his breath that so much respect should be accorded an uncouth boy no matter how strong he might be.

"You'll have to forgive my nephew," Tanuki said with a start and an elbow in Tarō's ribs. "He's quite hungry."

Just as Tarō could not take his eyes from Kamehime, she feigned interest in her food but took furtive measure of him as well, looking the brawny boy up and down, smirking as if she thought her father were playing some joke on her.

"Master Tokuyama, I owe you my thanks," she said suddenly.

Surprised, Tarō gave her a questioning look.

"You saved my father," she explained.

"Oh, yes," Tarō replied. "It was nothing."

"Nothing?" she repeated, taking insult just like her father.

"He really is quite strong!" Uncle Tanuki said, sensing a growing tension.

"If you say so," she said with a half-smile.

Just then, the collection of sliding doors that formed the partition behind Tarō and Tanuki opened, revealing a courtyard occupied by a raised, roofed stage and an adjoining covered walkway entering from the left. Tall *ikari* candles stood on iron tripods scattered throughout the courtyard and also placed at the corners of the platform, casting light and shadow across the open air theater. Crickets chirped in the courtyard, and Tarō's senses pricked as much as Tanuki's at the sounds and smells that wafted to them on the fresh air.

"Our entertainment begins!" the Karō said.

Servants doused the candles in the room, while Tarō and Tanuki and those guests who sat on the near side were obliged to turn to view the stage. Tarō turned only slightly so he might still see Kamehime, while Tanuki could not abandon his food or drink and continued to stuff his face as discreetly as he could manage.

"Ah! *Momijigari*!" Lord Tokugawa declared upon seeing the stage and the tall, cloth-covered frame symbolic of a rocky mountain crowned with maple leaves of burnished red and gold.

"Is it autumn already?" Lord Honda laughed. "How time flies like an arrow!"

The room nodded approval at his wit, just as the piercing whistle of a flute filled the courtyard, rising and falling, soon followed by the percussive knock of a hip drum, then accompanied by ominous, resonant chanting. Tarō did not fully understand the song, although some words sounded familiar.

The flute and the knocking continued, accompanied by the uneven plunking of a shoulder drum. Tarō listened, transfixed, even though he could barely see the ensemble of musicians seated in the shadows, and no one had appeared on stage as yet. The music gained apace, pitching up and down like a feverish dance, then slowed to ominous chanting. From the adjoining walkway, the actors entered the stage, wearing the masks of young women. A noble lady and her retinue of ladies-in-waiting, in fine, richly patterned *kimono* of red and gold silk, sang of coming to view the brilliant autumn colors of the mountain.

"Autumn drizzle darkens golden leaves," they sang, "Entering in the deep mountain, shall we enjoy the crimson leaves before the autumn rain falls?"

Tarō thought their song so lonesome. They sang of how long they had lived in this melancholy world, their house in ruin.

"Days pass and the fall has come quietly. The white chrysanthemum fades in the garden, reminding me of myself, alas, tearful, mournful."

They chanted on about their delight at the rich brocade of autumn colors spread across the mountain range, and the patterns of the falling leaves in a stream, where they stopped to behold the autumn splendor.

Tarō felt odd, watching from the sidelines when he usually stood in the arena, but he was completely engrossed in the spectacle. Tanuki took advantage of everyone's diverted attention to sneak the last morsels of his food—with more *sake* to wash it down, of course.

More chanting, shrill flute, and percussion accompanied an unmasked actor, dressed as a *samurai* with a tall cap, and armed with bow and arrow, as he entered the stage with his hunting party. The *samurai* sang of hunting deer deep in the crimson mountains.

"How sublime the autumn view!" he declared.

Encountering the noble lady and her attendants, the *samurai* directed a retainer to investigate. Announcing the presence of his Lord, Taira no Koremochi, the *samurai* inquired, but a lady-in-waiting answered only cryptically, "A certain noble woman."

Not wishing to disturb them, the *samurai* Koremochi and his hunting party moved to leave, but the noble woman stopped him. Speaking of their chance meeting as fate, she invited him to join her. Although Koremochi refused at first, she enticed him to stay.

"In this hidden mountain path, why should I hesitate to share a cup of chrysanthemum *sake*, said to be the elixir of long life?" the chorus chanted Koremochi's assent.

The offer of *sake* garnered Tanuki's full attention, although he had been yawning only moments before. The chorus continued to sing of autumn leaves scattered over mossy rock, and of the lady's face, shining amid the scattered autumn leaves.

"How ethereal her beauty!" the *samurai* declared.

"Koremochi's heart pounded like a mountain cherry tree in a storm."

The chorus sang of their fated meeting, as the lady poured more *sake* and danced, swaying gently, flourishing her golden fan, while the *sake* softened the *samurai*'s resolve.

"Oh, beautiful mountain leaves!" the chorus chanted.

"Beautiful autumn leaves," the noble woman echoed the chorus as she danced, casting a spell on Koremochi, who grew sleepy from the warm drink and the enchanting rhythm of her dance until he fell fast asleep.

Upon seeing that her spell had worked, the noble woman began to dance faster and faster, until finally she disappeared into the wooded mountain to the sound of chanting, drums, and flute. Tarō watched the dim stage, wondering what came next.

As the *samurai* slept, another figure approached along the covered walkway. Holding a sword aloft, the deity Hachiman, his mask that of an old man with a large forehead, flat nose, and growing whiskers, entered the stage to the plunk and knock of drums and whistling flute. Chanting in the *samurai*'s dreams, the deity warned Koremochi that the noble woman was but a demon in disguise.

"How fitting," Lord Honda said during a lull in the music, "that our diversion should mirror our Lord's recent encounter!"

Lord Tokugawa looked to his Karō who bowed, grateful that anyone had acknowledged his homage to his Lord's deliverance. His Lordship nodded quiet approval, and everyone's attention returned to the stage as the music rose.

Bestowing a holy sword to vanquish the demon, and with a stamp of his foot, the deity urged Koremochi to wake before it was too late. Starting awake, Koremochi spoke of his drunken sleep and how a revelation came to him in a dream.

Seizing the divine sword gifted from Hachiman no Kami, Koremochi steeled himself. He wrapped his head with a white *hachimaki* to prepare for battle, while the chorus chanted about the terrible lightning coursing across the sky, and the thunder rumbling so it shook the earth, and an ill wind blowing.

"How frightening to be alone in the middle of nowhere!" the chorus chanted.

Amid this tempest, the noble woman and her ladies-in-waiting returned, dressed in scarlet and gold, their heads covered with matching hooded capes. As they crept along the covered walkway toward the stage, Tarō leaned forward in rapt anticipation.

The strident chanting, drums, and flute quickened until the demons shed their hooded capes, revealing bright red, bushy hair and fearsome masks with golden horns and fangs, their mouths twisted in evil grimaces, while they brandished burning maple branches. Seeing them, Koremochi calmly drew his divine sword.

The music sharpened. The demons stamped their feet and whirled around the *samurai* in a furious dance, as the chorus sang of the battle. Watching the whirling demons, Tarō reeled from the *sake* in his head, as Koremochi sprang into action, slashing at the demons with his celestial sword until, one by one, he vanquished all but the chief demoness. She was the hardest to defeat, as she locked limbs with him in mortal struggle, intent on tearing him to pieces until, at last, he wrenched free and stabbed her torso.

The she-devil grabbed Koremochi by his hair, trying to fly away with him, but he slashed at her with Hachiman's holy sword. Then she cringed and climbed atop a rock, but he dragged her down, slaying her, and she fell dead with a resounding thud.

Koremochi struck a stance, stamping his feet triumphantly. As he turned, the audience clapped their hands rhythmically, punctuated by enthusiastic shouts.

Servants lit the candles in the room again. The doors behind Tarō and Tanuki remained open to the pleasant spring evening, but they turned their attention to the table again, as servants brought dessert of fresh strawberry and loquat fruits, and *sakuramochi*, a pink rice cake filled with sweet red bean paste and wrapped in a cherry blossom leaf.

"An auspicious end to this celebration, but there is still the matter of the attack on our Lord—" Lord Honda said abruptly.

The other *daimyō* grunted soft agreement. The Karō looked to his Lord who drew a breath but said nothing.

"The *kappa* dressed as a monk?" Lord Honda pressed.

"No," the Karō corrected. "The monk transformed himself into *kappa*."

"It does seem far-fetched, a human turning himself into an animal," said Lord Ii, who sat beside Tanuki.

Uncle Tanuki shifted nervously on his cushion, feigning agreement. The talk of human politics bored Tarō, who helped himself to Tanuki's *sake*, which Kamehime and Nun Tokiko observed with disapproval since it was considered very bad manners to serve oneself.

"If he had turned into a monkey, I would not have been surprised," Lord Sakai said.

The other lords and the Karō grunted amused agreement.

"I think we all can assume this was no coincidence," Lord Sakakibara stated, "the only question, 'Who gave the order?'"

"The monks have grown powerful again in their stronghold on Mount Hiei," Lord Honda offered, "but they have no quarrel with our Lord. So, who stood to gain?"

"Lord Oda has no love for the monks," Lord Ii replied.

"True," Lord Sakai said, "but what of Lord Monkey?"

"We do not know this to be true," Lord Sakakibara said.

"But surely Hashiba is suspect," Lord Sakai replied.

"For the time being we must keep an even more watchful eye than before," Lord Tokugawa said at last. "Fortunately," he added, "I have a new bodyguard."

This praise for Tarō drew a frown from Kamehime. Her father saw her look but feigned ignorance.

"Of course, Tarō must receive training in the ways of *samurai*," Lord Tokugawa said. "Tomorrow, my sword master will take charge of your training here in the castle."

Tarō shrugged, drunk and unimpressed. "I don't need a sword," he said boastfully.

"There's more to being *samurai* than a sword," Kamehime snapped, forgetting herself.

Her nurse leaned close to quietly remind her of her place, and Kamehime frowned at the censure.

"It's a pity Lady Kamehime was born a girl," the Karō said, trying to mend the awkward moment for all but Kamehime, who continued to fume, fanned by the perceived slight, though the Karō made amends by adding, "To see her ride with bow and arrow or spar with spear or sword, one would think she stood among the noblest of *samurai*."

At this unexpected praise, Kamehime bowed gracefully.

"But she's so small and skinny," Tarō said unwittingly, without the slightest notion of etiquette or diplomacy, especially where girls were concerned.

"Well, you're—" Kamehime glared, stuttering, "*baka*!"[6]

In that moment, Tarō realized why Kamehime looked so familiar. *She* was the handsome young *samurai* he had seen the day he bested the *kappa*. Tarō stared, speechless.

"You must forgive My Lady," Nun Tokiko interjected, speaking for the first time in her gravelly voice, "it is hard to raise a daughter without her mother."

As soon as she uttered the words, Nun Tokiko froze, glancing at her Lord and bowing her head to the ground in mortification. Kamehime bowed diplomatically and rose quickly.

"My Lady will retire," Nun Tokiko said hastily, pausing for Lord Tokugawa's assent.

Her Lord nodded without expression, and she turned to follow Kamehime, who left with a curt bow but without even a backward glance at Tarō. He hung his head, quietly chiding himself through the rest of the evening without a care to join in the conversation, drowning his shame with more *sake*.

*Musashi Province*

*Spring, Year of the Rat*

Still wounded from his embarrassing encounter with Kamehime, and half-drunk, Tarō stumped after Tanuki in human disguise with his belly sloshing side to side as he waddled over Nihon Bridge and through the dark streets of Edo. Uncle Tanuki stopped to take a swig from his jug

---

[6] [馬鹿], "horse-deer," idiot or fool, especially as an expletive.

of rice wine, then catching sight of his destination just ahead of them, he nudged Tarō to follow.

"This should cheer you up!" Tanuki encouraged, quickening his pace.

They arrived at a tall wooden gate under guard, the only entrance to the infamous pleasure quarter of Edo. The sign over the gate read, "*Yoshiwara*."

At the entrance, an ugly old man dressed in a shabby monk's habit accosted them.

"Prayers," he crowed, "prayers for *ichi mon*."

"Ha!" Tanuki laughed, his belly rippling under his *kimono* as he quizzed Tarō on human speech. "*Ichi mon*?"

As Tarō puzzled, Tanuki pointed to the great gate.

"You don't need to pray when a few coins will get you into heaven's gate here," Uncle Tanuki said with a lecherous wink, nodding toward a courtesan just inside the gate.

Tarō still looked confused. Tanuki laughed, waving it off.

"Prayers," the monk crowed again, "prayers for a copper."

Uncle Tanuki nodded. Reaching into his *kimono* sleeve, he produced a purse and gave the monk a coin.

"Thank you, good sir," the old monk said with a grin, which only made him look uglier still.

The monk gave Uncle Tanuki a wooden plaque painted with the Buddha of the Western Paradise. Tanuki huffed sacrilegiously and passed the plaque to Tarō, who studied the Buddha's serene face, intrigued. The old monk watched as Tarō and Uncle Tanuki passed through the gate into the pleasure quarter.

"Welcome to the floating world!"[7] Tanuki declared.

Tanuki moved eagerly and quickly on his human legs. Tarō had to skip to keep up with him, as they traversed the red-lantern-lit back

---

[7] *Ukiyo* [浮世], a term referring to the urban lifestyle, especially its self-indulgence, also ironically alludes to a homophone [憂き世], "sorrowful world," the earthly plane of death and rebirth from which Buddhists seek release.

streets crowded with common folk and *samurai* in search of a good time. The latter could be recognized by their *daishō,* the long and short swords thrust in their sashes, although many tried to maintain some anonymity and discretion by covering their heads with wide-brimmed sedge hats like mushroom caps or umbrellas of brightly colored, oiled paper. Still, some were not so discreet, already drunk with wine and lust as they lasciviously perused the courtesans on display behind the grated windows of the various establishments, while hawkers in their mushroom caps noisily plied their trades to passersby.

The peddlers squatted beside the way, and customers paused here and there to purchase their wares, tobacco, candies, and *bentō* meals among the most popular items. The mix of aromas made Tanuki's head spin, and Tarō had a good laugh at his expense.

Many of the women in the quarter wore lavishly patterned and colored *kimono*, their gorgeous sashes knotted in front, their large black wigs adorned with hairpins standing out like pegs on a *shamisen*, and their bare feet in wooden *geta*, as was the custom and fashion for women of their station. The *oiran*, the highest-ranking courtesans, had entourages of young apprentices in matching *kimono* to complement their mistresses, strolling the streets like floating floral bouquets. Tarō's eyes grew big, as Uncle Tanuki whispered lewdly to him, rubbing his fingers together as he pointed out the rich merchants and well-to-do *samurai* whose measure could be taken by the beauty of the women clinging to them.

"Come on," Tanuki whooped, "let's splurge until we drop!"

Uncle Tanuki led the way as if by smell, raising his nose to take in the myriad aromas of the street vendors, but he nearly lost his partner when Tarō stopped to listen to a woman plucking on a *shamisen*, her exquisite features and extravagant *kimono* partially hidden behind a grated window. A small crowd had gathered to listen to the plaintive twang of her instrument, a solitary note that rushed headlong into a frantic and passionate poem. The audience applauded fervently when she finished.

"Is she—" Tarō started to ask, but Tanuki rebuked him with a frown and led him away.

"No," he said, "she is *geisha*. The *geisha*'s beauty is in her skill to delight. The others—" Tanuki paused, then grinned, "well, I guess their skills also delight!"

Uncle Tanuki guffawed at his own joke. He stopped to take a big swig of rice wine from his jug and caught sight of courtesans waving to him from the windows of yet another brothel.

"Ah! I know what will lift your spirits," Tanuki said with a randy grin. "Come on!"

Tarō frowned, but he faithfully followed his friend, who had already bounded across the street toward the brothel.

"What is this place?" Tarō asked naively.

"It's a tea house."

"I don't like tea."

"You'll like this tea!"

Uncle Tanuki ducked through the *noren,* the split curtain over the open door. A lovely young woman in a colorful checkered green *kimono* and a bright orange sash greeted them.

"Two esteemed guests, welcome!" the hostess said, inviting them into the earthen foyer.

They removed their *zōri*, which she carefully arranged among the footwear of other patrons who had already gone inside. She guided them into the house, down a long corridor and into a raised great room of *tatami* mats arranged with many low tables surrounded by cushions, some of which were occupied by guests engaged in conversation, eating, drinking, smoking, and gambling on *sugoroku* boards, all of which delighted Uncle Tanuki.

The air smelled of perfume, stale wine, and smoke. Even the women smoked from long, delicate pipes. At one end of the room, a square space accommodated a sunken hearth in the floor, over which hung an adjustable pot rack of iron and wood carved in the likeness of a carp. Smoke rose from the firepit, mingling with the patrons' burning tobacco to weave its way around the ceiling in an undulating cloud, a shadowy dragon stalking the room.

Their guide paused to allow another servant, a young man carrying a paper lantern, to pass into the dim hallway ahead of them, followed by an elderly gentleman in commoner's clothing. They quickly disappeared down the hallway into darkness.

"Where are they going?" Tarō asked innocently.

Tanuki peered down the hall and nodded.

"Tea time."

Staff and patrons paused to stare as Uncle Tanuki and Tarō entered. Some gave them dirty looks, but all soon resumed their conversations when the lady of the house greeted them.

"Isn't he a little young," the madam said of Tarō.

Tarō frowned.

"He has a boyish face, that's all!" Uncle Tanuki said with a laugh, flipping a coin in the air. "Just a couple of drinks," Tanuki said with a grin.

The madam deftly caught the coin.

"Are you sure that's all you want," she asked, flirting and tickling his chin. "You're just my type, you know, big man!"

Tanuki chuckled. The madam clapped her hands and a servant brought *sake*, smoked squid, and pickled vegetables.

"Ah!" Tanuki said, his face lighting up. "Just the thing!"

Still morose, Tarō greedily grabbed the pitcher of *sake* and turned it up, chugging it in one go, which only piqued Tanuki.

"That's the spirit!" he laughed, then laughed again, pleased with his joke. "Get it? You know, spirit. Spirits. Rice wine? Good one, eh? We'll need another pitcher," he said to the waitress, "better make it two!"

Already drunk, three boisterous, off-duty *samurai* in Tokugawa colors, the hollyhock crest on their *kimono*, sat nearby. Impatient for the waitress' return, Tarō swiped the *sake* pitcher from their table and helped himself, downing it straightaway.

"Hey, boy!" one *samurai* growled and stood drunkenly.

Tarō's eyes narrowed. Uncle Tanuki shook his head, sensing trouble, as Tarō rose to the challenge. The *samurai* stepped back in alarm at this "boy" who stood as tall as he. The *samurai* reached for his sword, but Tarō quickly grabbed him by his collar and tossed him like a straw doll toward the back of the brothel. The *samurai* landed on a servant carrying a tray of drinks that hit the floor with a crash and clatter.

His cohorts jumped to their feet, but Tarō grabbed the table in front of him, holding it up as a shield just as the two men plunged their swords into the wood. While they tried to pry loose their blades, Tarō used the table to corral both men, forcing them out the window with a crash.

The first *samurai* got to his feet, reaching for a bottle from a nearby table, intent on breaking it over Tarō's head, but he tripped over debris on the floor and fell headlong into a courtesan's bosom. The young woman screamed, slapping the clumsy *samurai* so he reeled into another man who jostled yet another. Soon an all-out fight broke loose between the patrons.

The madam yelled for help in vain, jumping up and down in frustration as she watched tables and cushions and dishware take flight all around the room, while patrons put holes in walls and latticed windows and doors. Incensed, the madam broke a pitcher of *sake* on a rowdy patron as he plowed through one wall, his head the perfect target.

Tanuki led Tarō to the far side of the firepit, out of the fray, and they both plopped onto cushions to watch as the commotion continued. Tarō discovered a full pitcher of *sake* and, up-ending it until the last drop had fallen on his tongue, he suddenly dropped the pitcher and fell backward in a deep, drunken sleep.

When Tarō awoke, he found himself sitting next to a bashful Uncle Tanuki, who was trying hard to prop him up, but Tarō kept slumping this way and that. Slowly, the room came into focus, some chamber within Edo Castle. Tall candles lit the four corners, two more on either side of Lord Tokugawa, who sat on the raised floor at the head of the room. Dressed in a light robe and clutching a folding fan, he looked down on Tarō and Uncle Tanuki with a furrowed brow. Several guards knelt on either side of them. Tarō tried to sit straight but continued to teeter, so Tanuki had to tug frequently to keep him upright.

"My nephew never could hold his wine." Tanuki shrugged his shoulders apologetically.

"When I said fight," Lord Tokugawa shouted, annoyed, "I meant for me!"

"Yes, yes," Uncle Tanuki said, patting Tarō. "A thousand pardons, my Lord. He's just a boy. He only wanted to blow off a little steam. He'll be ready for work by morning."

"We shall see," Lord Tokugawa said, shaking his head.

He waved them away with his fan, and Uncle Tanuki quickly obliged, although Tarō nearly fell on top of him when they stood. The guards carted Tarō off. Uncle Tanuki smiled nervously and bowed profusely as he backed out of the room to follow.

Tarō slept fitfully that night, moaning so it kept Tanuki awake. While Tanuki tossed and turned, trying to stop his ears with his hands, Tarō dreamed again of Fūjin and Raijin, the Gods of Wind and Thunder, their crystal eyes flashing at him through some terrible tempest.

5

# ISLAND BOY

*Musashi Province*

*Spring, Year of the Rat*

Tarō lay sprawled across the *tatami* floor so he might have been mistaken for dead. Uncle Tanuki lay on another *futon* beside him, snoring like the roar of an ocean on a rocky shore. A shadowy man stood over them, shaking his head scornfully. With a sword made of split bamboo and a snap of his massive wrist, he gave Tarō a smart rap on his skull. Tarō groaned and stirred, rubbing the knot on his head.

"I am Yagyū Jūbei, son of sword master Yagyū Munenori," the man said imperiously. "Lord Tokugawa has ordered me to tutor you, and I shall obey." He frowned at his so-called pupil. "If you are to serve our Lord, you must train as *samurai*."

"*Samurai*," Tarō scoffed groggily.

Master Yagyū gave Tarō another smart rap on the head with his bamboo *shinai*.

"Training begins and ends with respect!" he said, lowering his sword, inviting Tarō to attack.

Tarō rose slowly, his head swimming from his hangover. Thinking of Yama Uba's mirror, he panicked and quickly felt for it, but finding it in his *kimono* sleeve, he sighed.

He stood, annoyed by his needless panic at his waking and the pounding in his head, especially when he saw his tormenter, a solid man of middle age.

Master Yagyū did not stand quite as tall as Tarō. Although he dressed as *samurai*, in a plain, light brown *kimono* and dark brown *hakama*, and he wore the long and short swords in his sash just as *samurai*, he did not have a topknot. Instead, his head was as bare as a priest's, except for the stubble covering the back of his pate to his crown, and he wore a thin mustache and beard running along the edge of his jaw to sideburns that wisped backward over his ears, giving him a foxlike appearance.

Tarō mustered himself and faced off, striking an angry, arrogant pose, arms folded over his chest, looking down his nose at Lord Tokugawa's sword master. Uncle Tanuki broke the tension when he woke himself with a tremendous fart. He rolled over, opening his eyes and smacking his lips.

"Breakfast?" he asked, smiling sleepily.

Master Yagyū's definition of breakfast disappointed Tanuki terribly: a single bowl of steamed rice, pickled radish and eggplant, and smelly, sticky fermented soybeans with soy sauce and yellow mustard that pinched Tarō's nose and made his eyes water.

"That's all?" Uncle Tanuki asked sadly.

Master Yagyū only huffed and grunted, "Training!"

Tarō tugged uncomfortably on his training clothes, a *kimono* and short *hakama* trousers bound by leggings. Spring had vanished overnight, and the morning already sweltered as they followed Master Yagyū to the training ground where the castle garrison had been drilling since first light. They marveled at the hundreds of men sparring hand to hand, or with sword or spear, *samurai* on foot or on horseback with bow and arrow, taking perfect aim at straw bale targets on wooden stands, and *ashigaru* foot soldiers firing their *tanegashima* matchlocks in formation, with flashes and thunderclaps that surprised Tarō and Tanuki and made them jump.

"So," Master Yagyū said perfunctorily. "Let us begin with the basics." He nodded to a bare patch of ground in one corner of the training area. "Wrestling."

Although he still winced from his pounding head, Tarō managed an assured smile. On one earthen paddock nearest them, a *samurai* extended his hand to a thrown opponent to help him to his feet. They bowed and quickly ceded the ring to Master Yagyū, who motioned for Tarō to follow him onto the paddock.

"So," Master Yagyū said, "let's see what you are made of—"

Tarō took a step back and hunkered down, facing Master Yagyū, who frowned and shook his head. He turned to the opposite side of the ring, where Kamehime stood, dressed as *samurai* again—in *kimono*, *hakama*, and leggings—hands on her hips and a resolute smile on her face that seemed to say, "karma."

"I'm not going to fight a girl," Tarō huffed.

Kamehime's eyes narrowed. Tarō fixed his eyes on Master Yagyū, but his boyish impudence only drew a thin, inscrutable smile from the sword master who waved his hand in invitation.

"You will not be finished with your training until you have bested her in each of the *samurai* arts," Master Yagyū declared.

Tarō stared back with foggy disinterest.

"I'll fight her if it means we get an early lunch!" Uncle Tanuki offered.

Master Yagyū waved his hand once more in invitation for Tarō to enter the ring. Tarō sighed and shook his head, wincing again from his hangover.

"I don't want to hurt you."

"I'll try not to hurt you," she replied with a half-smile.

As if on cue, the morning turned overcast and the sky rumbled. They faced off, Kamehime relaxed and ready, Tarō foggy and unsteady. As she feigned entry, Tarō lunged, but Kamehime slipped behind him and shoved on his back. He lost his balance for an instant but quickly recovered and wheeled. Annoyed with himself, he shook his skull to clear it.

Kamehime smiled and cocked her head as if to say, "point!"

He did not show it, but Master Yagyū smiled as the sky darkened and rumbled again. Tarō slapped his muscles beneath his *kimono* and squared off. This time, he took a menacing step forward and feigned entry, but again Kamehime deftly countered.

"She is not a bad student," Master Yagyū told Uncle Tanuki who jumped at the chance to make a wager.

"Not bad?" she protested over her shoulder, as she narrowly dodged another lunge by Tarō.

"Precisely," Master Yagyū said, smiling.

Still, try as he might, Tarō could not get a hold on Kamehime who countered again and again until, finally, his head pounding obstinately, he succumbed to frustration and lunged in anger. Just then, Kamehime slipped her hips beneath him, grabbing hold of his arm to throw him over her back with such flowing force that he hardly felt his broken balance until he toppled and hit the ground so hard it knocked a tremendous belch out of him. Kamehime recoiled in amused disgust.

"Well, I did not see that coming," Tanuki sighed, surrendering a few coins to Master Yagyū.

When Tarō recovered, he quickly checked the safety of Yama Uba's mirror. Satisfied with its apparent indestructibility, it only made him lament his loss all the more. *Beaten by a girl,* he thought, as he clutched his pounding head and groaned, and the sky rumbled once more.

"I'm not all here," Tarō offered in his defense.

"So," Tanuki said, looking at the forbidding sky, "lunch?"

"Spears!" Master Yagyū snorted.

The sword master took two strides to grab *mochiyari*, which he tossed to Kamehime and Tarō, but the heavens suddenly thundered overhead as lightning flashed across the sky like *gintsukuroi* silver on the cracks in a black *raku* bowl, and Tarō flinched in surprise. Kamehime snatched her spear from the air, but Tarō's fell at his feet.

Master Yagyū shook his head, unimpressed, which only goaded Tarō further. He snatched his spear from the ground to face Kamehime.

Rain came hard as the heavens flashed and thundered above them. Tanuki bounded for cover, but Master Yagyū stood his ground, oblivious to the storm, scrutinizing Tarō and Kamehime as they sparred, each striking at the other, slashing and stabbing, advancing and retreating in turn, targeting the other's openings, each barely dodging the sharp, flashing points of their spears. All the while Master Yagyū watched Tarō with a discerning eye, as a great teacher recognizes a prodigy, but Tarō's natural talent only made the sword master all the more suspicious. *Who was this boy?* he wondered as he stroked his mustache pensively.

Lightning flashed again, zigzagging across the sky as Kamehime stabbed over Tarō's shoulder, the steel tip of her spear glinting just beside his face. A vision of Raijin's flashing eyes surprised and blinded him for an instant. With one hand, he lunged and thrust wide, and Kamehime dodged his stab. Grabbing his spear with one free hand, she wheeled and rolled her body along the spear's length, wrenching it from his hands and tossing it to the ground. Then, grasping the handle of her spear close to its tip with both hands, she stabbed for Tarō, grazing his arm as he narrowly dodged the blow, but not before she drew first blood.

"Good!" Master Yagyū congratulated Kamehime again.

"I told you," Tarō growled, "I'm not feeling so sharp today."

"Empty cups at night will fill the head in the morning!"

Tarō snarled.

"The best lessons are self-taught," Master Yagyū countered.

Kamehime smiled, even though she was exhausted from the effort. As Tarō sulked, clutching his pounding head, the heavens suddenly poured on them.

Although the lightning and thunder eventually subsided, the deluge did not abate. The rainy season had come to Edo, but it did little to deter Master Yagyū, who insisted on Tarō training with Kamehime from dawn to dusk, day after day, throughout the relentless rain. Hand to hand, sword and spear, bow and arrow, Tarō's aptitude for the *samurai* arts of *jūjutsu, kenjutsu, sōjutsu,* and *kyūjutsu* surprised and pleased the sword master, who wore his sedge hat and bushy rice-straw raincoat as he stood scrutinizing their matches in the pouring rain, but it annoyed the sodden Kamehime, who soon realized that only her devotion could compete with Tarō's natural talent.

In the evenings, long after their training had ended, when they dined or sipped roasted barley tea after dinner, while the rain pattered obstinately outside and poured from the castle eaves and the frogs croaked loudly in the castle moat, Tarō barely attended Master Yagyū's rambling talk of martial philosophy. From time to time, Kamehime, who hung on her *sensei*'s words, would catch Tarō daydreaming and elbow him to pay attention.

"There is much more to being *samurai* than a sword," Master Yagyū continued.

Tarō sighed. "I don't care to be *samurai*."

"You like to fight?"

Tarō nodded.

"Why?" Master Yagyū pressed.

"I like to win!" Tarō said.

"To live by the sword is to die by the sword," Master Yagyū responded with his inscrutable smile.

Tarō cocked his head quizzically.

"Martial training is *bushidō,* a way of life," Master Yagyū said. "It is not a series of contests to be won or lost, but an aspiration for self-refinement and harmonious existence that transcends animalistic warfare." Master Yagyū was deadly earnest in his lecture as he continued, "Otherwise, one's life is condemned to the perpetual uncertainty of physical struggle, to win against lesser opponents, lose to stronger ones, and draw against equals."

"At least, you know who you are," Tarō said.

"By comparison with others, yes," Master Yagyū conceded, "but who are you, Tokuyama Tarō?" he countered abruptly, scrutinizing his enigmatic pupil, his question more than rhetorical.

Tarō had no answer, and long after they went to bed he gritted his teeth that Master Yagyū had got the best of him. His thoughts kept him awake through the night. When at last he slept, he dreamed fitfully of lightning and thunder, while he battled some imagined foe that strangely resembled himself.

The warm rains and Tarō's training continued through midsummer's day when Kamehime and Tarō took to horse to compete with bow and arrow. A long, low roofed gallery and thickets of hydrangea bordered the castle's archery track. Frogs croaked loudly from their hiding places around the muddy grounds. Without question, Tarō had an affinity with his horse, which Master Yagyū recognized immediately, and Kamehime watched curiously, enviously, as Tarō spoke to his animal, seemingly in conversation, the horse whinnying and stamping in response.

"Are you coming?" she shouted, mounting her steed.

Tarō spoke, and his horse whinnied his reply. He leaped astride it to gallop into the field after Kamehime, each taking aim with their turnip-shaped arrows as they passed the wooden targets at regular intervals along the course, their horses kicking up mud as they raced along the flooded track through the driving rain.

Taro and Kamehime Compete

Kamehime demonstrated exemplary poise in *tachisukashi*, holding her hips just slightly above the saddle to maintain her stability so her torso barely moved even at full gallop. She struck and split all three targets. Tarō seemed to have met his match, for although he had some talent with bow and arrow he could not compete with Kamehime, who had been training in the bow nearly all her life and *kyūba no michi,* mounted archery, since she could ride.

The competition exasperated Tarō. Round after round, Kamehime struck each target with skillful precision, while Tarō, despite his talent, missed his marks here and there. As they circled back for their final pass, Kamehime sensed Tarō's mounting frustration, which amused and touched her.

"Don't try so hard to hit the target," she offered. "Look inside yourself. Clear your mind. Put yourself in the target. You, your horse, your bow and arrow, the target, all one," she recited, looking gratefully to her master, who nodded approval.

Kamehime's kind words surprised Tarō. He nodded and spoke to his horse, rubbing its neck, and it snorted its assent.

Tarō nocked another arrow to his bowstring. He closed his eyes, breathing deeply, summoning all of his *ki*, and urged his horse to gallop forward into the driving rain, kicking up mud around them. Eyes still closed, Tarō felt the rain stinging his face, he felt the horse galloping beneath him as he steadied himself in the saddle, he felt as one with bow and arrow, raising them overhead and pulling downward with his powerful muscles to draw the hefty bow until the arrow lay against his cheek and the bow itself looked as though it might explode from the strain.

As his horse galloped past the first target, Tarō opened his eyes, but a sudden flash of lightning blinded him. In that instant, he saw a ghost from his past. General Toramasa knelt once more in front of him, gasping from the arrow in his bloody neck. Tarō let loose his arrow in surprise. He missed the target, but the arrow struck the post with such force that it split the timber in two.

Thunder cracked above them, and Tarō's horse balked in fright. Even Master Yagyū looked at the heavens in surprise.

Kamehime rode to inspect the sundered post, and servants ran forward to bear witness, murmuring anxiously. No one had ever seen such a display of strength. Kamehime watched with wonder, as Tarō calmed his frightened horse, and Master Yagyū studied him with even greater interest.

"He is no ordinary boy, that much is certain," Master Yagyū later reported to his Lord.

"We must keep an eye on him," Lord Tokugawa replied, clapping his *tessen,* an iron folding fan, against his other hand.

Master Yagyū grunted agreement and bowed dutifully.

太

*Yamashiro Province*

*Summer, Year of the Rat*

Standing upon the great veranda of Pure Water Temple, surrounded by some thirty courtiers who had accompanied His Imperial Majesty for the view, the prince tried to ignore the blackened hulk of the once august temple. Fire was common, as common as monastic clashes, but the recent incident at Honno-ji had marred his perfect city. The many wide tree-lined avenues and white stone-walled buildings of Kyōto had been neatly laid out so, from this distance, the capital looked like a grand checkerboard for the Emperor and his noblemen to play. The sun had just risen over the main hall behind them and shone brightly upon the elegant, walled city nestled in the midst of verdant hills that rolled toward the horizon like a rumpled, richly brocade *kimono.*

No finer vista of the capital could be had than standing upon the great veranda of Pure Water Temple, the intricate scaffold of timbers beneath the tall wooden stage of its main hall blending gracefully with the wooded hillside. Lush gardens of blue hydrangea grew throughout the temple compound. Nearby, Otowa Falls cascaded into the forest, its torrent rushing toward the glittering track of Duck River as it flowed alongside the city's eastern wall.

"It is still lovely, is it not?" the boy said in a voice that bespoke his life of delicate and refined idleness.

His courtiers were quick to agree. They dressed similarly, like so many gaudy birds, in *eboshi*, their tall, black crow-caps with waving crests, and finely patterned *kimono*, each befitting their relative stations, but the boy stood out among these men, and not simply because of his much smaller stature.

Although he had not yet seen his tenth birthday, he wore the Crown Jewel around his elegant neck, a jade pendant of extraordinary beauty and divine power. He also spoke with a melancholy, educated air, as if he were much older than his age, older even than his noblemen who nodded and bowed fawningly at every opportunity, each of them vying for favor in the boy's eye.

The boy had grown accustomed to obsequious courtiers. He did not truly know who to trust, and many mistook his quiet, aloof demeanor for arrogance, when in actuality he suffered from a crushing loneliness under the weight of a birthright without any real power.

The boy sighed relief as he beheld his handsome imperial palace safely situated to the north, unharmed by the recent fire, its outer wall surrounding a number of Chinese-style buildings with white walls, vermillion pillars, and tiled roofs, and enclosing the separately walled inner palace, the entire complex presiding in perfection over the symmetrical city that lay to the south. The Vermilion Bird Gate, the main entrance to the palace, opened onto a wide avenue that ran through the city center all the way to the Rajōmon, the main gate in the southern city wall. A cloudbank obscured the sun and cast a momentary pall upon the gate.

"The light changes so quickly," the boy said plaintively.

Once again his noblemen were quick to agree, but no sooner had the Emperor uttered these words than he beheld a dreadful sight, as an army of black-clad *samurai* entered the Rajōmon, marching into the peaceful city to the din of ominous horn blasts. The soldiers spilled into the wide Vermilion Bird Avenue and its side streets like ink spoiling a pristine painting. The boy gasped in disbelief.

Cries rose from the city below, as the citizens, *his subjects*, fled before the invading army. The boy stuttered, trying to find any words, while his noblemen clucked anxiously, darting around the veranda like so many frightened birds.

"Your Highness, we must flee the city," said a particularly nervous courtier.

"Where shall we go?" said another.

"We should pray," the boy said at length.

His courtiers quickly agreed, although not without backward glances. Hours passed, and smoke rose in clouds from the incense brazier before the main hall, while the Emperor sat on a cushion of purple silk, meditating in solemn, plaintive prayer to the small gilt statue of the eleven-faced, thousand-armed Kannon that stood behind the brazier.

His noblemen shifted uncomfortably throughout the Emperor's vigil until, at midday, they heard shouts from the wood, followed by the sound of marching feet approaching the temple entrance. The din of their footfalls quickened as a number of black-clad *samurai* in full armor, brandishing their Lord's golden gourd standard, rounded the three-tiered pagoda to overrun the veranda. The fearsome *samurai* quickly corralled the fluttering courtiers.

Wearing full armor and his helmet with its spiked fantail like some evil peacock, Lord Monkey strode forth, his squire at his heel and, one step behind, armed with his cruel *naginata*, the shadowy figure of the *Ikkō-ikki* monk who conferred with Lord Monkey at Enryaku Temple. His squire and the monk paused at the entrance to the oratory, but Lord Monkey strode to the Emperor, who was still praying to the Kannon.

"Your Highness," Lord Monkey said in a grave voice, bowing by habit, though he did not genuflect. "I bring ill tidings."

"Lord Hashiba? I—I thought we were being attacked," the boy said haltingly when he turned and saw the monk looming behind Lord Monkey's squire.

"On the contrary, I am here to protect you." Lord Monkey feigned concern, adding, "Lord Oda is dead."

"Lord Oda?" the boy gasped, staring in disbelief.

"I suspect—well, it is best not to speak of these things until I have safely escorted you back to the palace. Come!"

Although he did not lay a hand on him, Lord Monkey cast some spell of influence on the boy, who rose as if in a trance and meekly allowed himself to be guided from the main hall to his palanquin waiting beside the great veranda. The boy hesitated at the door to his carriage, then climbed inside. With a shout, Lord Monkey waved for his men to depart.

On horseback, Lord Monkey led the way to the imperial palace, callously expecting his foot soldiers to keep pace at double time, which they did without question, arriving at the Courtesy Gate in the Hour of the Sheep. They passed beneath the unpainted, pillared cypress roof into the outer courtyard of the imperial palace, the plastered walls of its buildings bright white in the afternoon light, its crimson columns supporting tiled roofs. Carefully cultivated, venerable pine trees, their twisted limbs braced by timber posts, decorated the courtyard here and there. Otherwise, the palace appeared empty, abandoned. The prince looked out of his carriage anxiously.

They marched quickly to the vermillion Chinese-style Consent Gate, which led to a courtyard of white gravel surrounding the stately Ceremonial Hall with its massive timber pillars and a hipped and gabled roof of brown cypress. On either side of the great hall stood a sacred tree, a cherry to the east, a bitter orange to the west.

The bearers halted at the base of the short flight of stairs to the hall, and the Emperor stepped timidly from the palanquin to meet Lord Monkey who had already dismounted. Again, Lord Monkey bowed from habit but did not genuflect.

"Where is everyone," the prince queried.

"I took the liberty of removing all persons from the palace until we could safeguard your Highness," Lord Monkey explained as they mounted the stairs.

The prince hesitated on the stairs.

"Your majesty?" Lord Monkey coaxed.

Lord Monkey had removed his helmet, but his notoriously ugly face did not inspire trust. Despite his youth, the boy stood almost as tall as the warlord, but he shrank instinctively in the presence of his armor-clad chaperone. Dutifully, he followed Lord Monkey into the Ceremonial Hall.

A long, narrow hallway separated the outer and inner chambers of the great hall. Within the inner chamber, in the middle of a wide open space of wood floor, upon a three-tiered dais, stood an octagonal canopy, supported by vermillion balustrades and veiled with bejeweled curtains. A small statue of a phoenix decorated the apex of the canopy, beneath which an elegant bamboo blind hid the Chrysanthemum Throne from mortal view.

Lord Monkey escorted the Emperor into the throne room, followed by numerous armed guards, his squire, and the monk, who lingered nearby like Lord Monkey's untethered shadow. The monk's presence troubled the prince, who furtively watched the shadow with mounting disquiet.

Lord Monkey nodded, and his *samurai* raised the bamboo blind so the boy could ascend the dais to sit upon the throne, a solid chair of black lacquer. Small lacquer tables flanked either side of the throne. Lord Monkey's *samurai*, his squire, and the monk withdrew to the fore of the great hall, watching the silhouettes of Lord Monkey and the Emperor behind the bamboo blind.

"Lord Oda's death presents a troublesome question, your Highness. Who sought to gain from it? Lord Ishida? Mōri? Tokugawa? Where did this treachery begin. Where will it end? Until we know for certain, your safety is our paramount concern."

"I thank you, Lord Hashiba," the boy said timidly, uncertain, but cowing obediently to the formidable warlord.

Lord Monkey bowed with as much charm as he cared to muster. "My troops will remain in Kyōto for as long as necessary to ensure the safety of your throne."

Speechless, still struggling with his disquiet, the Emperor nodded agreement.

"You look tired, your Highness. How thoughtless of me not to notice sooner. I am certain it has been an exhausting day for you. Perhaps you should retire until dinner?"

The boy nodded meekly. He took his leave after the usual formalities and ate alone that evening, taking no pleasure in the meal, attended only by servants who quietly saw to his needs but dared not speak for fear of the black *samurai* who stood guard outside the prince's chamber.

Meanwhile, Lord Monkey helped himself to the palace library, looking disdainfully through the archive of scrolls by flickering candle light. His squire knelt beside him, while his *yōjimbō*, the monk, stood in a shadowy corner of the room, invisible but for a glimpse of his white cowl in the candlelight.

The Emperor lay awake into the night, still troubling over the day's events when he heard Lord Monkey's muffled voice. The prince slipped from his bed to a corner of his chamber. No one heard him quietly open the hidden door, or when he crept along the secret passage from his bedroom to the library.

As he neared the library, the prince moved even more cautiously, for he saw the faint glow of candlelight at the cracks around the hidden door to the imperial archives, and he heard Lord Monkey's voice behind it. Ever so carefully, the boy leaned close to the door to eavesdrop.

"Are there no maps in this accursed library!" Lord Monkey said angrily, hurling a scroll across the room.

As the scroll unfurled its poetry, his squire leaped after it.

"Leave it!" Lord Monkey snarled, sweeping the table clean with his arm so more scrolls clattered onto the floor.

"My Lord!" a voice called, and a runner appeared, puffing from exertion, accompanied by two of Lord Monkey's bannermen.

"What is it?" Lord Monkey spat.

Aware of the risk, the runner delivered his news with a dry gulp, "My Lord, our spies report—the same peasant who aided Tokugawa on Mount Fuji has taken up residence at Edo Castle."

"Peasant?" Lord Monkey repeated the word distastefully, glaring at the messenger, who immediately dropped from one to both knees. "Lord Tokugawa has an ally who must be dealt with—that is all that matters!"

"My Lord," the messenger said, scrambling backward, but not timely.

Lord Monkey's sword separated his head from his body with one swift cut, and the head tumbled across the floor.

"Now who is the serf and who the nobleman?" Lord Monkey muttered, watching the head of the hapless messenger come to a stop beside the secret door.

When he saw one lifeless eye staring at him through the thin crack in the door, the Emperor recoiled in surprise and fell backward into the secret corridor with a thump.

Hearing the noise, the monk appeared from the shadows, instantly transforming himself, his neck elongating and striking with serpentine agility. His ghastly head crashed through the secret door and, spying the prince, the monk quickly coiled his unnatural neck around the boy, constricting him so he could not move. The monk's hideous head hovered close to the boy's face, teeth yawning menacingly, prepared to strike.

"Hold!" Lord Monkey said to his bodyguard, then to the Emperor in a smooth tone, "my prince, did you have a bad dream?"

The Emperor lay helplessly bound by the monk's coiled neck, staring in disbelief and horror.

"Priest," Lord Monkey said, "there is no need for your protection, the prince is safe," whereupon the monk immediately released the Emperor and resumed his human form.

"*Rokurokubi!*" the boy gasped in terror.

"My prince," Lord Monkey said, looming over the boy. "As I said, you had a bad dream, that is all. You must not worry about your safety in these difficult times. We will always be close at hand. Come now, it is time you get some sleep."

Lord Monkey coaxed the traumatized boy from the secret passageway, taking him under wing to lead him back to his bedroom, but the terrified boy could not sleep. The sun had not long risen when two of Lord Monkey's men came to collect him, tired, unfed, and wearing the same *kimono*, which hung unkempt on his thin frame.

"Ah, good morning, my prince," Lord Monkey said with a smooth smile. "I hope you slept well."

The room was filled with Lord Monkey's *samurai* and the nobility of Kyōto, including the Emperor's skittish retainers from the day before, who murmured anxiously among themselves as the prince took the throne. Lord Monkey knelt dramatically at a distance, hunching forward to keep an eye on the boy's face, although the boy could not look him in the eye.

"My prince," Lord Monkey began loudly, for everyone's benefit, "I have more ill news. It appears that one of the principal clans may have acted in the plot against Lord Oda. It is indeed fortunate I found myself so close to Kyōto that my army could come to your aid."

"What should I do?" the boy asked at last, his voice shaking.

"Under the circumstances, I believe it would be best if you retire to Momoyama Castle, just until this threat has passed."

The boy did not respond. He looked uneasily past Lord Monkey to a corner of the room where the monk stood in shadow.

"Your divine person should not be sullied with politics. Just leave affairs of state to me—for your protection," Lord Monkey said slyly, offering his open hand. "My prince?" Lord Monkey pressed.

Suddenly taking Lord Monkey's meaning, the Emperor looked at the Crown Jewel that hung from his neck.

"I could not appoint thee *Shōgun*—" the Emperor said with naïve superiority.

"My prince," Lord Monkey interrupted, his eyes flashing, but he restrained his temper and continued diplomatically, "No, I could not possibly accept such an appointment. Let it suffice for me to act as Lord Regent in your stead during these difficult times."

The Emperor glanced at Lord Monkey, then hesitantly at the monk standing guard in a shadowy corner of the hall. The boy faltered. Slowly, he removed the pendant from around his neck and held it up, and Lord Monkey quickly bent forward to take it.

Clutching the jewel in his hand, Lord Monkey struck an imperious stance. He surveyed his men, paying no attention to the courtiers, who huddled together like frightened pigeons. His squire scurried forward and knelt.

"Lord Regent!" his man loudly proclaimed, and Lord Monkey's bannermen roared approval.

"Send word to Lords Ishida, Mōri, and Tokugawa—the Emperor commands their presence in Kyōto!" His eyes narrowed in thought. "Lord Katō!" he called to one of his bannermen.

"My Lord!"

Wearing black armor with gold and purple lacing, Lord Katō stepped forward and knelt, his slender, refined face accented by a meticulously trimmed mustache and goatee.

"You know Tokugawa—you will deliver the summons."

Lord Katō glanced at the wan prince and bowed low so his head almost touched the floor. Lord Monkey looked around the great hall and grunted.

"Make ready, your Grace," he said imperiously. "While your life remains in danger, you are best protected from Momoyama Castle." Turning, Lord Monkey gave the boy a stern look. "We shall leave within the hour," he commanded. Then slyly, he gave his own reply, "As you command, your Highness."

Lord Monkey retreated from the dais, striding purposefully through the main hall, leaving the anxious Emperor behind.

"If Lord Tokugawa resists, you must be ready," Lord Monkey threw his command at the shadow as he passed, and the monk stepped forward from the shadows to obey.

*Musashi Province*

*Summer, Year of the Rat*

The rainy season had ended. Beneath the summer sun, Edo Bay shone like a jewel, a glittering, blue-green crescent set in the prongs of land securing it from the dark mantle of the great ocean beyond the bay. The little boat swayed on sloshing sea swells half a league from the nearest landfall. A little island on the southwest side of the bay presented itself at this distance as no more than a dark rock jutting just above the horizon, utterly dwarfed by the imperial profile of Mount Fuji rising over the distant shoreline.

"I don't understand why I have to do this," Tarō groaned.

His chin thrust in the air, face beading sweat from the relentless summer sun, Tarō stood astride the boat, one foot on each of the gunwales at the bow, pumping his brawny legs to keep his balance against the undulating waves rocking the boat. He held his fat wooden sword in one hand, arms folded indignantly over his chest.

"Exactly," Master Yagyū said beneath his sedge hat, as he fanned himself with his *uchiwa*. "That is why it is called 'training.'"

Tarō rolled his eyes. If they weren't so far from shore, he thought he might just dive into the cool water and swim away and be done with all this *samurai* nonsense.

Master Yagyū sat at the stern of the boat, studying his two pupils. Facing Tarō, Kamehime stood between them, with equal footing on each of the gunwales.

"You have tried each other in contest, but winning is the easiest of the three tests we all must pass in life. Now you must try each other in concert. That is the training, to spar in unison, blending with each other's movements, positive and negative as one harmonious exercise, the sum greater than its parts. But if either of you gets my feet wet—" he added, "you both lose! Now," he said, clapping his hands, "continue!"

Upon Master Yagyū's pronouncement, Kamehime did not hesitate but immediately struck Tarō with her oaken sword. Crack! Tarō barely ducked beneath the angle of his own *bokutō* to deflect the heavy blow at the last instant.

Tarō scowled at her as the crack of the wooden swords resounded over the bay, setting sea birds to flight from the rocky shore of the little island. He quickly countered, and the sparring began in earnest as they took turns striking and blocking each other.

Crack! Their swords crashed upon each other, clapping loudly in Tarō's ears. They pumped their legs from side to side, each working to stay balanced on the gunwales.

Crack! The din resounded toward the little island, startling more seabirds to flight.

"Anyone can do it standing still!" Master Yagyū scoffed. "Circle around the boat—but mind you don't get my feet wet!"

"Is that all?" Tarō said haughtily.

"How can you know without trying?"

Tarō and Kamehime intuitively chose to sidestep in opposite directions, each to the left, around the gunwales of the boat, measuring each other's steps to balance one with the other, all the while accounting for the swaying of the boat on the water.

The boat drew nearer to the island, no more than a spit of sandy beach between two rocky points. Jungle covered the rest of the islet, except for a dark cave in the rocky face of the western point. Sea birds cried out, as they wheeled over the rocky promontory, and waves crashed white against the black rock.

"Come, come!" Master Yagyū mocked, "you look like a couple of egrets stalking frogs! Pick up the pace! Attack each other!"

"Caw, caw," Tarō muttered to himself, thinking the sword master as annoying as those squawking sea birds.

Kamehime and Tarō began moving at a quicker pace, striking at each other from opposite sides of the boat, the crack of their swords sounding across the bay again. Kamehime was light of foot, but she envied Tarō's animal prowess. As the little boat yawed over the undulating sea, she was forced to hold out her arms to stay balanced. Even Master Yagyū held fast to the sides of the boat as it slipped into a deep wave, while Tarō seemed to adjust instinctively like a cat on a ledge.

All of a sudden, Tarō leaped to Kamehime's side of the boat to deliver a blow with his wooden sword. Crack! She managed to block the strike, but he leaped back to his side of the boat before she could counter, and she lost her footing.

She pitched and fell into the water with a yelp and a tremendous splash, and the boat rocked and took on a bucketful of water. Master Yagyū quickly stood, but not in time to avoid getting his sandals wet.

Tarō laughed, pleased with himself. He smiled down at Kamehime treading water, and she frowned and splashed him.

"I won!" he proclaimed.

"No," Master Yagyū corrected from his perch on the stern of the boat. "You lost."

Tarō frowned petulantly as Kamehime pulled herself into the boat like a wet cat. She wiped away the tresses of hair plastered to her face and wrung her sodden clothes.

"You lost your partner," Master Yagyū explained. "And you got my sandals wet!"

"Enough training," Tarō said, sweat pouring down his face. "I don't need to train. Just show me who to fight!"

"There is more to being *samurai* than fighting," Master Yagyū corrected. "Action is meaningless without thought, as meaningless as thought without action."

"More than a sword, more than fighting," Tarō muttered. "It sounds like a lot of talk and no action to me."

"You know nothing of true swordsmanship," Master Yagyū scoffed. "Ultimately, every battle is won or lost in one's own mind."

The boat had drifted much nearer to the island. They heard the sound of the waves crashing upon the landfall. The cave yawned black in the rocky face of the western point, where the shrill cries of the sea birds pierced the relentless sigh of the surf. Master Yagyū turned to take in the island.

"You don't know yourself, Tokuyama Tarō," he pronounced sternly. "You are not virtuous. Honor, loyalty, duty to one's family, Lord, and Emperor, to neglect these virtues is disloyalty toward humanity.[8] You are like Sarushima—that island over there," he said, nodding as they drifted closer to shore, "a solitary rock in a vast ocean. You think yourself special because you see only yourself. Your talent is wasted on selfish pursuits."

Tarō fumed, setting his jaw. Master Yagyū was unarmed, but Tarō had tired of this old crow always cawing. On a mean whim, he lunged with a quick overhead strike from behind, thinking to give this "sword master" a gentle rap and a taste of his own "training," but even Kamehime could not follow Master Yagyū's swift response, as he sidestepped Tarō's lunge. In an instant, he reached over Tarō's forward arm to grab the hilt of the *bokutō* between Tarō's hands, his other hand on the spine of the blade, and the reversal came with such force that it tore the sword from Tarō's hands. He lost his footing and fell from the boat into the choppy, cold waves. Disdainfully, Master Yagyū tossed the sword in the water near Tarō and wiped his hands.

Kamehime chuckled, while Tarō splashed and thrashed the breakers with his wooden sword. He found his feet in the shallows and growled and chattered unintelligibly, humiliated and furious as the waves buffeted him in defeat.

Master Yagyū frowned and shook his head. They were close to the island, the boat rocking with the tide breaking against the shore. He moved forward and took hold of the oars. In just a few powerful strokes, he steered backward through the breakers, leaving Tarō to splash around in the shallows until he realized the boat was departing.

"Hey!" he yelled. "What are you doing?"

"Leaving you to yourself," Master Yagyū shouted.

---

8 *Giri* [義理], "right reason," duty encompassing a moral obligation, loyalty, honor, and self-sacrificing devotion.

Tarō waded deeper into the waves, stamping angrily.

"Cool your head!" Master Yagyū declared over the crashing waves. "You cannot hope to subdue another unless you first learn to control yourself." Looking at the island, he added with a smile, "Think on that, Sarushima Tarō!"

Kamehime raised her hand to wave a helpless goodbye, as Master Yagyū continued to row the boat away from the island. Tarō slumped in defeat, the waves crashing around him. Fuming, he watched the boat grow smaller, then retreated to the beach and threw down his wooden sword.

"Go on, go! I don't want to be a *samurai*!" he yelled, but the crashing surf drowned his cry, so no one heard him but a troop of red-faced monkeys chattering wildly in the jungle behind him so it seemed everyone was laughing at him.

6

## THE MIRROR AND THE SHADOW

*Musashi Province*

*Summer, Year of the Rat*

Walking the lee shore of Sarushima, sweating miserably in the sticky heat, Tarō kicked at the surf and sand in anger and frustration. The boat carrying Master Yagyū and Kamehime was long gone, and there was not another soul in sight. Over the steady crashing of the waves, red-faced macaques chattered in the jungle of spiky palms and bushy sea grape trees growing close to the beach. One monkey ventured from the tangled shade of the jungle, curious about their visitor as he stumped past in his dark mood, but Tarō paid no heed, so the monkey retreated once more to the shady jungle.

The beach gave way to an outcropping of rough black rock where the air smelled especially fishy from kelp baking in the sun at low tide. Where the sea had washed over the rocks, it left tide pools filled with myriad sea creatures—starfish, sea cradles, snaky anemones, hermit crabs, mussels, clams and sea urchins. Gulls targeted the latter, grabbing their black spikes to drop them on the rocks and break them open. Their excited cries pierced the air, as Tarō, driven by hunger, robbed them of their prizes, tearing open the spiny globes to scoop out the salty, buttery, golden treasure.

Soon enough, Tarō grew terribly thirsty, which drove him in search of fresh water. Leaping onto the rocks, he saw the cave yawning in the jungle-covered hillside. A big wave crashed and sprayed close beside him as he bounded off toward the cave, the surf hissing below as it tunneled its way into the rocky point, occasionally spouting through fissures and holes in the rocks.

At the mouth of the cave, Tarō found a pool of rain water and drank his fill like an animal dying of thirst. When he recovered, he stared into the dark grotto. Curious, he made his way inside.

The cave was not deep, but the roar of the surf echoed around him. He turned to take in the view from the mouth of the cavern, the sky a disc of deep blue fading upward from the horizon.

Tarō sighed, his lower jaw sticking out defiantly. Without a care for his breeches, he sat with a thump on the damp cave floor, crossing his legs, fists on his knees, staring out of the cavernous porthole into the distant blue beyond, as the surf roared and echoed again.

All day and night, Tarō sat in silent indignation, listening to the relentless sigh of the surf crashing on the rocks outside, watching the mouth of the cave, where first the fiery eye of the setting sun, and then the cold white orb of the moon, stared back at him. The more he stared, the angrier he grew, his chest rising and falling with shorter breaths as he fumed about his predicament. Yagyū Jūbei's words haunted him.

*"You don't know yourself, Tokuyama Tarō."*

The sword master's judgment faded with the returning roar of the surf. Tarō looked at the eye of the moon staring back at him, lighting the cave as it shone through the entrance. Looking at himself glowing in the moonlight, a thought took him. He reached in his *kimono* sleeve and drew forth Yama Uba's little mirror.

*"This will protect you," she said. "Keep it with you always, but listen to me—" she warned, "You must never look in this mirror."*

The mirror was small. He weighed it in his overgrown hand, struggling in debate. He had promised her.

*"But why not?" he asked.*

*"Never mind. Promise me you will never look in the mirror."*

*Yes, he had promised, but why did she not answer him? What secrets had she hidden from him? Where was his father?*

Tarō raised the little mirror. First tentatively, then deliberately, he held it to his face, hoping for some oracle.

Out of the cloudy depth of the mirror, an image swirled, but the silver disc let out a sudden, terrible shriek as the monstrous reflection of Yama Uba, her white hair and piercing black eyes staring at Tarō with cold rage, leaped from the mirror.

"You promised!" she screeched.

The apparition vanished as quickly as it had appeared, but Tarō dropped the mirror in surprise. It clattered onto the rocky cave floor but did not break.

Tarō looked around. If indeed it had been Yama Uba, she was gone. He snatched up the mirror to inspect it for damage. Then he saw someone else's hand on the mirror handle.

Tarō held up his other hand in shock and amazement. He turned the mirror to his face to look at his reflection: It was him, still the same boyish face, but not as big, still the same *kimono*, but hanging loosely on his body. He was no longer big and brawny. Who was this in the mirror? Was it him? Where were his muscles? He looked so small, not his old self at all. By some witchcraft, his power was gone, lost. He was just a scrawny boy, swimming in his oversize clothes.

The surf roared once more outside the cave. Tarō rubbed his eyes in disbelief. He looked into the mirror again: the same reflection, no change in his boyish face, but he looked half as big as his old self. He rubbed the mirror with his overbig sleeve and looked once more, still no change. He grunted in dismay.

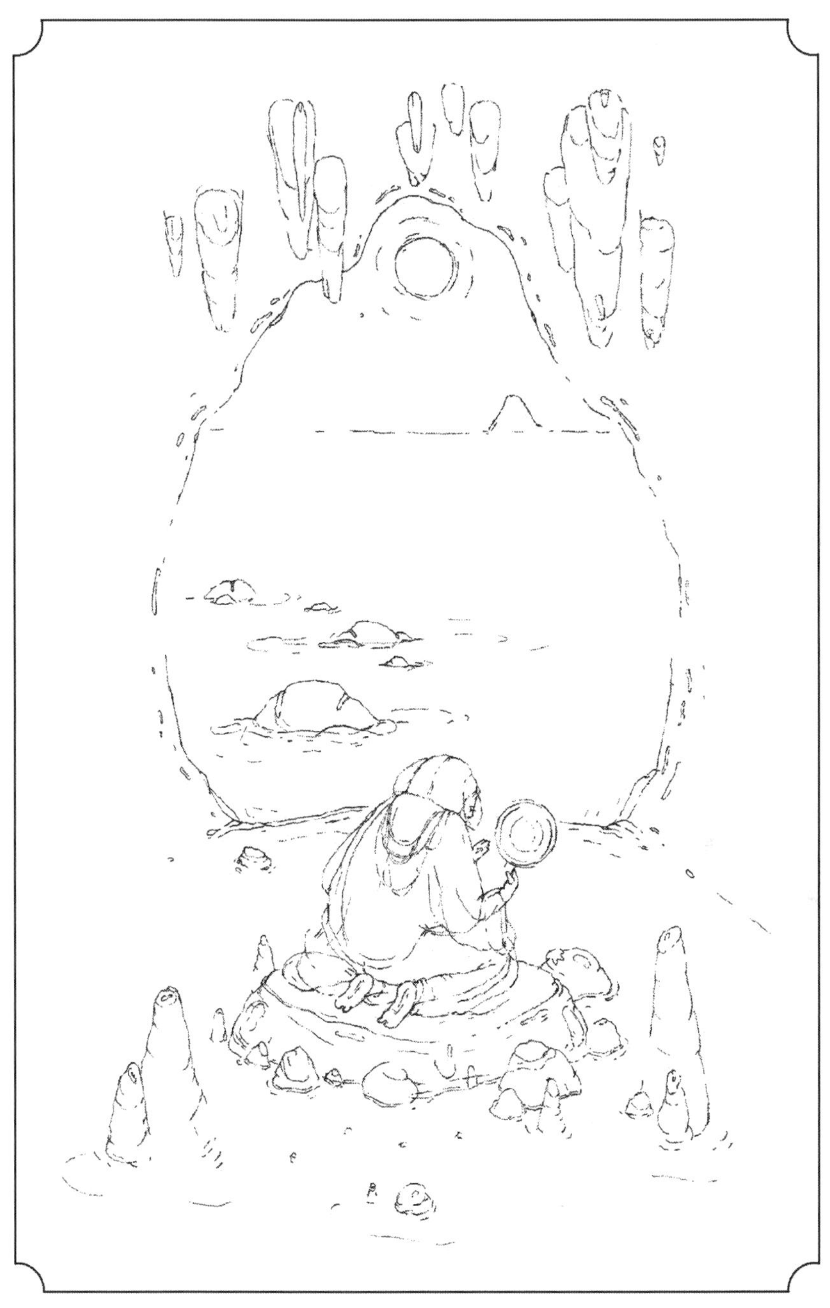

Taro Looks in the Mirror

Stuffing the mirror in his *kimono* sleeve, he stood up quickly. He looked at his hands. Without any doubt, they were smaller. He rolled up one sleeve of his *kimono* and felt his puny arm. Then he felt his thin legs hidden beneath his too big breeches.

"What happened to me?" he cried aloud.

*"Promise me, you will never look in this mirror," Yama Uba's voice echoed in his head. "Say it!" she ordered in her raspy voice.*

*"I promise," he said.*

Tarō looked around in bewilderment.

"No, no!" he cried, shaking his head desperately. "I'm sorry! I didn't mean to—"

The surf roared again, echoing in the grotto. He saw the moon sinking in the deep blue sky, swirling before his eyes until he saw himself in its silver face, just a small boy again, plunging into deep water. His face pinched as he focused, trying to fathom this mysterious vision, but it disappeared into the deep blue beyond.

Spurred by a thought, Tarō straightened. He started for the mouth of the cave, but he found it difficult to move in his oversize leggings and boots. He cast them off, then gathered his *kimono* and breeches and tightened their fit with his sash. Leaving the cave, he emerged in twilight.

Now that he was just a boy, Tarō found navigating the rocks back to the beach a little more difficult than before, but his feet were still tough from years in the wild, and he mustered some of his erstwhile skill, pleased to discover he still had his animal agility, enough to leap across the watery channels in the rocks and scramble back down to the beach.

Tarō made his way along the narrow strip of sand, back to the place where Master Yagyū had marooned him. When he got there, he discovered several red-faced monkeys deviling a giant sea turtle, chattering noisily and beating it with sticks for sport.

"Hey, stop that!" Tarō yelled angrily.

He seized his wooden sword from where it still lay in the sand and brandished it at the monkeys. They quickly took flight for the shadow of the jungle, chattering angrily at him from inside the green tangle.

Tarō smiled at the turtle. The turtle smiled quietly back.

"You're welcome," Tarō said.

"Thank you," the turtle replied, transforming into Tanuki.

"Oh! I didn't recognize you!"

"I didn't recognize *you*!" Tanuki said, looking Tarō up and down and shaking his head. "What happened? You look so—small. You look like you've been stuck here for weeks! You must be—" Tanuki shuddered at the thought, "starved!"

"I looked in Yama Uba's mirror," he confessed, shaking his head sadly.

Tanuki gasped, clapping his paws to his mouth.

"You promised!"

"I know—and now look at me, I—I'm just a boy."

"I guess her magic wore off. I suppose it could be worse."

"How could it be worse? I'm just a boy with no muscles at all! And I still can't remember who I am or where I came from!" Tarō exclaimed, hanging his head.

"Oh, right."

Tanuki shook his head, joining Tarō in a moment of silence.

"What are you doing here?"

"When you didn't come back with Master Yagyū and Kamehime, I thought I should come find you. Shall we go?"

Tarō nodded. Then looking at Edo in the distance, he said, "But not back there."

"What about Master Yagyū. And Lord Tokugawa?"

"Who cares? I don't want to be a *samurai*. I'm done with all that."

"Then where shall we go?" Tanuki asked, knitting his brow.

"There!" Tarō said, looking toward the purple grandeur of Mount Fuji rising above the sea to the south.

Tanuki nodded and smiled. In a flash, he transformed himself into the giant sea turtle again.

"I'll take you!"

Tarō gave the turtle a doubtful look.

"What?" Turtle Tanuki said, looking himself over. "I wasn't going to swim out here as myself!"

Tarō smiled and climbed on top of Tanuki's great shell. Then Turtle Tanuki lumbered toward the sea, and off he swam, paddling for Mount Fuji swelling above the blue ocean ahead of them.

太

*Musashi Province*

*Summer, Year of the Rat*

Chargers nearly ran down a child playing in the roadway—the child's mother pulling her to safety only just in time—as the brigade of *samurai* rode through the humid streets of Edo toward the castle. Lord Katō rode at the head of the contingent, wearing his black armor with gold and purple lacing and a helmet tall like a courtier's hat painted with two large golden circles, one on each side, and a golden crescent crest of metal on the brim. He gained entrance almost immediately when he displayed the imperial seal, but he was bade to dismount, and the bulk of his escort made to wait outside the Big Hand Gate.

A platoon of Tokugawa *samurai* escorted the warlord, his squire, and six of his close retainers from the main gate into the castle, through the maze of corridors and staircases, and finally to the Grand Reception Hall where Lord Tokugawa held audience. Candles lit the corridor. Sentries, ten in all, knelt quietly at their posts along the hallway outside the chamber. A guard slid open the door to the anteroom, where five more guards knelt in front of a second set of *fusuma* painted with gilt screens depicting bushy, twisted pine trees. A transom, elaborately carved with the same motif, spanned the breadth of the set of eight doors.

Two guards, one on each side, took hold of the gilt handles to slide open the central panels, revealing a large rectangular room covered with *tatami* mats running the length to a raised dais, the whole room lit by many candles. Behind the dais, an even more striking tableau greeted the castle guests—venerable pine trees and a noble hawk perched on one of the branches, its sharp eyes focused on the foyer. After the usual obeisance, Lord Katō entered the room, kneeling at a respectful distance from the dais.

"Come, come, old friend, let us not stand on ceremony!" his host said warmly.

Lord Tokugawa sat on a cushion on the dais at the far end, near an alcove equipped with an ornamental shelf and cabinets with decorative doors. The *fusuma* on either side remained closed, hiding other rooms or corridors, or perhaps a host of bodyguards waiting in the wings to come to their Lord's aid on a moment's notice. Beside Lord Tokugawa, his sword stood at the ready on a rack, and behind him sat his squire. Master Yagyū sat in a corner of the room, behind their guest and his men, but remained quiet.

Lord Katō bowed and took his place on the dais opposite his host. The great lords quietly regarded each other, welcoming a peaceful moment before the bad news.

With a courteous bow for disturbing the moment, Lord Katō produced a letter bearing the imperial chrysanthemum. He laid it on the floor with two hands. Lord Tokugawa nodded, leaning forward to take it. Before reading, he glanced at Lord Katō, who remained quiet, then he read without expression and placed the letter to one side. He regarded his guest for a tense moment before speaking.

"So, Oda is dead," he said rhetorically. "Do you stand with Hashiba?"

"I stand with the Emperor," his guest said after a moment's thought.

"As do I."

Lord Katō conceded the point with a half-smile.

Lord Tokugawa glanced at Master Yagyū, who met his look. Now aware of the sword master's presence, Lord Katō bowed in recognition, and the sword master responded in kind.

"Your answer?" Lord Katō asked politely.

"It would be—" Lord Tokugawa said slowly, "imprudent to travel in this heat. Respectfully, I must decline."

"Lord Hashiba will want to be informed immediately."

"I understand."

Lord Katō nodded. He laid his hands on his knees to bow and take his leave.

"It is a pity we cannot drink together."

"*Sake* reveals the true heart," Lord Katō replied.

The two men shared an ironic smile. Lord Tokugawa nodded, and his guest stood and bowed.

"Farewell," Lord Katō said, "old friend."

"Fare thee well—old friend."

"Does this mean war?" Master Yagyū asked, when Lord Katō had gone.

"Perhaps," Lord Tokugawa replied, "but responding to the call would not guarantee peace and could spell doom."

"Then we must be vigilant," Master Yagyū said, nodding grave agreement.

They doubled the castle guard that night, but no one saw the black-clad figure scaling the wall of the main keep in the Hour of the Boar. Ink-black clouds obscured the moon as if by some enchantment. The intruder slipped inside the keep, brutally dispatching first one and then another guard with his short sword. He quietly hid the bodies against discovery, then made his way toward Lord Tokugawa's sleeping quarters.

Slinking from shadow to shadow through the maze of corridors and staircases into the heart of the castle, the *ninja* assassin's pinched face remained covered by his black cowl until he arrived by some witchcraft intelligence in the corridor just outside Lord Tokugawa's chambers. He pressed against the wall to peer around the corner toward his objective—the same cold eyes and sallow face that shadowed Lord Monkey in Kyōto, only now the *Ikkō-ikki Sōhei* was clothed entirely in black, a black cloak hiding his face and a pitch-black *dō-maru* armored corselet covering his torso.

Four guards knelt at the ready just outside Lord Tokugawa's room, so no one could approach along the corridor without immediate detection, but spying open spaces on either side of the transom above the entrance, the *ninja* grinned maliciously. With both hands, the monk removed his cowl, and his head rose ghoulishly from his shoulders, his neck elongating until it curled upward like a serpent rising to strike. The neck continued to stretch unnaturally until its head touched the ceiling, then the *rokurokubi* slunk silently along the rafters toward Lord Tokugawa's chamber.

When it reached the transom, the head paused to grin down at the unsuspecting guards who, although awake, stared in boredom at the dim, empty corridor. The *rokurokubi* squeezed through the open space in the transom to snake into the dark room where Lord Tokugawa lay asleep on his pallet, his head lying on a lacquered headrest.

The *yōkai* assassin descended quietly to the *tatami* and crept along the floor. Nearing its prey, the face distended in hideous delight as it curled menacingly upward, swaying on its neck, poised to strike. Its teeth clicked hungrily and, but for this sound, Lord Tokugawa's life might have been forfeit in that moment. He woke abruptly, dodging in the instant the head struck. The *rokurokubi* missed him and bit into the lacquered headrest instead, its bite so deep that its teeth stuck in the wood. It wildly shook its head, trying to free itself for another strike.

Lord Tokugawa scrambled for his sword, but the *rokurokubi* whipped its neck to trip him up. With another violent shake of its head, it freed its teeth from the headrest, which fell noisily to the floor, alerting the guards.

Dismayed by this turn of events, the *rokurokubi* realized it would soon be outnumbered. As the guards threw open the door, the monk's body emerged from the shadows. With lightning swiftness, the arms whipped sharp *shuriken* from some arsenal within its robes, striking all four men from behind and killing them instantly. Another lash of its neck knocked Lord Tokugawa's sword from its stand and across the room, beyond his reach.

Lord Tokugawa wheeled to face his attacker, bracing himself as it coiled for another strike. Lashing out, its teeth snapped shut on Yagyū Jūbei's blade as he dove into the room just in time to shield his Lord from the deathblow. The teeth bit hard on the cold steel, but the sword master's extraordinary Masamune blade easily withstood the bite.

Master Yagyū tore his sword free with a powerful jerk that sliced the corners of the beast's mouth, and the head shrieked angrily. Before he could counterstroke, the *rokurokubi* struck, biting him across his face and piercing his left eye. Master Yagyū yelled in pain, dropping his sword and flailing his arms, as he wildly tried to free himself from the ghoul's grip.

Diving for his sword, Lord Tokugawa snatched it up and severed the neck in a single stroke, spilling its blood on the *tatami* floor. The neck instantly slumped across the transom and, in the corridor, the monk's body dropped to its knees.

# Lord Tokugawa and the Rokurokubi

Master Yagyū fell backward, clutching at the *rokurokubi* head, its jaws still locked on his face. With Lord Tokugawa's help, he freed himself, but the bite had cost him the use of his eye, rent as it was by the *rokurokubi*'s jagged teeth. Master Yagyū gathered the sleeve of his *kimono* and pressed hard against his face to stop the bleeding.

By this time, a number of guards had arrived to investigate the commotion. They gasped in awe at the slain *rokurokubi*, their lanterns casting ominous shadows around the room.

"My Lord is unharmed?" Master Yagyū asked stoically.

Lord Tokugawa grunted sympathetically. He surveyed the carnage, staring at the *rokurokubi* head, its lifeless eyes staring back at him. He looked again at his faithful sword master's wounded eye.

"*This* means war," Lord Tokugawa declared.

Clutching his eye, Master Yagyū grunted his assent.

*Kai Province*

*Summer, Year of the Rat*

The shrill chirping of cicadas filled the forest around them as Tarō and Tanuki hiked uphill, pushing their way through thickets of late-blooming purple wisteria hanging from the cryptomeria. Fog weaved through the tall cedars as they approached Yama Uba's cave, the shrilling of the cicadas reaching a crescendo. A curtain of lavender blossoms obscured the dark hole. Tarō stepped to the mouth of the cave and pushed aside the purple tendrils to enter.

"I—I think I'll just wait out here," Tanuki said.

Tarō felt his way into the dark cave, one hand on the rocky wall. The air was cool and moist, and the darkness quiet except for the tread of his feet. Once his eyes adjusted to the dark, Tarō saw the calcified stalactites again, hanging like battle spears above him. He was alone. The bats had gone. He closed his eyes. The darkness flashed, and a voice whispered and echoed in the cavern.

*"Tarō, we must hide—"*

Tarō looked around.

"Mother?" Tarō called, and the chamber echoed, "Mother?"

When no answer came, Tarō moved deeper into the cavern until the darkness lightened as he came to the blue luminescent chamber where Yama Uba once dwelled. There was no sign of her, just a dim, bare chamber, and the faint sound of water dripping into a shallow pool somewhere deeper within the cavern.

"She's gone," Tarō said, when he rejoined Tanuki, who relaxed to hear it.

"Now what?"

"I don't know. I—I thought maybe she could—"

Tarō sighed deeply and headed back into the forest noisy with cicadas.

"That's okay, my friend," Tanuki said pluckily, as he bounded after Tarō. "I like a mystery!"

They heard the muffled thunder of the nearby waterfall, and soon they arrived at the great *torii* gate of Fuji Hachiman Shrine. Once again, Tarō heard the hollow plunk of the bamboo water hammer greet him from the shrine compound above.

Tarō wasted no time climbing the stairs two at a time to the Twilight Gate, and Tanuki followed, giving Raijin an evil eye as they passed inside. Raijin's shining eyes stared back unperturbed.

Tanuki sniffed the air. Sandalwood smoke wafted into the courtyard from an incense brazier, and they heard a faint chanting of many voices inside the oratory.

"The priests are awake now, you know," Tanuki said. "Maybe I'd better—"

Tanuki looked around, quickly transforming himself into Tarō's rotund uncle.

"How may I be of service?" a voice inquired behind them.

Tanuki barked in surprise, then coughed to hide it. Tarō turned to see the priest with the kind, insightful eyes who had once tried to tame him with rice balls. As the priest cocked his head in recognition, the bamboo water hammer plunked again.

"Are you lost?" he asked.

Tarō nodded hesitantly, then added, "Yes."

"So you *can* speak," the priest said, smiling. "I am the abbot of the shrine, Tenzaemon at your service." He bowed deeply.

"Tarō," the boy replied weakly.

The priest nodded. Tanuki shrank to the side, trying to look inconspicuous.

"You have me at a disadvantage," Tenzaemon said, turning to Tanuki. "Are you his—grandfather?"

Tanuki frowned and shook his head. "Uncle."

Tenzaemon nodded thoughtfully, leaning closer to look Tanuki in the eye, which made Tanuki squirm.

"Of course you are," Tenzaemon said, smiling.

The bamboo water hammer plunked again. As Tanuki smiled back, shifting uneasily beneath the priest's gaze, Tarō looked around the shrine, searching for some hidden clue.

"You look troubled, my son. Can I be of help?"

"No," Tarō replied, shaking his head glumly as he studied the faces of Fūjin and Raijin.

"I find it helps to pray," Tenzaemon offered.

Tarō did not respond.

"The gods do hear us," the priest said, looking up at the wooden deities.

Tarō looked puzzled.

"These wooden statues are but effigies of the Gods of Wind and Thunder—their eyes are windows to their true spirits."

Tarō huffed skeptically.

"You may scoff," Tenzaemon said, "but we all are joined by *musubi,* the binding force of the cosmos, even though we do not see this connection. Light and dark, good and evil, nothing exists that is not tied to the positive and negative energy of the cosmos. Everything is linked. The *shinkai*, the realm of *kami*, may be hidden by the veil of mortal life, but when you learn to look, you will see."

Tarō gazed thoughtfully at the guardians, as the chanting continued to rise and fall inside the oratory.

"Well, please do not hesitate to call upon me," the priest said, bowing politely, then he left them alone in the courtyard.

Fragrant smoke swirled above their heads and the chanting continued in the sanctuary. Tarō stood in thought a moment, then he shut his eyes. He bowed twice, clapped twice, and bowed again.

All at once, the chanting stopped. Tarō opened his eyes. At first, the shrine stood in eerie silence. He felt as if time had stopped, then he heard a whisper again, an echo from the past.

*"Tarō, we must hide—"*

The bamboo water hammer plunked. Tarō looked around, confused. Then all at once, a flood of memories assaulted him.

General Toramasa knelt in front of him again, gasping from the arrow in his bloody neck. Looking toward the Twilight Gate, Tarō saw his father and the black *samurai* with the devil mask, his helmet crowned with spikes.

*"Monkey!" his father called out, just before the black samurai stabbed him in the back.*

Tarō stood powerless as he relived his father's slaughter, realizing they would never be reunited. A voice chanted insistently.

*"Tarō, we must hide!"*

Tarō looked up the steps toward the main hall. Then he sprinted off between the buildings toward the rear of the shrine.

"Hey, wait for me!" Tanuki called, shuffling across the quadrangle in his human form, but Tarō had already outpaced him.

Tarō found the rear of the shrine. Clambering up the mossy slope into the dense wood, he retraced his mother's desperate flight to the river as she carried him—not Yama Uba but his real mother. The cicada shrilling rose and fell all around him.

*"Over here!"* a voice rang as if the past had chased him there.

He found the tangle of roots where his mother had fallen with him. The bamboo water hammer knocked louder.

*"Mother!" his small self cried, as he tried to revive her where she lay.*

The cryptomeria trees stood tall and silent around him. He heard the faint sound of rushing water. Running on, he found the small glade grown full of dazzling white lilies. He ran across the clearing, while Tanuki, in true, furry form again, puffed and chugged to keep up.

The bamboo water hammer plunked in its corner of the glade before pausing to fill itself from the chute fed by the river. Tarō saw his mother sobbing on the snowy ground again, as he knelt beside her, smoothing the tresses of her hair.

*"Don't cry," he said.*

*"Run," she replied with a wild look in her eyes. "Run!"*

Tarō pushed through another tangle of purple wisteria toward the rushing river. Vines and brambles tore at his clothes and bare skin, but he found the place where the priests hung their laundry. Close beside the river, he spied a washtub much like the one that carried him away from his mother.

*"Mother!" he cried out, as she gave the tub a shove with the last of her strength, and the river carried him away, but not before he saw Lord Monkey turn on her.*

As Tanuki caught up to him, the bamboo water hammer plunked once more.

"So?" Tanuki asked, not realizing how lost and alone Tarō looked in that moment.

Tarō closed his eyes. He saw himself drifting downriver in the little washtub and spilling over the falls, the water beating down on him, driving him deep into the pool, drowning him. Then he saw it—the sword his father gave him on that fateful day. It slipped from his sash to dart through the dark water.

Tarō opened his eyes, returning to the present. He bounded suddenly through the underbrush along the river's edge, headed toward the falls, leaving Tanuki behind.

Huffing and puffing, Tanuki caught up with Tarō at the cliff's edge where the thundering cascade threw clouds of cool mist into the air. Without a word, Tarō dove into the cold falls. Tanuki peered over the edge, looking after him, as Tarō disappeared into the pool below with a tremendous splash.

"Ah, I think I'll climb down," Tanuki said aloud to himself.

Tarō swam deep into the dark pool. Searching the bottom, he soon found his father's gift wedged between two rocks.

Emerging from the pool, clutching his *wakizashi* in hand, he studied it. Although the handle had rusted, the lacquer scabbard still shone when he rubbed it clean on his *kimono* sleeve, and when he unsheathed it, he found the blade was still keen, the traces of Lord Monkey's blood long since dried on its edge.

"Murakumo-no-Hoken," Tarō called his sword by name.

*"Tarō!"* the sword mystically whispered its reply.

Tarō closed the blade and held it to his chest. As he thought of his parents, gone forever, his face grew hard, hatred seething from his pores.

"What did you find?" Tanuki puffed, reaching the bottom of the falls as Tarō stepped out of the pool.

"My sword."

"I didn't know you lost one."

"It was a long time ago. I forgot about it, but now I know who I am—and what I have to do."

"What do you have to do?"

"Collect a debt," Tarō said in a cold voice that surprised and worried Tanuki.

"That sounds—like trouble," Tanuki stuttered, catching the look in Tarō's eyes. "You sure you don't want to rethink that?"

"There's nothing to think about. He killed my parents."

"Who?"

"Lord Monkey."

"A monkey?"

"No, Lord Monkey, a *samurai*."

"Didn't one of Lord Tokugawa's Four Generals say something about him?"

"He called him Hashiba, and I am going to kill him."

"You know," Tanuki tried, "when I said 'live for the day,' it wasn't just wishful thinking. It's kind of my number one rule."

"It doesn't matter."

"Of course, it matters! Listen, you're just out of sorts. You'll feel better if you sleep on it. Here, I know what'll help!" he declared, pulling out his *sake* jug. "How about a little pick-me-up?"

"You don't understand!" Tarō yelled, suddenly slapping the jug to the ground so it shattered.

"Hey!" Tanuki shouted angrily, dropping to all fours to lament his broken jug.

Tarō pulled out Yama Uba's mirror. He looked at himself, just a boy, then he looked at his sword. He threw a glance at Tanuki, who scowled at Tarō, muttering to himself as he squatted over the shards of his broken jug.

"You'll never understand," Tarō stabbed, "you're not—human."

Tanuki looked up, his furry chin dragging, mouth agape as he impotently tried to muster a response. Tarō's words had wounded his friend deeply.

"Here, take it!" he said, shoving the mirror at Tanuki. "It lost most of its power. Now it only shows you who you really are—why don't you take a look at yourself!"

Tanuki stared back, nonplussed. He took the mirror from Tarō as if in a daze.

As Tarō turned to leave, Tanuki started to speak but frowned and hung his head instead. He watched under hurt, angry eyebrows, as Tarō disappeared into the wood.

# 7

## ESCAPE FROM EDO

*Kai Province*

*Summer, Year of the Rat*

Evening had fallen by the time Tarō weaved his way through the last enormous stand of bamboo and arrived at the Eastern Sea Road. The road was empty, the air ominously quiet, but a sudden gust descended from the mountain, an ill wind that thrashed the bamboo grove so its giant spears and fronds crashed against each other. Tarō hesitated, blinking in the gale, waiting, but nothing else came. He checked his sword in his sash, then took off down the road, the bamboo grove waving wildly at his back.

When he arrived at the first fortified post station at Odawara on the road from Mount Fuji, Tarō found the guards on high alert behind their stockade. Shouts jumped up from inside the gate, and two *samurai* stepped out to bar the way with long iron cudgels. Tarō stopped some distance from the gate, only partially visible in the torchlight.

"I am Tarō Takeda," he announced. "I am going to Edo to speak with Lord Tokugawa."

"Permit!" the guard demanded.

Tarō searched his *kimono* sleeve, but he had forgotten Lord Tokugawa's seal.

"I am Tarō!" he said, "Lord Tokugawa's bodyguard!"

Tarō strode toward the guards. Seeing the boy, they took him for some fool.

"Seize him!" their commander shouted.

The two guards stepped forward, grabbing Tarō by his arms with iron grips.

"What's this?" one of the guards shouted, as he snatched Tarō's sword from his sash. He made an ugly face, grinning through his yellow teeth. "What did you mean to do with this?"

"That's mine!" Tarō shouted.

"This was a Takeda sword," the *samurai* accused, observing the scabbard's markings. "Where did you get this?"

"I told you, I am Tarō Takeda—"

"A lie," the *samurai* spat. "You're no Takeda. The Takeda were wiped out years ago."

"No—"

"A spy is more like it," the other said, "or an assassin—who'd suspect a boy, right?" he repeated, when they brought him before their commander, who studied Tarō beneath the torchlight.

"No, listen to me, I have to speak to Lord Tokugawa—"

Tarō struggled until the *samurai* with the yellow teeth struck him over the head with his cudgel. The blow drew blood.

"Hold!" their commander said.

The guards stood Tarō up, his head swaying as he reeled from his injury. He tried to focus. The commander, a squat man with a large flat face and nose and a thin mustache, leaned forward to look into his face.

"I must speak to Lord Tokugawa," Tarō pleaded, "Lord Monkey killed my father—"

The commander struck Tarō across the face with the back of his gauntlet, drawing a cry and blood from Tarō's mouth. The guards grinned cruelly. Half-conscious, Tarō groaned.

"Boys will be boys," the commander said with a sadistic smile, playing to his subordinates. "Throw him in the pit," he pronounced, and the guards dragged Tarō off.

Tarō's jailers heaved him into a large muddy pit with several other half-clothed, hapless prisoners huddled in the dark. He fell into the mud with a thump and lay half-conscious with his face in the putrid muck. When his jailers replaced the bamboo cover over the pit and the hole grew even darker, Tarō felt his shadowy cellmates draw near. He smelled their stench as they growled like animals, picking over his body for spoils. They stripped him bare except for his loincloth, and Tarō lay shivering half the night in the mud and filth, unable to move.

At first light, Tarō coughed and spluttered awake, remembering where he was. The iron taste of blood was in his mouth. With a groan he raised himself, clutching his swollen face and feeling the tender back of his head where the blood had dried and caked on his wound. His cellmates huddled along the walls of the pit. Looking at himself, half-naked and filthy, he grew angry.

"Hey!" he yelled up through the bamboo cover. "Hey!" he yelled again and again.

"What are you bleating about?" one said, as two *samurai* removed the bamboo cover over the pit. "You want a skinning?"

"Take me to Lord Tokugawa!"

The *samurai* laughed.

"You, you're smart!" Tarō said, recognizing the yellow-toothed man.

The accusation caught his jailer by surprise.

"What do you mean?" the *samurai* said, his eyes narrowing.

"You recognized my sword. How many men could do that after so many years? You know your history."

Hooked, the ugly *samurai* nodded. His cohort started to speak, but Yellow-Teeth waved him off.

"You must know Lord Monkey killed Lord Takeda."

"Everyone knows that."

"Of course," Tarō encouraged, "I knew you must—but did you know Lord Takeda's son escaped?"

"The Tiger of Kai was your father," he said, cocking his head, sniggering through his yellow teeth, and his friend joined him.

"Yes, but what if I survived—I mean, what if Lord Takeda's son lives?"

"Again with your blathering—" Yellow-Teeth said, nodding to his cohort to help him replace the bamboo cover.

"A smart man would want to be sure Lord Tokugawa was not looking for me," Tarō said quickly.

"Wait a bit," Yellow-Teeth said to his cohort.

"A smart man knows information is valuable," Tarō said slyly. "There would be a reward."

"Not for a spy's lie," Yellow-Teeth spat.

"The sword does not lie," Tarō said, giving the man pause.

In spite of Tarō's flattery, thinking did not come easily to the lowly foot soldier, who squinted at the boy long enough for his cohort to grow annoyed.

"Leave him! " the other said, as he started to replace the bamboo cover.

"No," Yellow-Teeth said at last, "get the ladder. If the commander doesn't buy the rat's squeak," he grinned, "we can always beat him."

太

## *Musashi Province*

## *Summer, Year of the Rat*

The next day, the commander of the Odawara post delivered the "rat" to Edo. The city streets lay forsaken under martial law, its citizens shut inside their homes and shops. They peered through their windows as the *samurai* rode past with Tarō on a leash, bound by ropes, his arms behind his back, stumbling on his bare feet, covered in grime and wearing only his loincloth.

When the Odawara *samurai* brought Tarō into the Great Reception Room, Lord Tokugawa did not recognize the dirty, scrawny boy. He looked up, his brow already furrowed from some ill news on a paper he had just received, and his first thought was that his men had brought him some street urchin, a peasant thief upon whom he must pass judgment.

Although his tormenters had cleaned him up a little, Tarō's face was bruised and swollen. He wore a rough burlap coat that scratched his skin where the ropes bound his body.

"Master Yagyū, what happened to you?" Tarō exclaimed when he saw the sword master kneeling nearby, his face bound with a fresh cloth to dress his wound.

"Tarō?" Master Yagyū said when he saw the boy with his one good eye.

Suspicious, Lord Tokugawa leaned closer for a better look.

"Are you Tarō?" he questioned. "Where have you been? Master Yagyū searched but could not find you. Why do you look so—small?"

"We caught this rat sneaking around our post," the commander said. "I think he's a spy. He keeps talking about Takeda, and he was carrying this—"

The commander held up Tarō's *wakizashi*. Lord Tokugawa's chin jutted forward as soon as he perceived the markings on the scabbard. The commander stepped forward and knelt, offering the sword to his Lord, who took it.

"I am Tarō, son of Lord Takeda Nobutora!" Tarō declared in a voice at odds with his appearance. "I am *samurai*!"

"He's been on about that tripe since we caught him."

Lord Tokugawa studied Tarō, speechless. For a moment he stewed in confusion, as he beheld the diamond emblem on the golden scabbard. In that instant, seeing the avenging spirit of his vanquished foe, the warlord's usually inscrutable face betrayed his astonishment, but he quickly recovered and responded in anger.

"A *samurai* who fails his lord would take his own life in shame," Lord Tokugawa accused. "Where were you when I was attacked and Master Yagyū lost his eye defending me?"

"I went back to the shrine."

"The shrine?" Lord Tokugawa said, cocking his head suspiciously. "You agreed to be my bodyguard. You left without my consent—"

"Father—" Kamehime interrupted as she appeared, but the guards barred her entrance. "Why—?"

"Quiet!" her father shouted sharply, his ire surprising and frightening her.

"I can explain," Tarō said. "I went to the shrine to find—" he paused, "my sword."

"How is it that you are so changed?" Lord Tokugawa demanded. "A spy's disguise?"

"No, I was—" he hesitated, "enchanted."

"The same enchantment from which you pretended to rescue me?" Lord Tokugawa accused.

"No," Tarō argued in vain.

"The same black magic that tried to kill me two nights ago!"

"No!"

"Tsukiyama or Takeda, your absence alone condemns you!" Lord Tokugawa adjudged. "Take him away!"

"You don't understand!" Tarō yelled as several guards started to drag him away. "Lord Monkey killed my parents! I am *samurai!* I want to help!"

"If you are *samurai*—" Lord Tokugawa bellowed so suddenly his guards stopped to attend their Lord's command, and a hush took the room, "then you shall take your own life at dawn."

"Father!" Kamehime blurted, but he silenced her with a harsh look.

She watched as the guards dragged Tarō down the corridor, then looked at her father again with pleading eyes, but he could not see her. Lord Tokugawa stared silently, thoughtfully, into the void where Tarō had stood, as if the warlord had seen a ghost. He turned the sword over in his hands. The air was tense, as the room waited for a word from their Lord and master.

"Make ready every man!" Lord Tokugawa declared suddenly, looking at the message he received earlier. "We have ill tidings—Lord Monkey has kidnapped the Emperor. We march to lay siege to Momoyama Castle."

"Father—" Kamehime tried.

"No!" he snapped. "You will stay here to defend the castle."

"Father, Tarō—"

"Enough!" Lord Tokugawa thundered, brandishing Tarō's sword. "The boy is Takeda! He is either a disgraced *rōnin* or a spy, but he shall have an honorable death if he be *samurai*."

Kamehime flinched, silently fuming at her father's judgment, but she did not debate him. She threw a glance at Master Yagyū who exchanged her look without a word, as he followed his Lord from the room and into the castle corridor bustling with *samurai* rushing to make ready for war.

Drums sounded the alarm through the castle. Alone in the Great Reception Room, as Kamehime fumed, a wave of resolve crossed her face. She set her jaw defiantly.

"How shall I help?" Nun Tokiko asked, startling her mistress who had forgotten her faithful shadow.

"What?" Kamehime said innocently.

"You need not play dumb with me. It insults my intelligence. I can tell when you've set your mind to something," she said, pursing her persimmon lips. "So? How shall I help?"

太

Tarō huddled in a corner of his windowless prison cell, a tiny room of stone and timber deep within the monolithic bowels of the Edo Castle donjon. Hearing the groan of wooden prison doors opening and closing, and shouts echoing in the corridors, and the low rumble of drums, he imagined the Gods of Wind and Thunder were looking for him, their eyes flashing in the darkness.

Tarō blinked as lightning flashed across the walls of his jail cell, the flickering drawing nearer. He blinked again, trying to focus.

"Tarō?" Kamehime whispered, raising her candle.

"Are you okay?" he asked.

"Yes, thank you," she said, amused, "I came to free you."

"I'm not a spy! Or an assassin."

"I know. Why would you hurt my father—you saved him!"

Tarō nodded. She unbarred his cell door.

"We can't stay here or you'll die. Come with me!"

Tarō jumped up and followed her into the hallway, their backs pressed against the wall, Kamehime shielding the candle with her hand as they made their way along the corridor to a flight of wooden stairs, then cautiously opening the door onto another hallway. Beside the door sat a guard, his head hung as if asleep. Kamehime moved quickly past him, but Tarō paused for a look.

"Is he dead?" Tarō whispered.

"No, but he will have a big headache in the morning."

Tarō grinned.

"What?" she shrugged, "'please' would not have done."

They crept quickly through a maze of corridors, their backs against the walls, but Kamehime never faltered as she led them on until she came to a dead end. Before Tarō could question her, she put her shoulder against the cypress paneling. As if by magic, a door creaked open. She put her finger to her mouth, indicating they should move even more quietly, then snuffed her candle.

It was dark and close in the secret passage, which ran at a steep decline, but they managed to make their way until they felt the night air on their faces. The passage ended at a very narrow opening in the slanted wall of the castle keep, at a height of five men above the lotus-filled moat below. She nodded for him to follow, and Tarō joined her as they squeezed through the opening and climbed out onto the castle wall, their fingers and toes clinging wherever they could to the crevices between the massive stones.

Their eyes adjusted quickly. Although the clouds hid the moon, they could see darker silhouettes against the night around them. Slowly, sure-footedly, they both made their way across the wall and down, only once pausing to wait for a sentry to walk his post. When the guard turned and headed in the opposite direction, they slipped into the moat and swam to the other side, pushing through lily pads and pale lotus blossoms.

Scrambling up the other side, they darted for a corner of the compound where Nun Tokiko awaited them in hiding with a bundle of provisions. Tarō watched, red-faced, as Kamehime wasted no time stripping in front of him to change into the clothes she had prepared—nun's habits. Seeing Tarō's look, Kamehime covered herself bashfully. Her chaperone took a menacing stride between them that made Tarō step back in alarm. She forced a bundle of clothes on him.

"I'm not wearing that," he said when he saw the nun's habit.

"It's the only way out," Kamehime said firmly.

Reluctantly, Tarō donned the simple gray *kimono* and white cowl, so he and Kamehime resembled Nun Tokiko's young acolytes. Tarō looked deeply embarrassed, but their ruse worked, and they passed through the many castle gates without detection.

"Nuns make me horny," one crude sentry said as they passed through Big Hand Gate. "You're a cute one," he added, giving Tarō a quick pinch on his bottom.

Nun Tokiko quickly intervened. Her look alone was enough to cow the man.

"Nuns are scary," the crude sentry muttered as she led her acolytes away.

Outside the castle, they followed Nun Tokiko to her convent, a temple on the outskirts of the city where they ate a quick meal of rice steeped in green tea with pickled plum and changed clothes again for their flight from Edo City. Kamehime had prepared a short *kimono*, breeches, and leggings for Tarō, as well as light armor made of lacquered steel, leather, and chainmail.

"It was mine a few years ago, but it should fit you now."

Kamehime looked a man in her usual *samurai* riding wear and light armor, as she pulled her hair into a pony tail top knot. Bidding Nun Tokiko goodbye and thanks, she shoved her sword into her sash and joined Tarō outside the convent.

"Here!" she said, handing Tarō his *wakizashi,* his father's precious gift. "I thought you might want this."

Tarō smiled, holding the sword tightly, gratefully.

"You can have a horse," she said, "Tokiko prepared two."

"Aren't you coming with me?" he asked.

She shook her head. "I'm going to rescue the Emperor."

Tarō started to laugh, but seeing her face he caught himself.

"You could help me," she said hopefully.

He shook his head. "Look at me. I'm not strong any more. I'm just a boy."

"And I am just a girl!" she said angrily. "Did you learn nothing from Master Yagyū?" She sighed, shaking her head. "My father and seventy thousand of his vassals are going to war to lay siege to Momoyama Castle and rescue the Emperor from Lord Monkey—"

Tarō's ears pricked at the mention of Lord Monkey. He looked at his sword, his only memento of his slain father.

"His Army numbers more than a hundred thousand. If I don't try to stop this war, many good *samurai* will die. So, I am going to rescue the Emperor if it kills me—"

"Then I'm going with you," Tarō blurted.

Surprised and moved by his words, and grateful for a companion on her grave quest, she smiled, nodding thanks and quickly turning to hide the cheer he had brought to her eyes.

"Come on," she said, wiping her face furtively. "This way!"

She led him to the stable where they found their sturdy ponies. Once again, Kamehime marveled enviously as Tarō spoke to his horse, and the horse seemed to bond instantly with him.

It was no small feat to travel the Eastern Sea Road undiscovered, but each time they came to a fortified post station, Kamehime simply held up her father's badge and shouted, "Urgent message from Lord Tokugawa for the Emperor!" and they spurred their horses through each turnpike and onward toward Momoyama Castle. In this way they passed quickly on their route, riding many leagues from Edo, long before the Hour of the Rabbit when Lord Tokugawa discovered Tarō had escaped.

"Find him!" the warlord stormed when his Karō brought the news. Lord Tokugawa was dressed in full armor, in preparation for the march on Momoyama Castle. "I will deal with him when I return!" he said, wheeling to storm down the corridor.

太

Uncle Tanuki arrived just as all Edo turned out to watch the Eastern Army sally forth from the castle into the humid streets and march by the thousands over Nihon Bridge toward Momoyama Castle, their standards and banners waving, rank-and-file foot soldiers in lacquered conical camp hats and bearing spears or *teppō* muskets, cavalry in *oyoroi*, baggage trains with porters, and large numbers of pack horses and carts drawn by men and oxen.

"What's going on?" Tanuki asked a grandfather watching the parade.

"I heard tell Lord Tokugawa marches on Momoyama Castle to lay siege and rescue the Emperor who was taken hostage."

Tanuki craned his neck, looking for Tarō. Still feeling guilty about their quarrel, he soon lost heart and slunk toward the forsaken, naked streets of Yoshiwara in daylight.

"Just a pick-me-up," he told himself. "That's what I want."

"Esteemed guest—" the madam greeted him anxiously, when he returned to his favored tea house. She looked around, wary, then relieved to see his brawny, bully boy was not with him. "Alone? How wonderful to see you again! Please do come in!"

Uncle Tanuki managed a smile, and she showed him inside.

"Perhaps a private room?" she suggested when she caught the wistful look in his eyes.

He produced a bag of coins seemingly from thin air, and the madam chuckled when she shook it and heard the jingle.

She led him through the smell of perfume, stale wine and tobacco to a plain *tatami* room furnished with a low black table and two scarlet silk cushions. With a clap of her hands, comely young attendants appeared and disappeared and reappeared, ferrying *sake* and plates of food—dried, salted sardines, smoked squid, charcoal-grilled eel, and buckwheat noodles. The ladies brought more cushions to make him comfy. Tanuki smacked his lips excitedly, determined to make the most of his stay.

"Instead of fretting over things of no avail," he sighed, "it would seem better to drink a cupful of cloudy *sake*!"

One young courtesan smiled at his wit as she poured him a cup of wine, which he quickly drank. A hollow sigh followed. He frowned.

He reached for the jug and held it up and drank the whole contents in a single draught. When he finished, he cocked his head expectantly, but no anticipated revelation came.

"It's no use," he lamented. He slumped and shook his head sadly.

This upset the ladies of the house terribly for fear they had displeased him and would have to answer to their madam. They brought more wine and food, soliciting Tanuki to try this and that, fanning him with *uchiwa*, but he waved them off.

"Shall I play for you?" one young courtesan offered, plucking on her *shamisen*.

"No," Tanuki said listlessly. "Leave me."

Bowing and warbling their apologies, the courtesans retreated. Alone at last, Tanuki looked listlessly around the room, noticing the only decoration, a woodblock print pinned to one wall, the portrait of a beautiful courtesan in the prime of youth, admiring herself in a mirror.

Tanuki sighed and shook his head. Then, spurred by a thought, he produced his treasure bag from thin air and began rummaging through it purposefully until, at last, he found what he had been hunting—Yama Uba's mirror. He held it up, frowning. He hesitated, his shoulders hunching anxiously, as he turned the mirror to his face.

Out of the cloudy depth of the looking glass, an image swirled. Slowly, inescapably, his likeness materialized: Uncle Tanuki stared back at him, but even as he studied his human form, the image faded and a new reflection took its place, still the same mischievous expression in his eyes, but his true, animal self, just a fat old raccoon-dog with a grizzled chin. His mouth hung even lower at the revelation.

His disguise dissolved, Tanuki rubbed his over-sized belly and frowned, shaking his head in disappointment. He looked around, disgusted with himself. Then another thought took him, and his face exuded sudden determination. He shoved Yama Uba's mirror in his bag just as the madam opened the door to the room.

"Apologies for disturbing you, good sir," she said, "but the girls said you were feeling out of sorts—"

Seeing Tanuki instead of the anticipated uncle she had known, the madam blinked in utter disbelief before she sounded the alarm with a terrified shriek.

"Sorry!" Tanuki barked in surprise.

He bounded past her, down the stairs of the tea house and out the entrance, dodging surprised citizens as he raced through Edo toward Nihon Bridge.

# 8

## THE PRINCE OF PEACH MOUNTAIN

*Musashi Province*

*Summer, Year of the Rat*

The ragged moon hung low in the sky like a half-eaten rice cake on a black lacquer tray as Tarō and Kamehime galloped their horses along a dark stretch of the Eastern Sea Road. In time, they saw the glow of torchlight from Odawara-juku. As they approached, Kamehime held up her father's badge and they rode their ponies through the fortified post, past the collection of inns that serviced travelers with food and lodging between checkpoints. When they came to the western gate, they found a large melon cart blocking the way, the idle farmer gossiping with one of the guards by torchlight in the early morning hour.

"Urgent message from Lord Tokugawa for the Emperor!" Kamehime shouted, directing her horse around the cart.

Each man stepped away from the cart with his back to the guardhouse wall to allow the ponies to pass. Kamehime directed her horse forward, holding up her father's seal.

Another guard stood near the front of the cart. Seeing him, her pony snorted in surprise. As Tarō followed, a familiar voice accosted him.

"Hey, you I've seen before!"

Tarō's nemesis, the *samurai* with yellow teeth, stepped forward for a better look. He reached for the reins of Tarō's horse, but Tarō spoke first, and his pony responded immediately, tossing its head so Yellow-Teeth could not catch the reins.

"Ride!" Tarō yelled, whinnying to Kamehime's horse, and her pony leaped forward, knocking the other guard to the ground.

Before Yellow-Teeth could react, Tarō kicked him square in the chest, knocking him onto his backside. Sprawling on the ground, the *samurai* scrambled to right himself. Tarō grabbed a melon from the farmer's cart and, heaving it as hard as he could, he brought it crashing down on Yellow-Teeth who had no helmet. The melon cracked on his bald head, knocking him unconscious.

Shouts rang out around the post and within the guardhouse. Grabbing onto the cart, Tarō urged his horse, and they leaped forward, dragging the wagon until it crashed into the gate and launched its cargo so the melons exploded everywhere they fell. Three *samurai* rushed toward the gate but lost their footing on the slippery melon shards littering the ground.

Tarō looked back, smiling to see he had covered their escape, but a flash and thunderclap of *tanegashima* came from one of the stockade towers. The whizzing musket ball missed its mark in the darkness, as Tarō rode for Kamehime who had stopped only a short distance ahead to make certain Tarō escaped.

"Nothing we can do now but ride hard!" she shouted.

Looking back at Odawara-juku bustling with torchlight as *samurai* mustered for pursuit, Tarō nodded. He paused only to pat his pony gratefully then, urging it with a word, the horse leaped forward, and Kamehime followed, as they set their steeds to gallop.

They rode into the morning, bracing for another fight when they came to the Hakone-juku checkpoint high in the mountains near Mount Fuji, but they had outpaced any news of their escape and passed easily. By this time their horses were lathered, and the sun had risen, so they left the road to rest, since many leagues lay ahead of them. In a lush vale below the road, they found a secluded spring where their ponies could drink.

"It isn't much," she said, reaching into the small bundle tied to her saddle to produce their snack, two rice balls wrapped in seaweed. "There's more—but we need to make it last."

Tarō wolfed his down. She offered him half of hers, but he refused, even though he could have eaten ten more with ease.

They sat with their backs propped against trees opposite each other until the sky grew light. Although he insisted he did not need to sleep, Tarō soon slept deeply, exhausted from his recent trials and haunted by them. He dreamed he was back in the pit in Odawara, clawing desperately at the muddy walls, crying for help.

*"I am Tarō! I am* samurai*!" he yelled in vain. "Let me out!"*

*"You are* samurai*," a voice boomed, "born and bound to serve and protect your Lord and Emperor unto death."*

Tarō saw himself in the courtyard of Fuji Hachiman Shrine, wearing a priest's white *kimono*. Many faces had come to bear witness—Tanuki and the forest animals, Lord Tokugawa, Kamehime, Master Yagyū, and Tenzaemon the priest watched as Tarō loosened his *kimono* and drove his sword into his own belly, spilling his bowels, his crimson blood staining his hands.

Tarō woke with a start.

"We should go," Kamehime said, looking at the morning sky, "It is already the Dragon Hour."

Tarō blinked and nodded. He sighed, shaking himself awake. Still troubled by his dream, he did not speak as they made ready to depart.

"Should we risk it in daylight?" she asked, when their horses had climbed out of the vale.

"Do we have a choice?" he said, looking both ways along the Eastern Sea Road.

"Not if we hope to stay ahead of my father's army."

"Then we risk it!" Tarō said, urging his pony forward until both horses broke into a gallop.

They raced along the road with a warm wind in their faces. Although they worried that word of their escape had reached the next post station, they passed easily with Kamehime once more declaring their mission under her father's seal.

Emboldened by their good fortune, they rode hard and fast, slowing only to pass through other stations, and stopping only to rest their horses every few hours, always leaving the road to avoid any interaction with other travelers, always alert for the sound of hooves beating the road behind them. In this way, they traversed the Provinces of Sagami, Izu, and Suruga, skirting Suruga Bay in the span of another day. Kamehime marveled at Tarō's skill when he supplemented their meager provisions with trout caught fresh with his bare hands.

By silver moonlight, they bathed bashfully in the same stream, each stealing glances at the other, both tongue-tied as they quickly dried themselves and dressed to sleep in turns. Even then, Tarō slept little, but long lay awake, thinking of Kamehime's nakedness, the goddess of his heaven, while the hell of his dreams awaited him when at last sleep took him.

They traveled mostly by night, not only to avoid detection but to hide from the relentless summer heat that weighed heavily on them and caused their horses to lather quickly. In another day they crossed the brackish lagoon of Lake Hamana in Tōtōmi and reached Mikawa Province by nightfall.

"This is my father's homeland—I was born there," she said pensively, looking at Okazaki Castle pale in the distance, but she would not say more, and she did not wait for Tarō to ask, as she urged her horse forward. "It's not much further now, less than ten leagues, I think."

Off they rode on the last leg of their quest, but each had a very different vision: Kamehime imagined rescuing the Emperor and receiving her father's praise, while Tarō thought only of Lord Monkey and revenge, wrestling with his self-doubt, wondering if he could succeed without the power of Yama Uba's enchantment.

*Ise Province*

*Summer, Year of the Rat*

Their horses were thoroughly lathered by the time they passed the Miya-juku checkpoint above Ise Bay and came to a place where the Eastern Sea Road turned away from the sea. Kamehime stopped to look down the rocky slope at the surf roaring against the pale, crescent-shaped shoreline, as the first light of dawn filtered through a thick fog over the bay.

Ise Bay lay at a strategic point on the Eastern Sea Road, a natural bottleneck connecting the eastern and western provinces, where three rivers, the Kiso, Nagara, and Ibi, descended quickly from the mountains into a narrow valley and grassy plain known as Sekigahara, before spilling into the foggy bay enclosed by sheer black cliffs on either side.

"The Tortoise Mountains," Kamehime said, calling Tarō's attention to the range of rolling humps—the head, legs, and shell—enclosing the valley and bay, while the plain and delta resembled the silver fantail of a giant turtle crawling from the sea.

"Your second home, my princess?"[9] Tarō joked.

---

[9] Kamehime [亀姫], "turtle princess," considered a lucky name as turtles were said to live 10,000 years.

"This is Owari Province," she said, shaking her head and smiling, "part of Lord Monkey's domain." She looked around. "It's getting light. We should leave the road."

Kamehime dismounted and led her pony into the scrub beside the road, and Tarō followed until they stood on a rocky shelf overlooking the steep slope to the sea.

"It's all we have left," she said, offering Tarō one of the last two rice balls. "Over there—" she directed, munching on hers and pointing above the fog to a mountain on the opposite side of the bay, the head of the Tortoise Mountains, "Momoyama Castle."

The castle was no bigger than his thumbnail at this distance, but Tarō's sharp eyes could see the two tall keeps, pale in the ethereal, foggy light of morning, standing side by side on the mount. Tarō followed Kamehime's lead, as she directed her horse to descend through the fog and twisted pines to the seashore below.

Their ponies chose the way carefully, and they did their best to guide them, but the going was rough, and the horses stumbled often on the scree, which sent rocks clattering into the sea below. They skirted the hill through tall clumps of sea oats, directing their ponies down to the beach, where the black waves shone white as they crashed against the sandy shoreline. As their horses trotted onto the beach, a steady rain began to fall, punctuated by distant rumbling thunder.

The beach ran ahead for a great distance, their horses' hooves kicking up the surf and sand as they rode along the glowing, crescent between the foaming black water of the bay and the twilit delta, the rain and salt air in their faces. They slowed only to cross the wide, shallow mouths of the rivers spilling into the dark sea.

The rain had stopped by the time they reached the opposite side of the bay, and the fog rolled inland, dashing itself into tattered clouds that trailed upward into the folds of the wooded hills above the cliffs. Tarō spied the striking vermillion lines of an arched *torii*, the gateway to some distant shrine, perched upon the edge of the cliff overlooking the entrance to the bay, but Kamehime pointed instead to the wooded mountain rising above the cliffs. Surging from the twilight, the double-donjon castle loomed on the summit.

A great wave crashed upon the beach beside them, startling their horses. They each drew a deep breath before bidding their ponies forward and up, traversing the rocky slope and sand dunes and sea oats to gain the cover of the wooded hills beneath Momoyama Castle.

*Yamashiro Province*

*Summer, Year of the Rat*

Their horses were thoroughly winded when at last Kamehime and Tarō stood beneath the eaves of the forest, cautiously observing Momoyama Castle. Cicadas chirped in the oppressive heat, and crows cried raucously as they circled the sweet-smelling peach orchards surrounding the castle. The white walls and stones of its two towers, one a little taller and broader than the other, shone brilliantly beneath the morning sun. Atop the walls and towers, Lord Monkey's black banners emblazoned with the golden gourd stood stock-still in the stagnant air.

"What now?" Tarō asked.

"Now we wait for nightfall," she said, "then we sneak in and get the Emperor out."

"Is that all?" Tarō said skeptically.

"I've been inside," she said. "I was younger, but I still remember it. I think I know where to find the Emperor. We just have to get up there."

"Without getting caught," Tarō said, still smarting from his recent imprisonment.

"Lord Monkey is expecting my father's army, not the two of us. We got out of one castle. We can get into this one."

Tarō smiled, admiring her courage. He thought her beautiful. He longed to sit beside her, to touch the black tresses of her hair framing her delicate face.

"What?" she said, catching his look.

"Nothing," Tarō said, as coolly as he could manage, but blushing boyishly beneath his ruddy tan.

Kamehime nodded, but she sensed his reserve and mistook it for resentment.

"I'm sorry about my father," she offered. Then, confronted by a darker secret, she started to confess, "Tarō—"

"What?"

"I don't know what to say—"

She struggled for words. He looked so innocent. She could not bear the thought of losing his trust, and not just because she needed his help to rescue the Emperor, for she had grown fond of this wild boy. *What if he should hate her when he heard the truth?*

"We should rest while we can," she said with a sigh. "I'll take first watch."

"I don't need to sleep," he said. "You sleep. I'll keep watch."

Kamehime nodded, ashamed of her weakness. She moved to curl up between the roots of a large tree with her back to Tarō, and he took a seat beside her. She did not sleep immediately but lay staring pensively, still troubled by the dark secret she could not bring herself to tell. Tarō sat with his eyes on the nape of her neck above her *kimono*, studying her smooth black hair pulled into a pony tail and the delicate wisps of hair at her neckline. He longed to curl up beside her and cursed the tree root between them.

While Kamehime slept, and the relentless sun passed overhead, Tarō's stomach began to grumble. It had been hours since they last ate. He was just wishing they had more rice balls when he smelled the peaches.

The outermost trees of the orchard lay but a quick sprint from the woods over a low stone wall. Tarō stood. Another deep breath brought the scent of ripe peaches to his nose again, making his stomach growl even more. He checked Kamehime—still sleeping between the tree roots—and determined to risk a foray.

Looking around for any sign of movement, Tarō saw only the circling crows, their ugly cries spoiling the otherwise idyllic orchards. He bolted for the stone wall and, hurdling it with ease, darted for cover beneath the nearest peach tree.

Tarō's sudden appearance caused a murder of crows to take raucous flight. He froze, listening for any alarm from the castle.

When no other alarm sounded, Tarō relaxed. He looked around at the many ripe peaches littering the ground at his feet. The air was sticky sweet with the smell of the fruit rotting from neglect, and flies buzzed everywhere.

Tarō scrambled into his tree to pluck several fresh peaches, all of them bigger than his fist. Stuffing them in his *kimono*, he jumped down and sprinted back to the cover of the wood.

Kamehime was still asleep when he returned. He slipped close to her, pausing a moment to admire the delicate curve of her neck again and the soft wisps of hair that had not been gathered into her pony tail. Entranced, he held out his hand, longing to touch her cheek.

Kamehime awoke with a start. Mistaking his affection, she slapped him hard across his face. He recoiled, embarrassed, rubbing the sting from his cheek.

"What are you doing?" she asked, eyeing him suspiciously.

"Nothing—" he said guiltily, stuttering. "I only—are you hungry?" he quickly offered.

He knelt before her, opening his *kimono* to let the peaches tumble onto the ground at her feet. Kamehime smiled and snatched up the lovely, blushing fruit, biting into it with delight.

They shared surprised laughter as they ate, their peaches bursting with juiciness, their hands and faces dripping with sticky, sweet nectar. When they finished, Tarō fed the other peaches to their grateful ponies, telling the horses to wait for their return since the sun had already disappeared behind the castle.

Night fell quickly, but they waited until the white stone walls of the castle keeps stood out against the surrounding, humid darkness. Studying the torchlight upon the castle walls, they plotted a course to avoid the well-lit areas. Taking a coil of rope over her shoulder, Kamehime and Tarō left their horses and the cover of the woods to dart through the orchard, ducking from tree to tree as they made their way toward the first wide moat that separated the orchards from the castle grounds.

At some distance, a troop of *samurai* marched across the bridge that spanned the moat. Tarō and Kamehime picked the darkest point and slipped into the mossy-smelling, inky water to swim across. Climbing up the other side, they darted to the base of the first of many walls that encircled the mountain fortress, taking care not to expose themselves to view from the guard towers.

The wall was high but they managed to climb it without being seen. When they dropped to the ground inside the fortress, they found it littered with more spoiled peaches, desecrated by Lord Monkey's *samurai* who had used the trees for target practice, many of the peaches pierced by arrows and left to rot in the summer heat. Flies buzzed everywhere, and Tarō and Kamehime wrinkled their noses at the smell of the sticky, rotten air.

As they approached the next enceinte, Kamehime raised her arm to stop Tarō. Signaling him to stay still, she crept forward, stalking a sentry whose silhouette she saw against the dark of night.

# Taro and Kamehime Raid Momoyama

When she had stolen within striking distance, she cautiously stepped to the side and, drawing her sword, gently tapped the ground near the sentry. Startled, the guard stuck out his head, peering into the darkness for an instant before Kamehime cut him down. Quickly and quietly, Tarō helped her prop the corpse against a tree to conceal it from discovery.

They wasted no time moving through the tree cover, swimming the next moat, and climbing the next wall, always using the cover of the peach trees that grew throughout the castle grounds. When they crossed the third moat and wall without being noticed, they climbed into a tree to catch their breaths and survey the last massive barrier that guarded the inner courtyard. Lord Monkey's *samurai* patrolled the base, so Tarō and Kamehime had to wait for the patrol to pass. As soon as they saw an opening, they both leaped from the tree cover and bolted for the wall, nimbly leaping onto its stonework and clambering up the face as quickly and quietly as they could manage before the patrol returned.

Just as Kamehime had hoped, Lord Monkey's *samurai* were focused on their preparations for war. The castle courtyard swarmed with activity. Even at night, Lord Monkey's *samurai* toiled furiously, the grounds lit everywhere with flickering torches. Tarō and Kamehime hesitated, debating how they would traverse the inner courtyard to the keeps, and what was the best approach to scale the tower, and what if the Emperor was not there?

Fortunately, several startled horses raised a commotion at the other end of the compound nearest the main gate. Tarō and Kamehime wasted no time traversing the courtyard to a tall, twisted pine tree beside the larger keep. Then, as quietly as shadows they crept to the steep stone wall that formed the foundation of the tower. With but one look at the five, elegantly tiered roofs stacked upon each other, their plaster walls pale against the night, they pulled themselves onto the stones to begin their climb.

Scaling the steep wall was not easy, but not as difficult as it had been to negotiate the much larger stones of Edo Castle. As skillfully as spiders, they clung to the crevices between the stones, pausing every now and then to make certain they were not discovered, while the castle remained preoccupied with reinforcements arriving at the main gate.

When they reached the top of the stone wall, in order to remain hidden from the windows above, they were forced to negotiate a corner of the first tier. This they did by leaping from their footholds on the castle wall to grasp at clefts in the jointed timbers. Tarō nimbly managed with his animal agility, but Kamehime slipped and would have fallen if not for Tarō, who quickly grabbed her arm to pull her up beside him.

They both glanced at the ground below. Discovery was the least concern since a fall from that height would mean certain death.

They did not pause long to ponder the risk. Tarō led the way as they clung to the timbers, wedging their bodies against the braces to pull themselves onto the roof. In this way they negotiated the first two tiers, and it was much less difficult to climb the crisscrossing hipped and gabled roofs of the remaining two levels.

They took care not to spend too long in the slices of light that fell from the slatted windows in the gables. When, at last, they climbed over the railing of the outer parapet on the topmost level, they sat with their backs against the wall to catch their breaths.

Dim light and the plaintive twang of *koto* music filtered through the slatted window above them. Standing cautiously, Kamehime and Tarō peered through the window.

A narrow inner parapet ran beneath the windows that encircled the top of the chamber, with a ceiling tall enough to accommodate a man standing at full height upon the parapet. At the moment, no one stood guard, but a number of men and women in noble attire could be seen sitting on cushions in the chamber below, variously engaged in muted conversation or playing games, while a blind court musician played the *koto* to pass their time in house arrest. A princely boy sat at the head of the room, surrounded by attendants.

"The Emperor!" Kamehime whispered to Tarō, both grinning proudly at their good fortune.

As Tarō looked around, searching for a way inside, a door opened suddenly on the chamber below. Lord Monkey strode into the room, accompanied by his squire and a dozen *samurai*, including one uncommonly large and ugly bodyguard, so big he had to duck his head to keep from hitting it on the doorway as he entered the room. He was a massive man, much larger than any of his clan, so large that he walked with a permanent hunch so as not to hit his head on ceilings, which made him appear all the more brutish, and he wore armor of black and brown leather, his left side leaning on a heavy wooden hammer, its handle twisted at the end like a cane. His sallow ogre-face rivaled Lord Monkey's ugly countenance, so much so that one might have thought his Lord kept the brute around to make him look handsome by comparison.

"Lord Monkey!" Tarō muttered, his hands curling into fists.

Cowed by Lord Monkey's *samurai* and especially his ogreish *yōjimbō*, the nobles huddled together. A tense moment followed, as the warlord surveyed his audience, his eyes narrowing, until he turned once more to the Emperor and bowed for effect.

"Your Grace, as I suspected, Tokugawa marches on Kyōto. It is indeed fortunate that you could arrive here safely. His spies are everywhere."

"Kyōto has known only peace," the prince said plaintively.

"When the country is rid of these traitors and united under your rule, then we will have peace," Lord Monkey retorted. "Tokugawa has defied your order, your Grace."

"My order?"

"Your Grace commanded Lords Ishida, Mōri, and Tokugawa to appear for inquisition regarding Lord Oda's demise. Tokugawa marches on Kyōto with an army of 70,000 *samurai*. I would call that defiance of your order."

"I never gave such an order—" the Emperor said naively.

"Yes, your Grace, you did," Lord Monkey interrupted, taking a document from his *kimono* sleeve. "I have it here," he said, quickly stashing the paper again before the Emperor could ask to see it. "As I said, you must not trouble yourself with affairs of state. Such mean activities are beneath your Grace."

His eyes fixing on a heavy *Go* board with black and white stones for game pieces, Lord Monkey smiled in amusement.

"Now, what was I saying? Ah, yes, spies everywhere." Lord Monkey surveyed his audience again. "Did you know a sickness may spread among pigs that feed at the same trough, your Grace?" Lord Monkey glanced at the Emperor. "No, of course not, such trivia is beneath your Majesty."

Pacing the room, Lord Monkey paused before a handsome young man in noble finery.

"The key to safeguarding the herd is in isolating the infection," Lord Monkey said, striking an imposing stance, glaring until the young man hung his head, terrified.

The Emperor watched tensely as Lord Monkey held out his hand palm up. When he did not respond, Lord Monkey struck the young man with his gauntleted hand so hard he fell to the floor.

Kamehime tensed, ready to spring into action, but Tarō held her back, shaking his head. She sighed anxiously, and they stood fast, watching tensely.

Lord Monkey nodded to one of his *samurai* who stepped forward to jerk the courtier to his feet. Again Lord Monkey shoved his palm in front of the suspect. The young man raised his head. He could not meet Lord Monkey's gaze, but he reached into his *kimono* and drew forth a letter. Lord Monkey smiled as he received it. He studied the young man contemptuously.

Without turning, Lord Monkey beckoned to one of his *samurai*, who brought forth a basket. Uncovering the basket, he revealed the severed head of a young woman. Seeing it, the man cried out and fell to the floor.

Clutching the letter in one hand, Lord Monkey grabbed a blood-clotted clump of hair on the severed head and drew it forth. His audience gasped in recognition. A few noblewomen cried out and fell sobbing to the floor. Some courtiers lost their stomachs. Lord Monkey callously dropped the head, and it hit the floor with a thump and rolled a short distance. The Emperor stared in horror and disbelief.

"Sometimes," Lord Monkey continued, "an infected limb must be cut."

He turned his gaze on the paralyzed Emperor. Raising the letter, his eyes fixed on the Emperor, he slowly opened the note. His eyebrows peaked with interest as he read.

"This almost looks like your Grace's hand," Lord Monkey said, "but I know such base politics are beneath your grace and divinity. Rest assured, your Majesty," he added, his eyes flashing, "I am sworn to protect you from such treason."

"I know—" the Emperor said.

"You do *not* know—" Lord Monkey spat, then quickly checked himself, finishing in a silky tone, "what is best for you. But I do, your Grace."

"How could a farmer's son know what is best for the son of a goddess?" the boy blurted naïvely, striking a nerve.

Lord Monkey's head twisted, his lips writhing like a viper poised to strike. He studied the boy with a look of disgust.

Drawing a knife from his sash, Lord Monkey took one step toward the young man who had hidden the letter and opened his throat with the blade. Blood spilled over the young man's *kimono* as he sank to the *tatami* floor.

A united cry of grief and terror rose from the audience as the nobility scrambled for safety. Even the *samurai* who had restrained the young man quickly released the dying body, stepping back to avoid the blood as it stained the floor. Kamehime tensed to spring into action, but once again Tarō held her back.

The Emperor stared as someone who had never seen death until that very moment.

"The Prince of Peach Mountain!" Lord Monkey mocked, when he saw the Emperor's expression of innocence violated. "You see, your Grace, I know you better than you know yourself," he added with a spiteful sneer. "And now, your Majesty, I must prepare a traitor's welcome."

As Lord Monkey turned to leave, he heard a creak in the wood above him. Tarō and Kamehime froze. Lord Monkey paused, a thoughtful look on his face, then he strode from the room, followed by his men and the lumbering ogre.

Tarō and Kamehime sighed relief when Lord Monkey had gone. They listened for a moment, then checked the window. It was strong, but together they managed to snap out first one and then other slats until they made a hole large enough to squeeze through and climb onto the parapet inside.

"Shh!" Kamehime whispered to the babbling nobles below.

When the Emperor stepped forward, she knelt and bowed.

"Your Majesty," she whispered. "We're here to rescue you."

The courtiers murmured anxiously as the strangers descended the ladder from the parapet and Kamehime knelt again. Tarō hesitantly followed her lead, somewhat dubious of this prince who looked no older than he and a lot smaller.

"Your Grace," Kamehime whispered. "I am Kamehime, Lord Tokugawa's daughter, and this is Tokuyama Tarō—"

"Takeda," Tarō corrected.

Kamehime nodded a quick apology but continued insistently, "Your Grace, we must leave immediately."

The Emperor looked around at his courtiers. "What of my retainers and attendants?"

Kamehime shook her head. "They cannot come."

"But I cannot leave my people—"

"Your Grace," she interrupted, then realized her misstep when she saw the boy's face, unaccustomed as he was to being interrupted by his lesser, let alone a girl. She bowed, pleading with him, "my father's army marches here to lay siege to the castle. If it comes to battle, I fear for your safety, and theirs. Many good and loyal *samurai* will die, your Majesty—"

"But what of Lord Monkey? He will return and find me gone," the Emperor fretted.

"No, he won't," Tarō said, undoing his sash and *kimono.*

Kamehime frowned as if the plan had already been argued and conceded.

"I will find *him,* when the time is right," Tarō avowed with a cold light in his eyes.

"It is the only way, your Grace," she affirmed.

Reluctantly, the Emperor agreed when his retainers also insisted his safe escape was their paramount concern, but the nobility murmured with disdain as they watched his divine person disrobe to swap clothes with Tarō. Their transformation complete, the prince chuckled at himself in Tarō's garb and armor, while Tarō felt odd in the Emperor's luxurious *kimono.*

"At least you look the part from behind," Kamehime said as she looked Tarō over. "Now, we must go quickly!"

She turned and climbed the ladder, and they followed. Suddenly, the castle bell rang, startling them. They froze, until they realized it was only tolling the hour, but they waited for it to finish to be sure.

Tarō watched from the outer parapet as she crawled backward on her belly, down the tiled roof, followed by the Emperor, both of them holding her rope, which she had tied to the tower.

When she reached the eaves, she raised her head to look at Tarō one last time. Even in darkness his sharp eyes perceived her brief smile, just before she disappeared over the edge of the roof and out of sight, followed by the Emperor.

Tarō sighed. There was nothing for him to do at the moment, but he did not care to rejoin the clucking courtiers below, so he lingered on the parapet a little longer, even though he knew he must mingle with those humans, if only to keep up appearances.

Outside, Kamehime peered over her shoulder to get her bearings on the steep, gabled roof, which she negotiated quickly so she could watch out for the Emperor. He clung to the rope and hugged the roof, hesitant to trust his limbs, but he managed to ease himself down until he was close enough so she could brace his legs.

As soon as he had a safe footing, Kamehime directed him to crouch low. The prince stared at his stinging hands, unaccustomed as they were to hard work, while she looked around to make sure they had not been discovered.

The castle was still unaware of them hiding in the shadows. All they heard was the bustle of activity in the courtyard below.

Satisfied, she took out her knife and cut the rope, leaving the used length. The Emperor looked confused, but she silently reassured him with a raised hand. She pointed across the stripes of light that streamed from one slatted window to their next point of descent where the hipped roof crisscrossed with the gabled tier below. With a finger to her lips, she signaled they should cross.

They cowered as they traversed the light from the window but moved undetected to the eaves. There was nowhere for her to tie off the rope without risking discovery so she secured one end around the Emperor and directed him to follow closely as they negotiated the next tier, putting her shoulder into his descent while she did her best to steady her own footing on the slanting tiled roof.

When they both crouched safely on the second tier, she praised him with a cheerful nod. Signaling him to wait, she crawled down the sloped roof to one cornice to peer over the edge.

The activity in the courtyard sounded much nearer, even though they were still high up, but it was the noise of other pursuits in preparation for war. She tied off her rope on the cornice, testing it with a tug, then motioned for the Emperor to come.

Crawling toward her, the Emperor slipped on a loose tile. It skittered across the roof and fell with a faint crash on the ground far below. Almost immediately, shouts rose from the courtyard.

"Hurry!" she called, but the prince lay frozen with fright.

"Look! On the roof!" a voice suddenly shouted from a window overlooking their position.

Three *samurai* broke out the slatted window to climb onto the roof, as Kamehime crawled toward the Emperor.

"Get them!" Another man shouted from the window, as the three *samurai* bounded down the roof.

Kamehime quickly put herself between the Emperor and their enemies, drawing her sword. The center man was the first to reach them. He rushed headlong to deliver an overhead strike, but she leaned deeply to her right, presenting her sword horizontally to protect the entire length of her extended left side.

Sparks flew when their swords struck. No sooner had she blocked his strike than she swung her sword around to slice the man's side just below his armpit, cleaving deeply into his torso. With a jerk, she pulled her sword free of the man's meat, and he fell backward, his corpse blocking one of his cohorts, while the other came at her from the right.

Her first stroke passed fluidly into the second, as she twisted her hips back to cut the next man under his right elbow, hacking his limb so it hung from a single band of flesh, blood spewing from the wound. Still holding his sword, his left hand swung wide and struck the roof. He dropped, yelling and clutching his spewing limb. She finished him with a stroke that loosed his head, while the Emperor stared aghast, still paralyzed with panic.

As a fourth *samurai* climbed through the window onto the roof, Kamehime barely deflected a strike from the third as he hurdled his fallen comrade. They locked swords close to the handguards, but he surprised her with a sudden headbutt that sent her rolling down the roof.

Stopping herself, she scrambled backward as he pounced again, intending to cleave her down the middle. She received his strike, flowing with it until her sword rotated into a superior position. With a quick blow from the flat of her blade on his wrists, she knocked the sword from his hands. Even so, her assailant was too close. He came crashing down on her, and her sword fell onto the roof.

In an instant, his hands were on her throat. She could feel the bloodlust in his breath, and his grip on her neck made her heart pound in her head. She knew she had only seconds.

In a sudden burst, she twisted outside one of his arms, driving her forearm through his elbow and shattering it. The man reeled from his injury, lost his footing, and fell to the courtyard.

Spying her sword, Kamehime snatched it up just as the fourth *samurai* descended on her. Whipping like a reed, she snapped her hips to counterbalance the abrupt motion of her arms, dropping her sword hilt outside her body to deflect his strike.

Her parry was sure. As his strike went wide, she shifted her weight to spring forward, driving the tip of her sword just above her foe's gorget to penetrate his throat under the jaw. His mouth gaped grotesquely as her sword point drove deep into his brainpan. Snapping her hands to free her sword, the man toppled and fell.

"You must be Tomoe Gozen reborn!"[10] the Emperor exclaimed, staring at their vanquished foes.

Kamehime smiled, pleased to hear his praise, but she did not dwell on it. She quickly sheathed her sword and urged the Emperor to follow her to the eaves.

---

[10] A renowned, 12th century *onna bugeisha* [女武芸者], "female martial artist."

"I'll go first," she said, checking above and below.

Shouts rose from the courtyard, but no other foes appeared. She quickly lowered herself over the edge and nimbly dropped to the roof below, then she called to the Emperor to follow. All the while her heart and mind raced, wondering how they could escape now that they had been discovered.

# 9

## THE TIGER AND THE OGRE

*Yamashiro Province*

*Summer, Year of the Rat*

The castle bell tolled, and continued to sound the hour, a resonant bong reverberating over the din of battle preparations in the courtyard. A strong wind buffeting his face, Lord Monkey stuck his head out of the tower to survey the moonlit landscape. The view from the highest chamber in Momoyama Castle was as breathtaking as it was strategic. Crowning the summit of Peach Mountain, the castle commanded a panorama of the surrounding countryside, east and west along the Eastern Sea Road between Edo and Kyōto, as well as Ise Bay to the south, and Lake Biwa and the monkish stronghold on Mount Hiei to the north, thus guarding all approaches to Kyōto.

"He who controls Momoyama Castle, controls Kyōto—" Lord Monkey said aloud to himself, as he surveyed the view to the north and the road leading into the capital city, "and he who controls Kyōto, controls the country." The castle bell finished tolling. "Nine bells," he noted, "already Hour of the Rat."

The wider tower tiers partially obscured his view, but he could hear the sounds of his army mustering for war in the orange torchlight, which pleased him immensely. He drew a deep breath in anticipation of the realization of all his dreams and machinations.

He left the window, turning his attention to the chamber. The room was lit with candles in each corner and on a central table. A large campaign map occupied most of the table except for a number of scrolls heaped at one end. Lacquered, wooden tiles marched across the map, showing the positions of his forces and those of Tokugawa between Kyōto and Edo.

Three formidable warlords, Lord Monkey's chief generals, bent over the campaign map, while a number of attendant *samurai* stood or knelt around the room, and others passed in and out of the chamber by the staircase leading below. Hunched in one corner beside the stairs, the ogre-faced *samurai* stood guard.

"My Lord," General Katō solicited, "if Tokugawa knows the Emperor supports him—perhaps it would be best to deploy our forces above the plain. We outnumber his army. We should not sit idle and risk a siege."

"General," Lord Monkey said, looking sideways at the Lord of Kumamoto, "I care not for the Emperor's sympathies. He is a child—a divine child—but a simpering child nonetheless. He is hardly suited to govern. I alone know what is best for the Emperor, and the country. General Mōri, have the ships been made ready?"

"Yes, my Lord!" his general said, his mustache and goatee in the Chinese style making him look more priest than admiral.

"Good! They must be fit to depart Ōsaka on an hour's notice. General Ishida—" Lord Monkey turned to a shrewd-looking man cursed with a weak chin and a small brush of mustache. "Our forces will remain in the castle long enough to draw Tokugawa onto the mountain," he said, using a baton of lacquered wood with leather tassels to push a wooden tile across the map from Edo to Ise Bay just below Momoyama Castle. "Lord Mōri will sail our ships into the bay to cut off his retreat, and *then,* Lord Katō, *then* we will descend on his army—and crush it!"

Shouts outside the tower disturbed Lord Monkey's moment. He looked up as more shouts rose from below.

"My Lord!" a *samurai* shouted as he mounted the stairs.

"What?" Lord Monkey spat, irritated by the interruption.

"Intruders, my Lord! Outside the Emperor's quarters!"

Lord Monkey's eyes narrowed. He strode to the window and saw what appeared to be two *samurai* scaling the tower, his own soldiers sallying from a window to engage them.

"Bring me their heads!" Lord Monkey shouted.

"At once, my Lord!" the messenger replied, turning on his heels to run below.

As he watched his *samurai* bound down the roof to arrest the intruders, Lord Monkey's face twisted with a sudden thought.

"Generals, you have your orders!" he bellowed, turning on his heel.

Lord Monkey wore his short sword in his sash but motioned for his squire to fetch his longer *daitō* and follow.

"Come!" he ordered the ogre. "There may be work for you."

An ugly smile broke across the ogre's face, showing large teeth almost as long as animal fangs. Lord Monkey descended the staircase with quick intent, his squire at his heel, and the ogre dropped to his fists to follow, bent over and ducking his head, his hammer-cane thumping so he looked like an armored ape as he lumbered to keep up with them down several flights of stairs and into the corridor adjoining the two keeps.

When they came to the Emperor's quarters in the adjacent tower, Lord Monkey waited for his bodyguard. The brute stepped forward to throw open the sliding door, nearly tearing it off its track. Inside the chamber, the nobles backed away in fear.

Lord Monkey strode into the chamber, quickly surveying the room. His eyes narrowed when he perceived the back of the Emperor's elegant *kimono* among the cluster of nobility huddled at the far end of the chamber.

"Your Grace," he said, trying to get a better look at the Emperor. "There is an intruder in the castle."

Patient in his disguise, Tarō did not respond or move. He sat on a cushion with his head bowed, as if praying at a low table arranged for that purpose.

"Your Grace?"

Lord Monkey did not wait for an answer but strode across the chamber, followed by his squire and the ogre. The courtiers broke and cowered, murmuring in fright to see the ogre again at Lord Monkey's heel, but Tarō did not turn. He held his sword hilt with one hand, gripping the scabbard with the other, his knuckles white with hatred as he tensed to avenge his parents.

"Your Grace?" Lord Monkey called again as he drew near.

The warlord hesitated, sensing something amiss. He reached instinctively for his *wakizashi* but Tarō turned and slashed with animal swiftness. The strike glanced off Lord Monkey's breastplate as he sprang backward, but he did not draw his *wakizashi.* His squire stood at his side, offering his Lord's sword with one hand, while menacing Tarō with his own drawn sword.

"Hold!" Lord Monkey ordered as the ogre started forward.

His bodyguard swung back and forth, grinning hungrily, poised to pounce but waiting for his master's word. Terrified, the nobility scattered to the far corners. Only Tarō stood his ground.

Although he had grown since their last meeting and now stood taller than the warlord, Tarō was tiny next to the enormous ogre. Even so, his every muscle tensed, ready for the fight.

"Where is the Emperor?" Lord Monkey demanded, staring in disgust at this imposter.

"Gone!" Tarō said with a smug smile.

"Who are you?" Lord Monkey demanded.

"I am Tarō," he snapped, hatred in his eyes, "son and heir to Lord Takeda Nobutora—the Tiger of Kai!"

Lord Monkey's eyebrows furrowed but an instant then rose in recognition.

"So," he said scornfully, "you escaped me and the cold?"

"Even monkeys fall from trees," Tarō jabbed, robbing Lord Monkey of his sneer.

"Takeda cur! Has Tokugawa kept you secret all these years?" He paused in thought, then stabbed, "Obviously, he kept *his* secret from you."

Tarō made a face, confused. Seeing he had hit his mark, Lord Monkey laughed.

"Fool! Didn't he tell you his fireside story? Yes, I killed Takeda, but it was Tokugawa who burned his castle to the ground with everyone in it."

Lord Monkey's words struck Tarō like an armored fist.

"Liar!" Tarō yelled.

"Oh, no," Lord Monkey said with perverse satisfaction, "the truth is much sharper! Not that it matters—" he added with an evil grin. "Kill him!" he shouted over his shoulder to the ogre.

The ogre immediately lunged for Tarō. Already tensed, Tarō sprang upward as the brute charged, leaping over the heavy *samurai* to kick off his back and dive at Lord Monkey, slashing from above. The warlord did not expect such ferocity, and Tarō's stroke might have done more damage, but he cut short to evade the squire who sprang to defend his Lord. Even so the tip of Tarō's blade grazed Lord Monkey's unscarred cheek, drawing first blood.

Lord Monkey reeled, clutching his bleeding cheek, and retreated from the room. Tarō having dodged at the last moment, the squire's forceful cut struck the floor. Tarō crouched deeply and sprang off his feet like a fox, pouncing upward, both hands on his sword to drive into the man's throat. The squire reeled, spurting blood. Tarō did not pause, for he felt the ogre's shadow. He dove to the side just as the brute brought the full force of his hammer down, the blow splintering the floor beneath the *tatami.*

The ogre roared as he raised himself and turned, but Tarō dove and nimbly tumbled close behind him, slashing at his unarmored ankle, his sword cutting through the massive tendon. The ogre howled and dropped to his knee, his ankle no longer supporting his weight, but he swung wide with his arm, catching Tarō across his side with a force that cracked ribs. Tarō bounced across the floor and into the wall with a thud, only half-conscious.

The ogre grimaced with pain and rage. He used his hammer to raise himself, then limped toward Tarō, his hammer striking the floor with powerful thuds as he supported his injured side.

The nobility cowered in the corners. No one moved to Tarō's aid. He tried to focus as the ogre lurched toward him, struggling to raise himself and wincing from the pain in his side. He scanned the chamber for his sword. The scabbard lay many paces away and, not far beyond, his sword, but too far to reach.

The ogre loomed over Tarō, shifting his weight to his one good leg so he could raise his hammer overhead with both hands. Weakly, Tarō tensed for a blow that did not come, as a terrific roar filled the room.

The astonished ogre turned to see an enormous black bear rivaling his own size, standing on its hind legs, its forepaws raised to display razor-sharp claws and baring its fearsome teeth. It was the instant Tarō needed.

Clutching his side, Tarō bounded toward his sword. The bewildered ogre, deprived of his kill, turned on the bear, but the bruin quickly retreated toward the cowering nobility, men and women screaming and scattering before this new threat.

Tarō grabbed his sword, still clutching his side with one arm. He considered his injury, then his sword, then the distracted ogre, pausing only an instant in thought before placing the sword between his teeth. Bounding toward the brute, both hands outstretched at the last moment as he sprang onto the ogre's back, he dug his heels and wrapped his arms around his foe in the best chokehold he could manage on the brute's thick neck.

The ogre lumbered backward in surprise, crashing into one wall, knocking over a candle, which hit the floor and lit the straw *tatami.* Tarō grunted in pain but held fast, his sword tight in his teeth, thrashing his head back and forth against the rolls of flesh at the base of the ogre's skull.

The ogre howled as blood gushed from the wound. Taking hold of his sword, with a lightning stroke he opened the ogre's vein just below the jawline. Blood spewed fresh from the gash, and Tarō released the ogre, kicking off him to tumble safely away, although he winced in pain from the effort.

Tarō knelt and watched, as did the bear, its head sticking forward expectantly, while the courtiers cowered in the far corners of the room. Eyes wild in the throes of death, the ogre reeled and fell to his knees, then to the floor, and lay motionless as his life's blood seeped into the *tatami.*

The bear cast its eye on a lady crouching nearby, and she screamed. Surprised, the beast raised its paws, passively trying to reassure her, but she only screamed louder, and others joined her.

Tarō turned on the bear, who instantly became Tanuki, which only further confounded the frightened lady who fainted on the spot. Tarō stopped abruptly and sighed, for he had not seen Tanuki sneak into the tower.

"Friends?" Tanuki asked, hanging on Tarō's response.

"To the end!" Tarō said, grinning.

Taro Fights the Ogre

They embraced warmly, but their moment vanished when they saw the flames rising from the floor to take to the walls around them, smoke filling the room.

"Get out!" Tarō yelled to the cowering nobility.

The wailing nobles made for the entrance of the chamber, their panic thwarting a contingent of *samurai* who sought to enter.

"Come on!" Tarō yelled to Tanuki.

He ran for the ladder that led to the parapet, and Tanuki quickly followed as flame and smoke surged all around them. Both coughing, and Tarō wincing in pain, they climbed the ladder to the parapet. Punching out a window, they scrambled outside to bound down the roof, stopping at the edge to survey the courtyard.

Lord Monkey's *samurai* swarmed the grounds, raising torches, shouting and pointing toward Tarō and Tanuki, but their attention was focused on the flames leaping from the tower.

"Look!" Tarō said when he saw Kamehime and the Emperor sprawled on the first tier, cornered but not caught.

"We have to get to them."

Tanuki's eyes brightened with a thought. Instantly, he produced his treasure trove and hastily scoured through it.

"I knew this would come in handy!" he exclaimed as he drew forth the *tengu* feather that Tarō had won just months ago.

Tarō stared, puzzled.

"Do you trust me?"

Tanuki's treasure bag vanished as he offered Tarō his paw. With a quizzical look, Tarō nodded and held Tanuki's paw.

"Go!" Tanuki barked.

Holding the *tengu* feather aloft, Tanuki waved it with a flourish and pointed to the roof below where Kamehime and the Emperor crouched. A sudden gust of wind surprised Tarō, as it lifted them into the air to swoop toward the lowermost roof.

The sudden appearance of Tarō and his *tanuki* startled Kamehime and the Emperor. Lord Monkey's *samurai* having marked them, arrows whistled over their heads.

"Come on!" Tarō yelled. "This way!"

Crouching low, Tarō led them across the roof. He and Tanuki moved nimbly, but Kamehime took care for the Emperor so he did not slip again.

"Can the feather carry all of us?"

"How should I know?" Tanuki shrugged.

"There's only one way to find out—" Tarō said, turning to Kamehime. "Do you trust me?"

She nodded, mystified, as Tarō lifted Tanuki onto his shoulders and offered his hands to Kamehime and the Emperor.

"Go!" Tanuki barked.

Holding the *tengu* feather aloft once more, Tanuki waved it and pointed across Ise Bay to the east. Another gust of wind lifted them, and Kamehime and the Emperor gasped in wonder as the magical breeze carried them over the castle grounds, clearing walls and moats, until the cries of the enemy faded behind them.

Gliding over the outermost wall and moat, Tanuki steered for the cover of the orchards. Tower guards watched in amazement as they flew past, but one sentry quickly recovered his wits and, raising his bow, he took aim for Tanuki and let fly his arrow. Tanuki cried out as it pierced him just below his shoulder. The magical feather slipped from his paw and wafted away, and they all plummeted, crashing through the boughs of a peach tree.

A low branch caught the Emperor so he hung there upside down and unconscious. Tree limbs broke their fall as well, but Tarō and Kamehime hit the orchard floor, raising a cloud of flies that buzzed over them as they lay motionless amid the rot of fallen peaches.

Tanuki managed to cling to one of the higher branches and dragged himself, painfully, onto the branch. Looking at the arrow sticking through the muscle just below his shoulder, he felt sick. Squeamish, but mustering his courage, he pulled hard on the arrow and held it up triumphantly, then swooned and collapsed on the tree branch.

# PART THREE

---

# MOMO TARŌ

# 桃太郎

Lord Monkey

Momo Taro

# 10

## FLIGHT TO THE SEA

*Yamashiro Province*

*Summer, Year of the Rat*

The scar from Tarō's blade still fresh on his cheek, Lord Monkey glared in rage as he watched orange flames engulf the topmost story of the taller keep, throwing sparks and embers at the sickle of the moon as it swung low over the castle. A newly appointed squire stood behind him with his Lord's campaign map and several scrolls in hand. Generals Katō and Ishida stood nearby.

"My Lord—" A lieutenant rushed forward, kneeling to report, stuttering, "the Emperor is gone."

Lord Monkey glared so the man sensed peril. He bowed lower still but to little avail. Lord Monkey drew his sword and severed the man's head from body in a single stroke. Blood spurted and pooled from the headless corpse where it fell in a heap. The head rolled some distance before it came to rest among scattered peaches, a cloud of flies buzzing over the fallen fruit. Lord Katō regarded his Lord with disgust, but Lord Monkey did not see his vassal's disapproving look as he turned his face from the heat of the fire, snorting in rage.

"No doubt the Emperor is being escorted to Tokugawa as we speak! Patrol the area! Find the Emperor and bring him to me!"

"At once, my Lord!" General Ishida replied.

"My Lord," General Katō spoke, "our latest intelligence reports Tokugawa's army is encamped above the cliffs on either side of the Eastern Sea Road, presumably to secure his line of supply before laying siege."

"The castle is lost."

"My Lord?"

"Withdraw the men."

"What of your plan, my Lord?"

"Nothing changes!" Lord Monkey railed, his eyes flashing. "Tokugawa's rear may no longer be an option, but his flank will still be exposed from the sea. Deploy your troops on the left above Sekigahara. General Ishida, you will secure the right flank and the Eastern Sea Road at Kuwana-juku with the bulk of our army. Our divisions will draw Tokugawa's forces onto the plain, while our ships sail from Ōsaka into the bay for the pincer move. Send to General Mōri for the fleet to sail at once."

"Yes, my Lord!" the generals said in unison, quickly bowing and retreating to carry out their orders.

As Lord Monkey watched his generals depart, a figure approached in the orange firelight, his head swaddled in a white cowl, his arms folded in the sleeves of his dark robe. A cabal of similarly dressed *Ikkō-ikki* warrior monks followed him, wearing breastplates of black lacquer and leather over their gray robes.

The *sōhei* struck terror in the hearts of Lord Monkey's *samurai*, who parted before them, until their leader stood facing Lord Monkey, head bowed beneath the shade of his white cowl. The monk raised his head, his face still in shadow but visible, his pale bluish skin and red eyes staring back. Lord Monkey flinched when their eyes met, but the warlord stood his ground.

"Move your army into the wood, circle around to the north of the plain. Conceal yourselves there until I raise the signal. With Tokugawa's defeat, our agreement will be fulfilled."

"With pleasure," the monk hissed, eyes flashing as he grinned, revealing black teeth and fangs.

As the monk retreated into the night with his disciples, Lord Monkey threw a final furious look at the burning castle before turning on his heel.

"My horse!" he shouted as he strode for the main gate.

太

Distant shouts stirred Tanuki as he straddled the peach tree dappled in moonlight. Seeing Tarō lying on the dark ground below, he called to him. Then, painfully, he moved to climb down.

Tarō winced from his cracked ribs as he revived on the orchard ground, surrounded by rotten peaches buzzing with flies. Shouts invaded the grove. Lord Monkey's *samurai* were not far.

Tarō shook himself. He checked Kamehime lying motionless beside him, pausing only a moment, debating his conflicting emotions. He admired and loved her, but Lord Monkey's revelation about her father haunted him.

Shouts jumped up again in the orchard. Tarō shook Kamehime to wake her.

"Where is the Emperor?" she exclaimed the moment she regained her senses.

They looked around and saw the prince hanging upside down from the peach tree.

"Is he—" she asked.

"I don't know."

"Your Grace!" Kamehime whispered hoarsely.

The Emperor slowly opened his eyes and groaned, then flinched in fright at his predicament. While Kamehime coached the prince to safety, Tanuki was already backing himself down the tree, his claws scratching for a grip on the bark until he dropped into Tarō's arms, though not without a little yelp of pain.

Shouts in the orchard grew nearer. Pointing out the low stone wall encircling the grove, Tarō quickly led the way as the beat of galloping horses approached.

"We cannot outrun them, not like this," Kamehime said.

They stopped. Tarō nodded agreement and looked around.

"Go!" he said.

"What about you?"

"I'll be right behind you! Go!" he said, and turning to Tanuki he added, "You go with them. I'll catch up."

Tanuki nodded bravely.

"Follow me!" she said to the prince, and they sprinted for the wood beyond the orchard, while Tanuki struggled to keep up.

Tarō stepped behind a tree to peer across the dark orchard as several horsemen approached, their steeds weaving around the trees. He waited for them to draw near, then he cupped his hand to his mouth and neighed at the top of his lungs.

"Hey!" he whinnied in horse-speech. "I'm a friend! Can you help me?"

Confused, the horses stopped abruptly, stamping and champing, while their riders whipped them with their reins to drive them forward. The horses whinnied back at Tarō, then began bucking wildly, throwing their riders one by one. They reared over their *samurai* masters, kicking the air, threatening death with their hooves, until the *samurai* scrambled backward and fled, terrified of retribution for years of mistreatment.

Tarō tarried only a moment, enjoying a quiet laugh, although he felt it in his injured side. Satisfied, he crept swiftly away to rejoin his friends and found them beneath the eaves of the wood.

Although they called out hoarsely, their ponies did not come. Tarō and the Emperor quickly exchanged clothes. Tarō made do with his breeches, using strips cut from his *kimono* to bind Tanuki's wound. Kamehime helped Tarō bind himself, but they soon heard shouts again, so they were forced to move.

They quickened their pace in flight down the moonlit mountainside, weaving through cypress trees, crashing through underbrush, and sliding on scree until they came to a thicket of bamboo so dense they had to squeeze between the giant bars of their prison to escape. They emerged onto a steep, rocky grade studded with twisted pine, descending on either side of a gorge through which flowed a rushing stream glittering in the moonlight.

They used the twisted pines to traverse the rocky slope, but each footing proved unsteady and sent loose rocks clattering into the brook, while others fell upon large rocks beside the stream. Soon, a noise like an avalanche echoed in the gorge, causing them to cringe at the likelihood of their discovery and driving a cloud of chittering bats from their roosts to dart through the night.

"Go on!" Tarō said, as another thought took him.

"What about you?" Kamehime asked.

"Trust me! Go!"

Kamehime took hold of Tanuki's paw to help him navigate the rugged slope with the Emperor close beside her. All the while, the shouts of their pursuers grew nearer.

"Hey!" Tarō suddenly called into the night.

Kamehime gasped, shocked that Tarō would give away their position, but he waved her on. Once more, he peered from behind a tree to watch as the *samurai* approached, several of them with lanterns held aloft. Looking up at the bats still circling frantically, he put his fingers to his mouth and whistled in a way that caught the bats' attention.

"Hey!" he chittered. "I'm a friend! Can you help me?"

The bats darted close to listen, and Tarō twittered and clicked until they whirled suddenly upward and flew off toward Lord Monkey's *samurai.*

In a rush of beating wings, the bats descended on the men, harrying them into a craze until they dropped their lanterns in a frantic retreat. Tarō laughed quietly to see it, still wincing from the pain it caused him, then he turned to rejoin his friends.

All the while descending toward the sea, the four companions ran beside the mountain stream for more than an hour at the fastest pace they could manage with Tanuki wounded and the unseasoned young Emperor whose legs were unaccustomed to forced marches. The taste and smell of sea spray greeted them as they scrambled out of the wood and brush to stand unexpectedly on a moonlit, well-hewn path in a wide, rocky cliff above foggy Ise Bay.

Looking across the bay, they could make out diffuse torchlight from a great encampment, presumably Lord Tokugawa's army, stretching across the Tōkaidō from Miya-juku along the northeastern spur of the Tortoise Mountains. To their left, the cliff descended gradually to the beach, and the Eastern Sea Road, and the grassy plain beyond. To their right, the cliff and the path rose steeply toward the headland, and a flight of stone steps led to a massive *torii* gate, the very same that Tarō and Kamehime had seen the day before, although now enshrouded in fog.

"Ise Shrine!" the Emperor exclaimed.

Tarō and Kamehime did not respond. The Emperor pointed toward the *torii.*

"We must go to the shrine," he said.

"No, there isn't time," Kamehime argued. "We must go to my father. It isn't safe here."

Descent to Ise Shrine

Tarō scowled when she spoke of her father.

"No! We must pray to Amaterasu Ōkami," the prince insisted, his suddenly mature, commanding tone surprising them.

"Tanuki should rest," Tarō added.

"I'm fine," Tanuki said but faltered, and Tarō caught him.

Kamehime acquiesced and followed as the Emperor turned to ascend the stairs to the shrine, Tarō supporting Tanuki along the way. Large stone frogs adorned the cliff-side of the staircase, their bulging eyes and heads poking out of the mist as the companions climbed the stairs. They reached the top and passed through the shadowy gate guarded by familiar effigies of Fūjin and Raijin, their crystal eyes following them as they traversed the moonlit courtyard perched beside the rocky cliffs.

Sacred sentinels, a few ancient cypress and maple trees, their leaves already hinting of autumn, surrounded the shrine. Tarō brought Tanuki into the dark main prayer hall, an enormous, double-gabled, pillared building, adjoined by a complex of cypress wood with gilt ornamentation shining in the moonlight.

The Emperor stopped to purify himself at the hallowed reservoir, and Kamehime dutifully joined him beneath the open, covered well, its water spilling from the mouth of a large iron frog. As she bathed her hands, she looked toward the bluff. Beyond the bay, she could still see the diffuse, flickering light of her father's encampment. With an anxious, backward glance, she followed the Emperor to the oratory.

The main hall was dark and quiet. A large braided rope with alternating tassels of rice straw and lightning-shaped paper streamers garlanded the eaves of the wide entrance. Purple curtains emblazoned with the imperial chrysanthemum hung behind. Just inside the entryway before the altar, a long rope and tassel attached to a bell hung from the ceiling.

The Emperor stepped up to the rope and pulled, softly rattling the bell. He bowed twice, clapped twice, and bowed again.

"Amaterasu Ōkami watches over the imperial house," the Emperor explained hopefully.

Kamehime nodded, observing the same ritual for a brief but sincere prayer before they stepped into the hall, dim except for a little moonlight that slipped inside the wide room fragrant with sandalwood, cypress, and *tatami*, its ceiling supported by enormous timbers. A fine bamboo blind partially obscured the altar. Tanuki lay nearby on the *tatami* floor with Tarō tending him.

"You don't need to fuss," Tanuki chattered, trying to lick his wound.

"Let me have a better look," Tarō chattered back.

Kamehime and the Emperor marveled at Tarō conversing with the raccoon-dog, but they had not forgotten how this magical creature had rescued them from the castle.

"I must go and find the abbot," the Emperor said, concerned for the creature.

"No, I'll find him," Kamehime offered, looking around.

She disappeared into the complex through a hallway beside the oratory and soon returned with three bald priests dressed in white robes.

"Majesty!" the abbot exclaimed, bowing low when he saw the Emperor, and his disciples quickly joined him.

"Our companion is hurt," the Emperor said.

"Allow me, your Grace," the abbot said, bowing and moving to examine Tanuki, who snarled and bared his teeth.

"It's okay," Tarō said. "They only mean to help."

Reluctantly, Tanuki submitted to the priest's examination. The abbot whispered to his disciples, who left to do his bidding, returning quickly with water to wash the wound and herbal medicine to heal it. Another priest bound Tarō's ribs with clean linen and provided him with a fresh *kimono*, and the third brought food for their guests, simple fare—seaweed soup, dried mackerel, and rice—but their hungry guests eagerly devoured it.

As Tanuki ate, the abbot moved to tend his wound. Instinctively, Tanuki snarled again but instantly recanted.

"I can't help it," he chattered to Tarō.

Tarō reassured the abbot, who carefully washed and treated the wound, while Tanuki winced and muttered.

"You'd better let me do that," Tarō said when it came time to bind the wound.

The temple bell tolled suddenly, startling them.

"It is but the tolling of the hour," the priest said, reassuring all but Kamehime.

"Ox Hour?" she asked anxiously, although the bell had not yet tolled eight times.[11]

"You may leave us," the prince said, sensing her disquiet. "We are most grateful."

"May Amaterasu Ōkami bless and protect you!" the abbot responded, bowing deeply before withdrawing with his disciples.

Kamehime bowed as the priests left, then glanced over her shoulder toward the bay. She started to speak, but the Emperor left her to kneel before the altar again, so she slipped away.

Tanuki yelped as Tarō bound the wound.

"Sorry! Too tight?" Tarō said in human speech.

Tanuki shook his head. He smiled thoughtfully.

"I'm sorry," he said, responding in human speech, which caught the Emperor's wondering ear.

"Why?" Tarō asked.

The Emperor stared over his shoulder in amazement when Tanuki conjured his treasure bag. After a brief search, he held up Yama Uba's mirror, offering it to Tarō who took it reluctantly.

"I'm sorry I ever looked at it."

---

[11] The witching hour, between 1:00 and 3:00 a.m., based on a 24-hour day divided into twelve 2-hour segments, each based on a Chinese zodiac animal.

"I'm not," Tanuki replied. "Maybe it didn't give you muscles—maybe that was Yama Uba—but it still has magic. The mirror saw through my human form. When it showed me my true self—just like you—I knew I had to find you."

Tarō smiled, grateful for his friend.

"After all," Tanuki joked, "you can't go to a fight without your coach!"

"I failed," Tarō said, his eyes dark and dejected.

The Emperor listened keenly over his shoulder.

"I had one chance to kill him—Lord Monkey—and I failed. If only I had my strength back. And Tokugawa—he destroyed my home and my people—" Tarō trailed off, filling with anger and sadness in the knowledge of his patron's betrayal. He looked around for Kamehime and realized she was not there. He sighed heavily. "I should never have left the forest."

Tanuki laid his good paw on Tarō's arm to comfort him. "We should go home."

"Yes," Tarō nodded and sighed deeply. "Just rest a little, then we'll go—home."

"Oh, yes," Tanuki said, laying his head on the *tatami* and closing his eyes. "That sounds good to me."

Tarō stood. Seeing the Emperor before the altar, he slipped outside to look for Kamehime and saw her standing at the cliff's edge, looking into the fog over the bay. Although he wanted to confront her, he lost heart. He stumped across the courtyard to the main gate where Fūjin and Raijin stood guard, but she could not hear his deliberate footsteps over the sound of the waves crashing against the rocky cliffs below her.

Kamehime watched the ocean swell and crash with a flash of white foam. Not far from the bluff, encircled by fog and surrounded by water, two rocky sea stacks pushed up above the surf, one a little taller, both joined by a massive, braided rope with large tassels of rice straw. As the wedded rocks were a sacred focal point of the shrine, a small arched *torii* stood on the larger of the two islands. The ocean crashed against the coupled rocks and sloshed against the cliffs again, then ebbed into the dark sea.

Kamehime looked across the bay, straining her eyes for any glimpse of her father's army encampment through the fog. She followed the diffuse torchlight across the Eastern Sea Road to the army's left flank positioned below the tall Tortoise Mountains encircling the valley. Above and behind her, as Momoyama Castle belched flames like a small volcano, flickering fiery tendrils snaked their way down the mountainside. Suddenly, she understood. She turned, startled to see the Emperor behind her.

"Your Grace," she said. "It isn't safe here. We must join my father now."

Seeing Tarō standing near the gate, she started toward him.

"Wait," the Emperor said, "let me speak to him."

Once again, his mature tone surprised and puzzled her, but she obeyed. She watched as he joined Tarō at the entrance.

Tarō stood gazing out the portal at a partial vista of the dark wooded foothills above and below the shrine, bounded by the lighter night sky. He could not see the moon, but he knew it was there, its light seeping into the dark forest, illuminating the tattered strands of fog that crept up from the bay to wind their way into the wood. He glanced at the formidable effigies of Fūjin and Raijin, their crystal eyes staring back at him from the shadows beneath the pillared gate, but hearing the prince approach, he turned.

"I understand how you feel."

Tarō did not respond.

"I overheard you talking to the *tanuki*. I know—"

"You don't know!" Tarō said, his voice cracking with rage fighting grief. "Lord Monkey killed my parents, and I failed to avenge them, and Lord Tokugawa killed the rest of my family, and I *saved his life*! You know nothing."

The prince balked. No one had ever questioned or argued with him in this way. Even his advisors had always counseled him with strained—or feigned—courtesy.

"I know Lord Oda killed many innocent people—in *my name*," he responded, "and now Hashiba—Lord Monkey—has taken his place, but I do not believe the same of Lord Tokugawa."

"So Lord Monkey lied about him burning my home?"

"No," the prince said, shaking his head, "but Lord Tokugawa had no choice. He swore an oath of allegiance to Oda to attack the Takeda clan in the name of the Emperor—my grandfather," he added, seeing the look in Tarō's eyes.

"Oda persuaded my grandfather to give up the throne, but my father died suddenly. I became the Emperor, and Lord Oda was appointed as my regent. Then your father petitioned the other lords to unite against him, so he ordered Lord Tokugawa to destroy the Takeda clan. I was told Lady Tsukiyama's only crime was having corresponded with your father for some time, seeking a Takeda wife for her son, but after Lord Tokugawa carried out his order, Oda accused his wife and son of treason for conspiring to warn your father and ordered their executions."

Tarō listened grudgingly, unmoved by his explanation.

"When Oda perished, Lord Monkey accused Tokugawa, claiming it was revenge for killing his wife and son, but I never believed him—and now he is regent," he said, shaking his head sadly, "and I gave him that power. He holds the Crown Jewel."

"But why?"

"I was afraid," he confessed, downcast. "I don't have any real power." He sighed, his shoulders sagging. "'Carry yourself as a god,' my grandfather said, 'but be prepared to bend like bamboo in a storm if you hope to survive the tempest of life'—those were his last words to me."

His heart remained unmoved, but Tarō realized he had misjudged this boy who showed insight beyond his years.

"Lord Monkey's army is coming!" Kamehime cried when she could wait no longer. "We must go to my father, your Grace!"

The Emperor turned, but Tarō kept his back to her, staring at the implacable guardians, frozen in their fearsome poses.

"My father can protect us," she said, trying for his attention.

Tarō huffed sarcastically. "Protect us? Your father put me in a cage, remember?"

"He doesn't know you like I do—"

"He knows I'm just another Takeda," Tarō snapped and suddenly accused, "You *knew*, didn't you?"

He turned on her. Seeing the look in his eyes, she blanched.

"You knew he burned my home and killed my people—"

"I—I tried to tell you—I wanted to explain but I didn't know how."

"Explain?" he accused.

"You don't understand—"

"I understand your father—"

"He was ordered to—"

"So?"

"He is *samurai*, sworn to carry out his duty—"

"*Samurai*," Tarō mocked. "And what did he get for his precious *samurai* honor and duty? How did you feel when Oda killed your mother and brother?"

"She was not my mother."

Confused, Tarō stared at her.

"My mother was Lady Tsukiyama's lady-in-waiting." She stared past Tarō, troubled by her recollection. "When she discovered their affair, Lady Tsukiyama ordered my mother stripped naked and driven in shame from Edo Castle. They tied her to a stake for all to see. Since my mother could not return to the castle, Lord Honda took pity on her and gave her sanctuary. She died giving birth to me."

Tarō did not respond. Looking through the gate, Kamehime saw the flickering lines of torchlight snaking their way farther down the mountainside from the castle.

"Lord Monkey's army!" she said, pointing through the portal. "Please, your Grace, we must join my father. If we go now, he may still have time to withdraw and summon other lords to champion you." She paused. "Tarō?"

Tarō stared stubbornly through the portal. Faced with their impasse, the Emperor sighed heavily.

"In my short life, I have seen my country ravaged at the whim of ruthless warlords," the Emperor said. "I do not know Lord Tokugawa well, but I know he stands against Lord Monkey. The fate of my people rests in their hands, and I am powerless to do more than pray for our salvation. I will go to Lord Tokugawa in the hope that my presence will bless his cause, for if Lord Monkey should win, I fear my people will fall into darkness."

"Tarō?" Kamehime tried once more.

"Go! Go to your father," he said finally, "I'm going home. Yama Uba was right, the world of men is cruel."

Kamehime's head dropped in disappointment. She summoned her resolve and angrily brushed past him to leave.

"I am in your debt, Takeda Tarō," the Emperor said, "and yours, Master Tanuki," he added, as Tanuki hobbled across the courtyard to join them.

Tanuki smiled to hear his praise. With a gracious bow, the Emperor strode through the gate to follow Kamehime. Tarō watched the two of them start down the steep flight of steps, but she stopped suddenly and turned.

"Don't you get it? This isn't about you!" She choked, holding back tears. "A *samurai* is born to serve the greater good!" She started to leave, then jabbed, "You may be Takeda, but you will never know what it means to be *samurai*!"

She turned, wiping her eyes as she disappeared down the stairs with the Emperor.

"*Samurai*," Tarō repeated in disgust, looking at Tanuki who simply shrugged.

The sky was growing lighter with the approach of dawn, and a strong wind began to blow across the bay, driving the fog inland. As Tarō looked at the guardians again, their crystal eyes flashing, the sea crashed loudly against the cliffs below the shrine. A sudden wind gusted through the courtyard, stirring up little dust devils, harbingers of a coming storm.

## 11

# WIND IN THE WOODS, FIRE ON THE MOUNTAIN

*Ise Province*

*Autumn, Year of the Rat*

While the sea crashed against the cliffs below, the line of stone frogs along the bluff watched Kamehime and the Emperor descend the rough-hewn staircase toward the Eastern Sea Road. The sky grew lighter, and the wind blowing across the bay drove the fog ahead of them, but they hiked for more than an hour down the rocky grade. The path descended to its lowest point near the sandy shoreline before rising again to join the road, its course obscured by the fog. Kamehime turned there to descend the rocky slope to the beach.

"The road is ahead," the Emperor said.

"Lord Monkey controls the road. We must go this way."

The Emperor nodded and followed. She carefully picked the way down the slope, through sea oats and shifting sand dunes, but no sooner had they reached the beach than they heard shouts above them.

A squad of mounted *samurai* clad in black armor, and bearing Lord Monkey's standards at their backs, had seen them and gave chase. Kamehime and the Emperor broke into a run, kicking up sand as they raced along the shoreline toward the opposite side of the bay, the surf crashing beside them.

Looking back to check on the Emperor, she saw the *samurai* reach the beach and set their horses to gallop. She looked around in desperation. The beach ran ahead too great a distance. They had not even come to the first river.

"Into the water," she directed, veering to the right to splash into the breaking waves.

The prince hesitated. When she called to him again, he followed, but he grew anxious with each splashing step. Knee-deep in the breakers, he looked desperate to keep his feet, holding out his arms to maintain his balance.

"Be ready to swim when I tell you!" she said.

"I can't swim!"

Kamehime exhaled sharply. Gritting her teeth, she turned and drew her sword.

"Get behind me," she said, as the *samurai* charged their steeds into the surf just a few hundred paces from them.

As she faced the enemy with the Emperor behind her, a big wave struck his back, rocking his footing. Frantically, he clung to her so she fell to her knees, the sea splashing around her.

All of a sudden, arrows whistled from their right. The lead *samurai* in pursuit fell into the waves with a splash, then a second, and a third behind him. Their horses reeled and broke toward the beach, the bodies of their fallen riders tossing in the waves, while the remaining *samurai* were thrown into confusion.

Looking around, Kamehime saw a formidable line of horsemen, the blue triple hollyhock standards of the Tokugawa clan flapping at their backs as they raced across the beach from the east. Half the detachment rode forward to rout Lord Monkey's *samurai* and made short work of them with arrow and spear, although several escaped. Kamehime grabbed the Emperor to steady him and they waded toward the beach.

"My Lady," Master Yagyū shouted from his mount.

"Master!" she cried, and wept, but quickly wiped her forearm across her eyes to hide it.

"Your Grace," Master Yagyū exclaimed in surprise, leaping from his horse to stand in the waves, imposing in his black lacquer armor, his headgear adorned with an enormous golden crescent moon broader than his shoulders.

The prince balked at the sight of the redoubtable, one-eyed *samurai*, but Master Yagyū humbly knelt before his Emperor, without a care for the waves breaking against him.

"We must leave at once! Take my horse, your Grace," he said, pulling his mount forward by the bridle. "My Lady, you should ride with the Emperor."

Kamehime quickly mounted his horse, while Master Yagyū knelt again to offer his hand for the Emperor's foot. The prince climbed behind her, holding onto her waist as she took the reins.

Master Yagyū's squire rode forward and dismounted, offering his horse, and the sword master leaped into the saddle and held out his arm for his squire to ride behind him. Nodding to Kamehime, Master Yagyū spurred their retreat to Lord Tokugawa's encampment.

太

Although they stood on the bluff at Ise Shrine, Tarō and Tanuki could not see their companions' desperate flight as the fog rolled inland, but they had an uninterrupted view of the bay in the early light and, across the bay, the faint purple cone of Mount Fuji rising above the mist.

"We can't go home yet," Tarō said, "not the way we came, and you should rest."

"I'm fine," Tanuki said stoically.

"You can't swim with your wound," Tarō said, looking down at the ocean crashing against the cliffs.

"I can try."

Tarō shook his head. "We should stay a while," he argued, although he seemed preoccupied with competing thoughts.

They sat for a time, Tarō staring at the wedded rocks joined by their massive, sacred cord. Inside the shrine, the priests chanted morning prayers, and the sigh of the crashing waves mixed hypnotically with their chorus. Tarō drifted in thought, dreaming on a day, years ago, when he looked upon the rock garden in his castle home, the four large stones marching across the snow-laden gravel and, when he closed one eye, how the stones became one.

*"Smaller stones will sink beneath the Sea, but one great stone may withstand the tide—"* his father's voice echoed in his head.

Tarō saw his younger self again, a boy of seven years, transfixed as his father penned calligraphy for his birthday blessing.

*"Ni-hon-ichi," Tarō read the words aloud.*

*"You will be a great leader someday, first in all Nihon," his mother said, rousing the Tiger.*

*"Foolish woman, do not tempt the gods! That is not what it means. You'll fill his head with dangerous thoughts! Tarō is* samurai, *born and bound to serve and protect his Lord and his Emperor unto death."*

As Tarō gazed pensively at the wedded rocks, the waves crashing around them, another voice haunted him.

*"You are not virtuous," Master Yagyū accused. "You are like that island over there, a solitary rock in a vast ocean. You think yourself special because you see only yourself. Your talent is wasted on selfish pursuits."*

Tarō sighed heavily, but Kamehime's accusation had stung him even more deeply.

*"You may be Takeda, but you will never know what it means to be* samurai!"

Waking from his anxious reflection, Tarō beheld an awesome sight. The glowing red-orange aura of Amaterasu rose from the sea between the wedded rocks, her rays piercing ragged clouds on the horizon, but his heart welled with grief, anger, and shame, and he took no comfort in the beauty of that breaking dawn, as he thought of Kamehime's harsh words.

As dawn broke, Master Yagyū's detachment raised alarm, galloping through their lines toward Lord Tokugawa's command post perched on a rocky escarpment overlooking the foggy valley. Surrounded by his aides-de-camp on the grassy hilltop, wearing black armor with blue lacing and a short surcoat of the same color, Lord Tokugawa sighed relief when he saw his daughter but gasped in astonishment when he beheld the Emperor.

"Father!" Kamehime cried.

"Your Grace!" Lord Tokugawa knelt before the Emperor.

"My Lord Tokugawa, your daughter is a great *samurai*."

Lord Tokugawa bowed. He stood and nodded to his daughter, and she ran to him.

"My daughter," he said with misty eyes, "well done indeed!"

They stood proudly together on the brink of the eastern escarpment, the calm, self-assured leader, a veteran of many battles, and his young *samurai* daughter. The blue triple hollyhock banners and *jinmaku* camp curtains of the Tokugawa clan rippled in the strong warm wind blowing inland, the fog slowly lifting, shrinking from the red dawn to creep up the slopes of the bluff, until nothing remained but rags of mist that disappeared like wraiths into the wooded slopes of the surrounding mountains.

The valley looked blood-stained already, its grassy plain overgrown with countless red spider lilies, while the three rivers that poured from the hillsides to wind their way across the plain toward the Eastern Sea Road reflected the red-orange sky kindled by the sunrise. The Ibi joined the Nagara as the rivers approached the bay, and the Eastern Sea Road crossed the glowing rivers by two arched bridges on its way to Kuwana-juku, which marked the boundary to the western provinces. The road was ominously deserted. Kamehime drew a deep breath, as she looked toward the bay and Ise Shrine, thinking of Tarō.

"Father—" she started to speak, but the long, low blast of a battle horn sounded over the plain.

Distant drums beat an ominous, thundering response, as tens of thousands of men-at-arms, their black standards proclaiming Lord Monkey's golden gourd as well as the imperial chrysanthemum, marched slowly forward on the western escarpment, swarming the hillside like voracious insects.

"It begins!" Lord Tokugawa shouted, raising his *tessen* war fan. "Sound the call to arms!"

A herald ran forward, holding a large pink conch shell trumpet to his lips to blow a long, low horn blast. Drums awoke the lines on either side of the command post, prompting Lord Tokugawa's divisions to form ranks in haste.

"Kame," Lord Tokugawa said, "take the Emperor, join General Honda on the left flank. It will be safer there."

"Father, no!" she protested, "Let me be the first spear!"

Her request took him utterly by surprise. He stared speechless for a moment, looking at the Emperor, then Master Yagyū. He did not expect advice, and they did not offer any, but neither did they object in the slightest way.

He studied his daughter. *How she had grown.* He quietly reproached himself for his failure to raise her as a true lady—*and yet she had become twice the man of many male* samurai. *Indeed, who could have rescued the*

*Emperor from Lord Monkey's clutches? None of his bannermen would have even proposed such a seemingly insurmountable feat. Who was he then to direct—or deny—her destiny if the gods willed it so?*

"So be it!" Lord Tokugawa said suddenly, surprising everyone, and Kamehime most of all. "Runner!" he called, and a messenger ran forward with pen and ink and knelt. "Send to General Ii—Kamehime shall ride with the vanguard."

Lord Tokugawa personally sealed the message, and the messenger quickly took to horse. He turned to his daughter, his eyes moist, a thin wisp of bittersweet pride in the corner of his mouth. Kamehime smiled and bowed, grateful for her father's confidence, but she flushed from the flutter in her heart as she thought of the battle ahead.

"Jūbei," Lord Tokugawa said to his trusted sword master.

"My Lord!"

"Please make haste to escort the Emperor to General Honda at Miya-juku and return as quickly as possible—you would not want to miss the war," he said, smiling as he met Master Yagyū's one good eye.

The sword master smiled and bowed. Lord Tokugawa bowed deeply to the Emperor.

"May Amaterasu Ōkami and Hachiman no Kami bless your swords this day!" the Emperor said in parting, then turning to Kamehime, "My Lady, I am forever in your debt. Fare thee well!"

"Your Grace!" she shouted and knelt to bow.

Father and daughter watched, as Master Yagyū and the Emperor mounted their horses to ride toward General Honda's division above the Eastern Sea Road.

"We shall meet again when the battle is won," Lord Tokugawa said, turning to his daughter with a wistful eye.

"Yes, Father!" she shouted, her eyes watering with pride and sadness.

Lord Tokugawa watched as she took to horse. Waving farewell, she galloped away toward the right flank to take her post with General Ii's division.

The drums still beat a constant rhythm as Lord Tokugawa raised his *tessen* to signal the corps again. The herald stepped forward and blew several blasts on his battle horn, and other horns responded down the lines on either side.

One by one, Lord Tokugawa's commanders rode to the fore of their divisions, poised in their respective positions on the eastern escarpment.

In command of the left flank, riding forth on his magnificent black steed, General Honda, the "Yellow Devil," wore armor with golden yellow lacing, a huge Buddhist rosary slung diagonally across his breastplate, his helmet famously adorned with a massive crest of stag antlers, his infamous spear, Dragonfly Cutter, in hand.

The "Red Devil," General Ii, in his signature blood-red armor, his helmet adorned with a tall crest of golden horns, and carrying his spear Hachiman, commanded the right flank. His *samurai* wore various crests by which they hoped to be recognized on the battlefield, but all wore the same blood-red colors as their General—armor, helmets, facemasks, banners, even the horses' harnesses were lacquered in devil-red.

Lord Tokugawa's squire brought his helmet, a black steel cap fitted with a short neck guard, adorned with gilt ferns arranged in a circlet surrounding a golden, pouncing lion-dog. He waited patiently until his Lord finished reassessing the lay of the land and penned last-minute orders, which Lord Tokugawa gave to a rider.

"Deliver this at once," he said, donning his helmet.

"Yes, my Lord!" the rider shouted upon receiving his charge and, racing to his mount, off he rode at breakneck pace.

On either side of the plain, the armies, Eastern and Western, undulated in anticipation, the calm sea before the storm.

Wearing his helmet, its crest of fanned spikes newly painted with gold lacquer glinting so they rivaled the rays of the sun, the coveted Crown Jewel glowing green upon his breastplate, Lord

Monkey surveyed the battlefield from his command post cordoned by a *jinmaku* of black cloth on the western escarpment overlooking the Ibi River.

Lord Monkey's highest ranking generals commanded the Western Army's flanks—on the right, General Ishida, in black armor, his helmet adorned with a bleached white human spine and skull, a red tassel hanging from its teeth, and on the left, General Katō, wearing his helmet tall like a courtier's hat with the painted golden circles on each side and the golden crescent crest.

General Katō shaded his eyes to look across the grassy plain toward the eastern escarpment, watching General Ii's division surge forward with Kamehime in the vanguard. Down the sloping escarpment they rode to cross the wide but shallow Kiso River onto the grassy plain where red dragonflies flitted over the fields of blood-red spider lilies in the early light.

For a time, the armies regarded each other like arrows drawn on taut bows, banners and standards of both sides whipping in the humid wind gusting off the bay. Then Lord Tokugawa raised his iron fan to give the signal.

The battle began when Kamehime and General Ii charged the vanguard south across the Nagara River to engage the Western Army's left center. At the same time, General Katō suddenly turned his ranks to cross the Ibi, his arquebusiers attacking the left flank of Lord Monkey's central division. The thundering reports of their matchlocks echoed across the valley. This betrayal caught Lord Monkey's troops completely by surprise. In just minutes, they suffered heavy casualties before retreating in confusion.

"Katō, you sentimental fool!" Lord Monkey spat furiously. "Do you think your treachery will carry the day? Secure our flank! Signal the *sōhei*!"

A herald stepped forward to blow upon a black conch shell—three long horn blasts. General Ii's Red-Devil Division had crossed the

Nagara but slowed and wavered, as a rushing wind descended from the wooded northern slope above the plain.

Several thousand *Ikkō-ikki* warrior monks in white cowls and black armor charged suddenly from the forest cover to descend on General Ii's right flank, their leader deftly deflecting *samurai* arrows right and left with his *naginata* as he led their advance guard. General Ii's red-devil *samurai* fought bravely, but the warrior monks' cruel *naginata* cut them down like scythes reaping grass, until the flank collapsed south along the Kiso River.

"Tokugawa hesitates," Lord Monkey mused as he watched the Eastern Army's central division from his command post. "We must draw him out."

A runner took to horse, and Lord Monkey raised his tasseled baton, signaling to his right flank. General Ishida, his gruesome, red-tasseled skull crest swaying back and forth, waved his troops forward along the Eastern Sea Road, while Lord Monkey led his own division onto the grassy plain to cross the Nagara River, holding on the western bank of the Kiso.

Under previous orders, General Honda stood his ground since he had been entrusted with the Emperor. Whether he took the bait or by design, Lord Tokugawa rode forward with his division to face Lord Monkey.

A tense breath followed as the armies faced off from opposite sides of the Kiso River, each firing volleys from bow and *teppō* and wooden cannons bound with cord, arrows and bullets lodging in movable wooden barricades, while the unlucky fell under the deadly barrage and explosions on both sides. Then spearmen charged forward, meeting in a thundering clash across the Kiso, followed by cavalry from both sides.

Master Yagyū returned just in time to join his Lord, and together they rode into the fray. The grassy fields were muddy from the previous day's rain, and the battle devolved into a primal conflict on the sodden riverbanks, an undulating mass of bloodlust. Emblazoned with heraldic characters, flowers, insects, animals, or mythical beasts, the banners of both sides shook violently as men vied and fell in the brutal melee of bow, musket, spear and sword. Soon the bloody river swept into the bay to foul the seafoam.

The warrior monks of Mount Hiei had the advantage of surprise, inflicting heavy casualties on General Ii's *samurai*, but his division still vastly outnumbered them. With Lord Monkey's right center defending against General Katō's defection, General Ii and Kamehime rallied the troops to face the *sōhei.* The General made efficient use of a triple skirmish line to deliver volleys of musket shot that cut down nearly a hundred monks, while Kamehime commanded archers who dispatched nearly two hundred more.

Seeing this reversal, the leader of the *sōhei* removed his cowl, revealing his naked, pale blue head crowned with two knobby horns. His eyes flashed red, and his lips curled over his cruel teeth as he gave a blood-curdling *kiai* to rally his soldiers. A number of shamans in the *Ikkō-ikki* ranks responded, removing their cowls to take evil *yōkai* form—*kappa, rokurokubi,* and demonic *oni.*

The sight of these monstrous *bakemono* paralyzed General Ii's men, as the various *yōkai* descended on the hapless *samurai*, cutting them down with their cruel *naginata* or tearing them limb from limb, even feasting on their flesh while other *samurai* stared aghast or fled. Still, some of General Ii's men did not shrink from this new terror but proved true to their ferocious epithet, as they exacted Red-Devil revenge for their fallen comrades.

Inevitably, General Ii's division surrendered ground to the *Ikkō-ikki* sorcerers and their fierce warrior monks, until the battle waged on the slopes of the eastern escarpment, retreating toward the bay. Lord Tokugawa watched his elite vanguard fight a brave rearguard action against the monstrous monks.

General Ii himself faced the monkish leader, Red Devil against the blue, his spear Hachiman vying against the monk's vicious *naginata*, each thrusting, slashing, and parrying, until the monk forced the point of the General's spear to the ground. Then, leaping onto the spear, the blue devil ran its length on nimble, clawed feet, and slashed at General Ii with a downward stroke that cleaved his shoulder. The General lost his spear and fell to the ground, mortally wounded.

The blue devil loomed over its foe, savoring the moment. Seeing its prey powerless to defend himself, the fiend dropped its *naginata* and climbed onto the General's body, grasping his limbs with its clawed feet to hold him down. Tearing off the General's helmet, it clutched his top knot and bared its vicious teeth to rip out his throat, but the demon suddenly gasped, spurting blood, as an arrow protruded from its mouth. Kamehime had hit her mark. The *oni* fell lifeless over the General's body. She wheeled her horse to dismount and, with a detachment of Red-Devil *samurai* to bear the General away, they retreated across the river.

As the battle raged in the Hour of the Horse, Lord Tokugawa and Master Yagyū fought side by side, urging their troops onward against the center of Lord Monkey's host, their swords slashing left and right, splashing the blood of their enemies around them. Lord Tokugawa saw his daughter leading what remained of the Red-Devil division, less than a fifth of its original twenty-five thousand with the monstrous monks close on their heels. He swung his horse around to ride to their aid and was about to call Master Yagyū to his side when he spied his nemesis.

Astride his horse, the spiked helmet watched the melee from high ground across the river and well behind the crush of his advancing lines. Time stood still, and the distance shrank between them for an instant, as each regarded the other, two warlords in command of tens of thousands of their countrymen, each vying for ultimate power. Lord Monkey raised his war fan, signaling to his right flank, which responded with horn and drum.

General Ishida, his death's head crest rocking back and forth, suddenly charged his division forward along the Eastern Sea Road. Lord Tokugawa searched for General Katō, who still engaged Lord Monkey's left flank, but the General's division could do little against Lord Monkey's superior numbers.

Surveying the battlefield, Lord Tokugawa realized the same peril awaited his own forces if he did not act quickly. The center of Lord Monkey's army surged forward, across the Kiso, the hellish monks cutting a swath through Kamehime's rearguard, while General Ishida's troops pressed along the Eastern Sea Road. His army could ill afford to be cut off from General Honda's division. Raising his *tessen*, Lord Tokugawa signaled retreat.

As the Tokugawa lines fell back along the road toward Miya-juku, an Ishida contingent bulged suddenly forward, smashing through their lines and charging straight for their principal target whom they recognized by his golden lion-dog crest. Lord Tokugawa defended from his horse, cutting down two of his enemies right and left, but not before another foot soldier thrust his spear upward, stabbing just below the cuirass, barely missing the kidney. Lord Tokugawa grimaced in pain. Grabbing the spear, he pulled it from his side, then wheeled his horse to broadside his assailant, who fell backward into the enemy ranks.

Master Yagyū rode to his Lord's aid, deflecting arrow and spear with his sword alone, but the enemy closed on them. When all seemed lost, General Honda suddenly appeared, his stag horns thrashing wildly as he wielded the Dragonfly Cutter to carve a swath around his Lord and Master Yagyū. The enemy fled before the Yellow Devil, and his *samurai* charged forward to form a barrier between their Lord and the Ishida lines.

The Eastern Army beat a desperate retreat along the Eastern Sea Road toward Kiso Bridge, but the sight of the bay stole the blood from their faces. An army of ghosts marched across the horizon between the black water and the hazy yellow sky. Master Yagyū shouted, pointing at the tall warships.

As they strained their eyes to discern this new threat, Kamehime rode to join them, but a musket ball from the enemy ranks struck her shoulder, and she fell suddenly from her horse. Seeing this, Master Yagyū swung his steed around, rushing to her just as a number of *sōhei,* led by their evil shamans, broke the Red-Devil flank. Master Yagyū leaped over Kamehime to intervene, his fearsome Masamune blade striking down one foul creature after another, *kappa, rokurokubi* and *oni*, while the Red-Devil *samurai* valiantly covered their withdrawal.

Abandoning their horses, Master Yagyū lifted up Kamehime, and they beat a hasty retreat to rejoin their Lord, while General Honda marshaled the rearguard. All the while, Lord Monkey's horde pressed ever forward, forcing them toward the sea.

Tarō and Tanuki watched the battle rage from their vantage on the cliffs, although they could only see as far as the Eastern Sea Road where General Ishida's division had advanced, thousands of soldiers blotting out the road as they engaged the Tokugawa lines. The chanting inside the shrine had stopped. Priests appeared and disappeared, running this way and that around the shrine, obviously troubled by the proximity of the warring armies.

"So much hate," Tanuki said.

"Yama Uba warned me—I didn't understand."

"Humans!" Tanuki grunted. "Let them kill themselves!"

Still struggling with his thoughts, Tarō did not respond, but Tanuki's callous comment wounded his humanity. His eyes trailed from the battle to just below the cliffs where the waves crashed against the wedded rocks. The glaring sun had risen apace. He shaded his eyes, squinting, trying to get a better look at what appeared to be many stones marching across the glittering mouth of the bay, wondering that he had not noticed them before.

As the sun slipped behind the ragged clouds, Tarō immediately recognized the marching "stones" as ships invading the bay. Hundreds of warships in close formation, under billowing sails emblazoned with a solid black line above a triangle of three dots, General Mōri's fleet covered the wide sea to the horizon, and each ship carried many *samurai* warriors.

"Look!" he said, pointing at the black battle standards with the golden gourd. "It's him," Tarō fumed, "Lord Monkey!"

Tarō and Tanuki watched helplessly as the armada sailed into the bay, dropping anchor to dispatch longboats packed with General Mōri's *samurai*. Their oars beat the choppy water with furious intent, driving their bows forward to pierce the waves.

"I wish—" Tarō stuttered, "I wish I was my old self. I wish I had my strength back."

Tarō's sudden change of heart surprised Tanuki.

"You can't help it," Tanuki consoled. "You can't hide from yourself. Remember Yama Uba's mirror."

Wistfully, Tarō nodded, but struck by a sudden thought, he stiffened. Reaching into his sleeve he drew forth Yama Uba's mirror. Tanuki was still chattering beside him, but Tarō did not hear him. Slowly, he held up the mirror.

At first, he saw only himself staring back from the highly polished metal. Then, his image began to move and swirl, and Tarō saw his younger self again, his father leaning close to him.

*"The Takeda family was meant to unite this land," his father whispered. "It is your destiny."*

Tarō held the mirror close as his father corrected himself.

*"Only the gods can see your destiny," his father said aloud.*

Tarō stiffened with a thought, throwing a backward glance at the Gods of Wind and Thunder guarding the shrine.

"Hey!" Tanuki said, as Tarō suddenly stood to stride toward the entrance.

As he approached the guardians, Tarō remembered the priest Tenzaemon's words.

*"These wooden statues are but effigies of the Gods of Wind and Thunder—their eyes are windows to their true spirits. Everything is linked. The* shinkai, *the realm of* kami, *may be hidden by the veil of mortal life, but when you learn to look, you will see."*

Tarō moved closer to stand before the statues, their crystal eyes staring fiercely back at him, witnesses to time and space far beyond his ken. He heard the battle raging—from across the bay but also echoing in his memory. Guardians like these had seen his father slain by Lord Monkey. He looked at Yama Uba's mirror.

"Maybe there is still some magic in it," he said to himself.

He tucked the mirror in his sash and drew a deep, determined breath, summoning his faith. Holding up his hands, he bowed twice, clapped twice, and bowed again.

"Hear me, guardians!" he cried aloud.

He waited for an answer but none came. He wavered, desperate for a miracle. Then he remembered what had prompted him. He pulled the mirror from his sash.

Leaping onto the pedestal of one tall pillar that stood beside Raijin, he clambered up it and stretched out his hand to hold the mirror up to Raijin's fearsome visage. The statue's crystal eyes flashed at its reflection, and the image in the mirror swirled.

Tarō shook, his face twisting determinedly as he strained to hold fast to the pillar and steady the mirror. Just when he thought he could not hold on any longer, he heard a faint rumbling, and the air began to crackle with static electricity, teasing his hair.

Emboldened, Tarō slid down the pillar and bounded to the other side where Fūjin stood. He scrambled up the nearest pillar to hold up the mirror just as he had done to Raijin.

Meanwhile, the rumbling grew. The air around Raijin crackled angrily, and the sky darkened as storm clouds gathered, flashing and thundering overhead. Soon the warm salt air stirred with a divine wind, and the *kamikaze* gusted across the courtyard. Tanuki had come to check on Tarō and stared in awe as Raijin or, rather, its *kami,* suddenly awoke. A pale white apparition with a giant halo of rumbling thunder-drums, the very semblance of its wooden effigy, emerged from the giant statue to hover overhead.

As Tanuki shook and cowered before the fearsome deity, the air swirled and gusted around Tarō, and the very image of Fūjin awoke as well. Its *kami*, a pale green spirit, churned the air with a gale storm force from its windbag that bent and whipped the trees around the shrine. Priests scrambled to batten down the doors and windows against this holy typhoon as it blew tiles from the roofs of the shrine buildings.

Raijin and Fūjin hovered at the gate, regarding each other in bewilderment. Spying Tanuki, Raijin flashed and thundered.

"You!"

Tanuki cowered, stopping his ears with both hands, terrified of the lightning and thunder.

"Who are you to summon us thus?" Fūjin howled. "Have you come to honor your debt?"

Tanuki squirmed and stuttered, "Yes, well, about that—"

"He didn't call you!" Tarō yelled, blinking at the gusting wind and lightning flashes. "I am Tarō, *samurai* of the Takeda clan," he shouted, pulling his sheathed sword from his sash and holding it up in salute, the mirror in his other hand. "I beg your favor. In exchange, I offer my life, to do with as you will, even unto death."

Small though he was, Tarō's bold account of himself disarmed the guardians. Fūjin's billowing windbag ceased rippling, and Raijin's thundering drums hushed.

"What are you?" Fūjin bellowed. "What power have you to summon us thus?"

"Only this," Tarō declared, holding up Yama Uba's mirror.

At once, both guardians took keen interest in the shiny talisman, each vying for a look.

"There it is! Let me see myself again!" Raijin demanded. "How fierce I looked!"

"Let *me* see!" Fūjin interrupted. "I looked terrible indeed!"

Both deities rumbled and grumbled, Raijin flashed, and Fūjin blustered, and the air rustled and gusted and crackled and flashed and rumbled all around them as their argument flared.

"You can have it!" Tarō yelled over the din.

Once again, the blowing and thundering subsided as the demigods abandoned their stormy debate to hover close to Tarō, each god thrusting forth a sinewy arm to grab for the mirror.

"If you help me," Tarō said, holding the mirror to himself.

Fūjin and Raijin recoiled angrily but quickly relented, each coveting the mirror.

"What would you have us do?" Raijin thundered.

An ill wind blew across the bay, this wind that brought General Mōri's armada. Watching from his sequestered position on the eastern cliffs, as the battle turned from dark to hopeless, the Emperor recognized the General's insignia and his heart sank in despair at the sight of the invading fleet. He strode toward the cliffs before his appointed bodyguards even realized the boy might take his own life by flinging himself from the rocky precipice, but the prince stopped short, gasping in fear, and fell to his knees, breathing heavily, struggling to hold back his grief.

As he knelt in desperate prayer, the prince heard a rumbling thunder from across the bay. The sky grew dark and the heavens flashed. The Emperor raised his face to the sky. The strong wind blowing from across the bay made him blink, but his face hardened with determination as he stood and strode to the nearest bodyguard.

"A horse!" he demanded.

"Your Grace!—" the flustered *samurai* stuttered.

Seeing the look in his Emperor's eye, the look of a man facing death, the *samurai* quickly knelt. Moved by their plight, he took his short sword from his sash and offered it to the prince, who proudly took it.

Moments later, his bodyguards in close formation around him, the Emperor rode toward the battle, even as it surged toward him. General Ishida's division pressed General Honda across the Eastern Sea Road, while Lord Monkey drove against what remained of Lord Tokugawa's division along the Kiso River, and the monstrous *Ikkō-ikki* monks swept against the right flank, pounding their lines again and again. Each time the stalwart *samurai* drove back the waves, but slowly, inevitably, as steadily as the rising tide, Lord Monkey's army gained ground until thousands lay slain or wounded, Lord Monkey's troops stepping over corpses and writhing bodies, stopping only to take heads for trophies.

Master Yagyū had seen his Lord and Lady safely to the eastern end of Kiso Bridge. Wounded though they were, they both insisted they would not leave the field. Standing on Kiso bridge, its elegant arch framed against the hazy yellow sky growing dark from some new witchcraft, Lord Tokugawa surveyed the battlefield where half of his Eastern Army lay dead, while the other half formed a desperate rout across the eastern escarpment and the road, pursued relentlessly by Lord Monkey's forces. Although he was wounded, none could stop Lord Tokugawa from moving closer to the front lines to encourage his men in their darkest hour.

Riding forward and witnessing firsthand the horrible slaughter, and seeing his champion leading his *samurai* toward a glorious death, the Emperor pulled so hard on the reins that his horse nearly stumbled and fell.

"What have you done?" Lord Tokugawa shouted at the Emperor's bodyguards when he saw the prince there.

"No!" the prince quickly intervened, "I commanded them."

Lord Tokugawa looked up at the boy, proud in his saddle, but still a boy.

"Your Grace—"

"If I must die," the prince said, cutting him short, "I do not want to die alone."

Moved by the boy's courage, Lord Tokugawa nodded. His face hardened with pride and resolve, even as Lord Monkey's army engulfed the plain and all seemed lost. The skies darkened with great rumbling storm clouds, and the bay rose to meet the battle, the sea swelling toward the Eastern Sea Road. Branched lightning suddenly split the sky and smote the mountains, setting them ablaze, while the divine wind swept wildfire through the wood and down the mountainside. The storm unleashed a driving rain that dampened matchlock and cannon, but still the armies fell upon each other, sword and spear, while the monstrous *yōkai* flung hapless *samurai* over the eastern escarpment or fed upon the bodies of the fallen.

Lord Monkey raised his face to the sky, smiling at the warring symmetry of heaven and earth. He could see Lord Tokugawa—and the Emperor—just behind the eastern lines, his eyes narrowing in satisfaction, but even as he thought of victory, lightning suddenly struck the valley, setting the grassy plain ablaze beneath his army, and his horse reeled from the thundering sky.

As he struggled to rein his mount, Lord Monkey glimpsed the bay and the roiling ocean, the wind and waves angrily tossing his armada. Fūjin unleashed his colossal wind bag, and the divine wind stirred the sea until it rose as tall as the cliffs of Ise Shrine. The anchored armada slipped suddenly into the trough of a great wave rising ever higher until it peaked, and curled, and crashed upon the insignificant ships, crushing and engulfing them, and driving them to smash against each other. Then Raijin set the ships ablaze with lightning that crackled from his fingertips to the rumbling of his circlet of drums.

"What is this spell-craft?" Lord Monkey yelled in vain as he watched this calamity unfold.

太

Tarō and Tanuki watched from the cliffs as the sea swelled below them, the great waves rising nearly to the brink to roll inland where Tarō had set his gaze. Seeing the look in Tarō's eyes, Tanuki shrugged stoically.

"I guess we've come this far—why not finish it?"

Tarō smiled and nodded, and together they jumped into the churning sea as a great wave rolled past the cliffs. Tarō grabbed onto Tanuki's shell as he instantly transformed into his sea turtle self and swam for the shore as fast as he could manage.

At the head of Lord Monkey's forces battling across Kiso Bridge, General Ishida stared aghast. The sea had risen to meet the battle along the Eastern Sea Road, but suddenly it retreated, faster than a galloping horse, swelling into one giant wave, taller than the cliffs of Ise Shrine, and Tarō rode Turtle Tanuki on the crest of the *tsunami*, the sea spray in his face and the wind in his hair.

"Look! It's Tarō!" Kamehime cried suddenly.

Her heart leaped as she saw him surfing the crest of the great wave on his giant sea turtle, but Tarō could not hear her over the storm and the angry sea. Raijin flashed and thundered and Fūjin howled as Turtle Tanuki surfed the swell, Tarō directing him straight toward the warlord with his unmistakable spiked helmet.

"You!" Lord Monkey snarled when he saw Tarō atop the curling swell.

Taro Wakes Fujin and Raijin

The warlord raised his sword defiantly, but his horse balked, and he faltered as he fell under the shadow of the great wave. The *tsunami* curled upward toward the flashing thunderclouds, then fell, crashing upon the Eastern Sea Road and the plain, engulfing Lord Monkey's army. Lord Monkey rode forward in the last instant, leaping from his horse to grab hold of Kiso Bridge, as the great wave crashed and swept away his steed and all else not rooted to the plain.

Lord Tokugawa's *samurai*, most having crossed the Kiso River and fighting from higher ground, scrambled for safety from the sudden flood, but many good *samurai* were lost. Lord Tokugawa, Kamehime, the Emperor, and Master Yagyū would have washed away had they not also clung to the bridge.

Lord Monkey's forces occupied the breadth of the valley, and the great wave exacted karmic devastation upon his army. *Samurai* and *sōhei* floundered and drowned in the raging tide, swept away forever. Those few survivors fled the field.

As the great wave spilled over Kiso Bridge, Tarō and Tanuki leaped from the crest to grab hold of the rail. Tanuki transformed in midair but barely caught himself from slipping over the bridge, his claws digging into the wood to keep from being swept away. Tarō held fast and grabbed his friend by the scruff of his neck until the wave passed, but as he pulled his friend onto the bridge, Tanuki barked in alarm.

Lord Monkey struck suddenly from behind. Barely evading the warlord's sword, which split the bridge rail, Tarō rolled a safe distance to make his stand, clutching his tender ribs. Tanuki retreated in the other direction, leaping onto the bridge rail to run its length, but he came face to face with a waterlogged General Ishida, spluttering and coughing up sea water as he pulled himself onto the bridge through a broken portion of the railing.

The General's cruel helmet had been swept away, and his wet topknot drooped across his face. Seeing Tarō's companion, he grimaced. He snatched up a fallen spear and jabbed, but Tanuki quickly dodged his thrust and scrambled along the spear to jump on him. The warlord flailed, trying to get his hands on Tanuki who scrambled all over him. The General caught a foreleg, but Tanuki latched onto his hand and took a big bite. With a howl, he threw Tanuki to the ground, but stumbling backward, the General fell from the bridge into the churning river as it swept into the sea. Tanuki sighed and slumped to the ground.

Meanwhile, soaked and dripping, Tarō faced Lord Monkey, drawing his sword, which flashed from the lightning tearing across the skies. Sneering at the sight of the soggy boy and his little sword, Lord Monkey strode toward him, brandishing his long sword, the Crown Jewel glowing green atop his breastplate. All around them the heavens roared as they stalked each other.

"I should have killed you when I killed your father—" Lord Monkey said, holding his *katana* at his shoulder ready to strike.

Tarō bared his teeth. Grinning in response, Lord Monkey lowered his blade so it trailed behind him, inviting Tarō to attack.

"—And your mother," Lord Monkey snickered.

Tarō faltered, waves of sadness overwhelming him, then he flushed with anger, his ire rising so it threatened to usurp all his senses. Then, amid the din of the storm, he heard a faint cry, his mother's voice calling to him.

*"Courage, Tarō!"*

A sudden calm came over Tarō. Seeing that he failed to bait the boy, Lord Monkey lunged and slashed, but Tarō rolled beneath him.

Springing from his shoulders against the ground, Tarō kicked, his feet catching Lord Monkey beneath his chin, snapping his head backward with such force that the warlord's helmet flew off his head and landed on the ground behind him, the fan of spikes pointing at the flashing heavens. As Lord Monkey reeled, Tarō grabbed the jewel around his neck and pulled hard, snapping the chain and robbing the warlord of his prize.

"Takeda dog," he yelled, "this time I will finish you!"

Lord Monkey slashed, but once again Tarō nimbly evaded his strike, vaulting over him. In midair, he flipped the sword in his hand and sunk it deep into Lord Monkey's neck just above his breastplate, then landed squarely on the ground behind his foe.

Lord Monkey gasped and reeled, dropping his *katana* to clutch Tarō's sword, his hands slipping on the blade's razor edge so they bled as well. He staggered backward, disbelief in his eyes.

Pulling the *wakizashi* from his throat, Lord Monkey clapped a hand to his wound, blood spurting through his fingers. He stared at Tarō's sword and dropped it. He tried to curse but could not, as he choked on his last breath and fell backward on his helmet, its spikes rending his steel cuirass and piercing his chest.

Tarō stared at his vanquished foe. Retrieving his sword, he glanced at the Crown Jewel glowing in his fist, then stashed it in his sleeve and rushed to check on Tanuki, calling to him.

Tanuki did not respond. Cradling his fallen comrade in his arms, desperate at the thought of losing his best friend, Tarō rubbed Tanuki's furry face and called to him again. Opening his eyes, Tanuki groaned.

"Can we go home now?"

Tarō smiled and helped his friend to stand. The tempest still raged, but they watched from the bridge as the great wave receded from the plain into the bay.

Fūjin and Raijin appeared overhead. At some distance, Kamehime, Lord Tokugawa, Master Yagyū, and the Emperor watched in awe as the deities descended from the dark clouds to confront Tarō.

"Tarō!" Kamehime cried for fear the gods might smite him as well, but he could not hear her over the din of wind and thunder.

"So, Takeda Tarō!" Raijin rumbled. "Now we shall have our reward!"

"Indeed!" Tarō replied.

"Are you sure you want to give up the mirror?" Tanuki said, the little bit of his crafty old treasure-hoarding-self showing.

"It's mine!" the gods roared at once.

Each held out a huge hand, eager to receive the prize, and Tanuki cowered behind Tarō.

"As promised!" Tarō yelled.

Pulling the mirror from his sleeve, he threw it into the air. Fūjin and Raijin bellowed and thundered as they grasped and fumbled for the mirror, each batting it higher into the sky. Flashing thunderclouds whirled around them as they disappeared from view, and all eyes followed the gods into the heavens, the rumbling rising with them and traveling out to sea.

Holding her injured shoulder, Kamehime ran forward to join Tarō. The Emperor quickly followed, and Lord Tokugawa hobbled after, supported by Master Yagyū and General Honda.

Tarō managed a smile as he met Kamehime, and her eyes filled with joyful tears, but he stiffened when he saw her father over her shoulder, and she balked when she saw the look on Tarō's face.

The storm had subsided, but the air still crackled around Tarō and Lord Tokugawa. Everyone stood transfixed, bracing for a final showdown.

Tarō fumed, one foe vanquished, yet one remained. Kamehime looked first at Tarō, then her father, searching for words to help them reconcile their differences, before she lost one or both of them forever.

Tarō stood tall, no longer a boy but a young man, lean and confident, with some supernatural remnant of his surrogate mother, the white witch, still coursing through his veins, and the look in his eyes conjured some wild animal of the shadowy forest, or perhaps even the flashing eyes of the very guardians he seemed to command. Lord Tokugawa paused, but then he hobbled forward.

Tarō did not flinch. As Lord Tokugawa drew near, Tarō dug in his heels for the deathmatch, every muscle in his body tensed to spring, his fingers tingling for his sword, but before he could pounce, Lord Tokugawa dropped to one knee. Tarō's hands curled into fists, but he hesitated as Lord Tokugawa removed his helmet and laid it at Tarō's feet.

"Takeda Tarō, you have saved the country—you have saved us all," the warlord said humbly. "You are indeed a great *samurai*, the spirit of your father. You have good reason to hate me, and once again I owe you my life." He pulled his sheathed sword from his side and held it up. "This time, I shall pay it in full. Do with me what you will."

"No!" Kamehime cried, and her father's closest retainers tensed to intervene.

"No—" Lord Tokugawa said, gently rebuking his daughter. "I have seen this country united in the name of the Emperor. Now I may die in peace, if that is my destiny."

Lord Tokugawa held the sheathed sword up once more, and Tarō took it.

"Tarō, please don't—he is my father," Kamehime begged.

Tarō avoided her pleading eyes. He glanced at the Emperor. The prince did not speak, but his eyes appealed on her behalf. Tarō met Master Yagyū's inscrutable gaze, then he looked at Lord Tokugawa kneeling before him.

Setting his jaw, Tarō held the warlord's sword as if to draw it. He pulled on the hilt so a glint of steel escaped the scabbard, then he abruptly snapped it shut.

"Keep your life, and keep the peace," he said, striding past Lord Tokugawa to kneel before the prince, presenting the sword—and the jewel—and declaring, "In the name of the Emperor!"

A roar of approval answered him, thousands of *samurai* cheering Tarō, the boy *samurai*. As the sea slipped beneath their feet to ebb into the bay, washing away the blood of the fallen, Amaterasu's bright rays pierced the dispersing storm clouds to herald the dawn of a new day—a new era.

12

## PEACH BOY AND THE SHŌGUN'S JEWEL

*Yamashiro Province*

*Autumn, Year of the Tiger*

Many moons passed before Lord Tokugawa swept away the remnants of the Western Army that survived and fled the Battle of Sekigahara. To secure a peaceful Kyōto, he stormed and razed the monkish stronghold on Mount Hiei. Not one *Ikkō-ikki Sōhei* or evil shaman survived. As if in homage to Lord Tokugawa's triumph in service to the Emperor, the maple trees blazed red and orange on the surrounding hillsides, and the crescent jewel of Lake Biwa shimmered peacefully in the early morning light.

The scaffolded veteran, Momoyama Castle, kept watch over the valley, while laborers still worked to refurbish those parts ravaged by fire. As they passed the fortress and beheld the peaceful valley below, Tarō and Tanuki paused, drawing a deep breath of the autumn air.

Tarō wore a priest's white *kimono* and *hakama*, his golden *wakizashi* tucked in his sash. Looking back along the Eastern Sea Road, the sun glowed like a blushing peach rising over Ise Bay. Seeing this, he realized they should pick up their pace and bounded off toward Kyōto, calling to Tanuki.

"We must hurry!"

"They can't start without you," Tanuki argued, "you're the guest of honor!"

When they arrived at the Main City Gate of Rajōmon, an armed escort greeted them. Golden fan-shaped ginkgo leaves fluttered around the champions as they strode along the wide avenue leading to Kyōto Palace, and children ran beside them, shouting excitedly to see the fabled heroes.

"Momoyama Tarō! It's Momo-Tarō and *tanuki*!"

Tanuki puffed with pride, but Tarō just smiled and waved.

When they arrived at the enormous vermillion *torii* gate to Peace Shrine, the courtyard had filled to capacity, but the crowd gave way to the armed escort so they passed quickly to the main hall, a magnificent two-tiered building of vermillion posts and lintels, its green-tiled roofs with elegant upturned cornices stacked one upon the other. Crowding into the wide courtyard, peasants and nobility alike murmured excitedly, and again shouts greeted the champions as the multitude recognized the celebrated boy *samurai* and his curious *tanuki.*

Passing up the short flight of stairs and into the shrine, the heroes found the oratory dimly lit within. In contrast to the masses outside, the audience here was limited to three hundred representatives of the imperial court, Tokugawa vassals, and special invitees.

Expectant whispers filled the hall as Tarō and Tanuki marched toward the dais where the Emperor, Lord Tokugawa, and Kamehime awaited. Frowning upon their belatedness, Lord Tokugawa wore full armor and his famous helmet, its golden, leaping lion-dog and laurels glinting in the candlelight. Kamehime stood beside him, dressed in a richly colored *kimono* in the high-court style. Master Yagyū stood nearby, as well as Lord Tokugawa's generals. As he approached the dais, Tarō knelt and bowed his head, and Tanuki knelt beside him.

Taro and Tanuki, Banzai!

"Rise, Takeda Tarō!" the Emperor said, waving for them to ascend the dais.

Lord Tokugawa gave Tarō a nod in greeting, and Tarō returned his favor. As he took his place beside her, Tarō and Kamehime exchanged looks, her eyes quietly rebuking him. Tarō shrugged bashfully.

A resonant bell rang, and a drummer stepped forward, beating a solemn rhythm on the great drum beside the dais. The Emperor raised his scepter in blessing. Assisted by servants, the prince unfastened the Crown Jewel from around his neck, holding it up for all to see. The jade crescent glowed with rich green light.

"Behold!" the Emperor said in a voice surpassing his years. "The Crown Jewel of Nihon, the symbol of our land, the birthplace of Amaterasu Ōkami, the Sun Goddess. On this second anniversary of the great victory at Sekigahara," the prince said in a clear, confident voice, "by the divine power, I declare Lord Tokugawa *Shōgun*, Commander-in-Chief and Protector of the Realm."

Lord Tokugawa knelt to receive the pendant, bowing low, and the congregation cheered. With the ceremony concluded, the audience spilled from the dark hall into the sunlit open courtyard, and the multitude hailed Peach Boy and the Shōgun, the Crown Jewel glinting in Amaterasu's bright, blessed light.

Lord Tokugawa strode forward to stand at the top of the stairs, framed by the central massive vermillion pillars. As the Emperor joined him, Lord Tokugawa shouted.

"Long live His Majesty the Emperor!"

"*Banzai! Banzai! Banzai!*" the crowd roared in response.

Turning, Lord Tokugawa bowed to Tarō and waved for his squire. His man came quickly forward carrying a sword with gilt and black lacquered fittings, bearing the Takeda crest in gold leaf inlay on the scabbard.

"Your father's sword, recovered from Lord Oda's castle," he said, presenting it to Tarō.

Tarō instantly recognized the sword, his eyes misting as he received it. He bowed graciously and held it up in offering to the Emperor, and the crowd cheered again.

"Tarō!" Lord Tokugawa shouted, raising his iron fan.

"Tarō!" the crowd roared in recognition, their praise so loud it was later said that even Tarō's father himself, the Tiger of Kai, heard their tribute and growled approval.

All Kyōto celebrated throughout the day and into the night. Flute and string and drum and song set every citizen to dance. In the Hour of the Rooster, festive red lanterns lit the way beside Duck River, where weeping cherry trees marched and sighed and waved their trailing branches in the autumn breeze, and everyone gathered to watch the night sky flash and thunder with fireworks.

Tarō and Kamehime stood on Sanjō Bridge, watching the festive display. Nearby, Tanuki's eyes grew large and hungry as he received skewers of grilled, toothsome rice cake dripping with sweet soy sauce from a nearby vendor. He licked his lips at the skewers in each hand. Not knowing which to eat first, he shoved both in his mouth at once. Standing beside him, Master Yagyū took a step back in alarm at Tanuki's appetite.

Fireworks whistled and boomed and crackled overhead—magnificent orange, red and pink blossoms. Kamehime and Tarō gasped and nodded approval. She looked fondly at him, but when she caught his eye, she blushed.

Master Yagyū and Tanuki watched their friends with approval. From a new ever-flowing *sake* jug, Tanuki poured Master Yagyū a cup, cringing in alarm as he spilled a fair amount. Master Yagyū laughed and chided him.

"The gods must have their share."

Standing beside Tarō watching the night sky flash and thunder, Kamehime searched for words.

"Why don't you stay?" she blurted. "You could be of great service to my father. You are *samurai*—" She turned to look at him, adding, "You are a great *samurai*."

"As Master Yagyū said, 'There is more to being *samurai* than a sword.'"

Kamehime smiled, conceding his point.

"Not a bad student after all," Master Yagyū said to Tanuki.

Still stuffing his face with skewered *mochi*, Tanuki shrugged.

"Besides, what will *samurai* do now that the war has ended?" Tarō queried, to which even Master Yagyū had no reply.

"No, I am not suited to be a courtier—all that talk of politics," Tarō said, shaking his head, "I was born *samurai*, but I grew up in the wild. I don't belong here—maybe I don't belong there. I guess for now the shrine is my home—" he said, patting the railing of Sanjō Bridge and grinning easily, "my bridge between two worlds."

"What will you do?" she asked.

"I don't know yet," he said. He smiled pensively and added, "A wise man's stomach is never full."

She made a face, bemused, then pensive.

"I guess it's nice to have a choice," she said enviously.

She looked at Tarō as if she were seeing him for the first time—and the last.

"I expect you to visit me!" she burst out.

"I promise," he said with a bow.

She gave him a stern eye, and they shared a bittersweet smile. Tanuki rolled his eyes but kept his tongue.

They turned to watch the fireworks again, each stealing glances at the other as they raised their faces to the balmy embrace of the autumn breeze. They gasped in wonder as yet another glorious starburst boomed and crackled overhead. Master Yagyū and Tanuki watched their friends with approval, then regarded each other, contemplating some show of affection, but each thought better of it and settled for a nod.

太

## *Kai Province*

### *Autumn, Year of the Tiger*

Mount Fuji rose in snow-crowned majesty toward the azure sky as Tarō and Tanuki returned home, crossing the sacred bridge to hike through the fragrant green cypress and brilliant maple trees toward Fuji Hachiman Shrine. Tarō bathed his hands at the sacred reservoir before bounding lightly up the steps to the Twilight Gate.

The great wooden effigies of Fūjin and Raijin still stood silent sentinel. Tarō knelt in homage to the guardians. When he looked up and met their shining eyes, he smiled in greeting. Puffing behind him, Tanuki shrugged self-consciously.

"See you later, right?"

Tarō nodded and they bid goodbye, Tanuki waving as he bounded across the courtyard and into the forest. As Tarō turned, the hollow plunk of the bamboo water hammer greeted him.

He crossed the courtyard but stopped beside the votive rack crowded with prayer plaques of unfinished wood, the many tiles painted with the image of a tiger stalking through a bamboo forest, each inscribed with a prayer, hundreds in all, some granted, some still awaiting divine grace. Tarō smiled.

"Welcome back," a familiar voice said.

Tarō turned to greet the abbot. Tenzaemon smiled and offered him a broom, and Tarō took it cheerfully.

太

Much later, when the shrine slept beneath the spell of the dark, chirping forest, a door slid quietly open as Tarō, half-naked except for his loincloth, stepped into the crisp autumn night. Smiling at the full moon, he crept through the courtyard to the Twilight Gate where Fūjin and Raijin stood in shadow.

As he passed through the gate, lanterns all around the forecourt below began to glow with green torchlight that danced across the ornate facades of the shrine buildings and the tall, dark cypress trees encircling the shrine. The courtyard soon filled with the familiar chatter of his forest friends—bear, fox, badger, deer, dormouse, rabbit, fish owl, pheasant, crane, frog and toad, red-faced monkey—and Tanuki, of course. Tarō smiled in greeting to all. Then he slapped his muscles, ready for a fight.

Excited chattering filled the shrine courtyard long into the night, now rising, now falling, punctuated by grunts, growls, squeaks, squawks and howls as the enchanted audience watched the two silhouettes strain against each other in the torchlight, until yet again, loud and clear above the din, the referee shouted.

"Tarō wins!"

# GLOSSARY

*Amaterasu* or *Amaterasu Ōkami* [天照 or 天照大神], "heaven-shine," the Sun Goddess.

*Ashigaru* [足軽], "light foot," generally conscripted peasant infantry employed by *samurai.*

*Baka* [馬鹿], "horse-deer," idiot or fool, especially as an expletive.

*Bakemono* [化け物], or *obake* [お化け], "transforming thing," a preternatural, shape-shifting creature, including magical animals, and monsters, a species of *yōkai.*

*Sugoroku* [双六], "double-six," a game similar to western backgammon.

*Banzai* [万歳], "ten thousand years," a cheer roughly equivalent to "hurray!" often in reference to *Tenno Heika* [天皇陛下], "His Majesty the Emperor."

*Bentō* [弁当], "convenience," an individual, boxed meal.

*Biwa* [琵琶], "lute," a plucked, fretted, short-necked, pear-shaped lute with four or sometimes five strings.

*Bokutō* [木刀], "wood(en) sword."

*Bugeisha* [武芸者], "martial artist."

*Bushi* [武士], "warrior."

*Bushidō* [武士道], "the way of the warrior," a chivalrous code of honor for *samurai.*

*Chanoyu* [茶の湯], "hot water for tea," the tea ceremony, a transformative aesthetic pursuit for spiritual awakening.

*Chawan* [茶碗], "tea bowl."

*Daibutsu* [大仏], "great Buddha."

*Daimyō* [大名], "great name," a powerful feudal lord.

*Daishō* [大小], "long (and) short," the pair of swords, *katana* and *wakizashi,* worn by *samurai.*

*Daitō* [大刀], "big sword," a long sword.

*Dōjo* [道場], "training hall (for martial arts)."

*Dō-maru* [胴丸], "body wrap," a cuirass, a type of light armor generally used for fighting on foot.

*Eboshi* [烏帽子], "crow cap," the traditional black hat worn by nobility.

*Edo* [江戸], "bay door," the former name of Tōkyō.

*Fujisan* [富士山 or 不死山 or 藤山], "abundant mountain," or "immortal mountain," or "wisteria mountain, " Mount Fuji, located in Kai Province.

*Fundoshi* [褌], "loincloth."

*Fusuma* [襖], "sliding screen," opaque rectangular panels that slide on tracks to act as doors or redefine spaces within rooms.

*Futon* [布団], "cloth mattress."

*Fūrinkazan* [風林火山], "wind, forest, fire, mountain," an abbreviation for the motto, "Swift as the wind, quiet as the forest, fierce as the fire, firm as the mountain."

*Fūjin* [風神], "Wind God."

*Geisha* [芸者], "performing artist," female entertainers who perform traditional artforms such as song and dance.

*Genpuku* [元服], "coming into one's own," a coming-of-age ceremony generally celebrated on the 15th birthday.

*Geta* [下駄], "under board," wooden clogs.

*Gintsukuroi* [銀繕い], "silver repair," lacquer mixed with powdered silver (or *kin-* [金] "gold"), used to repair cracked pottery.

*Giri* [義理], "right reason," duty encompassing a moral obligation, loyalty, honor, and self-sacrificing devotion.

*Go* [碁], or *igo* [囲碁], "encirclement game," a game of strategy.

*Gū* [宮]," also *jinja* [神社], "god place," a shrine.

*Hachimaki* [鉢巻], "headband," often inscribed with meaningful calligraphy and worn as symbolic of courageous effort.

*Hachiman* or *Hachiman no Kami* [八幡 or 八幡神], "God of Eight Banners," the God of War.

*Hakama* [袴], "trousers," pleated, wide pants worn with *kimono*.

*Hashiba* [羽柴], "winged brushwood," the adopted name of the preeminent 16th century *daimyō,* one of the three Great Unifiers.

*Hara hachi bun me* [腹八分目], "belly 80 percent full," a proverb for health and longevity, loosely translated as, "A wise man's belly is never full."

*Harakiri* [腹切り], "belly-cutting," a vulgar term for ritual suicide.

*Honmaru* [本丸], "central circle," the innermost defensive citadel of a castle.

*Ichi* [一], "one."

*Ichi go, ichi e* [一期一会], "one moment, one meeting," an idiom expressing the fleeting, unrepeatable nature of a moment.

*Igo* [囲碁], "encirclement game," a game of strategy; see also *Go.*

*Ikari* [碇], "anchor," a bright, top-heavy style of *rosoku* [蝋燭], candle.

*Ikkō-ikki* [一向一揆], "single-minded rebellion," an uprising against feudal rule led by a zealous sect of Buddhist monks.

*Ise* [伊勢], "(spiritual) force," a province where Ise Shrine is located.

*Ji,* also *tera* [寺], "temple."

*Jinja* [神社], also *gū* [宮], "god place," a shrine.

*Jinmaku* [陣幕], "camp curtain," a cloth screen enclosing an army commander's headquarters.

*Jūjutsu* [柔術], "supple technique," a system of grappling using an opponent's force for advantage and employing throws, joint locks, and pins to subdue an attacker.

*-Juku* [宿], "inn," suffix denoting a fortified post or town, a station on a trunk road.

*Kabuto* [兜 or 冑], "helmet."

*Kagami* [鏡], "mirror."

*Kagami mochi* [鏡餅], "mirror rice cake," a traditional New Year's decoration.

*Kagemusha* [影武者], "shadow warrior," a body double or political decoy.

*Kago* [駕籠], "carrying basket," a litter.

*Kai* [甲斐], "fruitful," a province, ruled by the Takeda clan, where Mount Fuji is located.

*Kamehime* [亀姫], "turtle princess," considered a lucky name as turtles were said to live 10,000 years.

*Kami* [神], "gods," the gods and the forces of nature as well as the venerated spirits of the dead.

*Kamikaze* [神風], "divine wind," an unexpected spiritual power saving a seemingly hopeless situation.

*Kanji* [漢字], "Chinese characters," an imported component of writing.

*Kannon* [観音], "perceiver of (the world's) sounds," a bodhisattva, any person who is on the path to enlightenment.

*Kappa* [河童], "river child," a legendary supernatural being, half-turtle, half-human, a species of *yōkai.*

*Karō* [家老], "house elder," the chief retainer or steward of a castle or household.

*Katana* [刀], "sword," specifically a long sword.

*Katte kabuto no o wo shime yo* [勝って兜の緒を締めよ], "in victory tighten the helmet cords," a proverb warning not to rest on one's laurels but always be on guard.

*Kenjutsu* [剣術], "sword technique."

*Kesa* [袈裟], "monk's shawl," a rectangular cloth, scarf, or mantle worn diagonally over the left shoulder and under the right armpit, denoting Buddhist ordination.

*Ki* [気], "(life) force," cosmic energy.

*Kiai* [気合], "spiritual extension," a shout or short utterance intended to startle an opponent or focus effort.

*Kimono* [着物], "wear," a traditional garment, a formal robe.

*Kintarō* [金太郎], "golden boy."

*Kinō no boro, kyō no nishiki* [昨日のぼろ, 今日の錦], "yesterday's rags, today's brocade," an idiom for rags-to-riches success.

*Kirisute* [切捨], "cut and discard," the right to cut down anyone of lower class for an offense against *samurai* honor.

*Kohin ya no gotoshi* [光陰矢のごとし], "light (day) and darkness (night) fly like an arrow," a proverb meaning time is fleeting.

*Koi* [鯉], "carp."

*Komainu* [狛犬], or sometimes *shishi* [獅子], "lion-dog," mythical, magical creatures believed capable of warding off evil spirits and symbolic of strength.

*Kōan* [公案], "matter for (public) thought," a paradoxical anecdote or riddle, used in Zen Buddhism to demonstrate the inadequacy of logical reasoning and to provoke enlightenment.

*Koto* [箏], "zither," a 13-stringed, musical instrument.

*Kubibukuro* [首袋], "neck bag," a netted bag used to carry the heads of defeated enemies.

*Kuso* [糞], "shit," crap, bullshit, damn, or fuck, depending on the context, and as a modifier such as in *kusobaka,* "damned idiot."

*Kyōto* [京都], "capital city," formerly known as *Heiankyō,* "capital of peace and tranquility," the seat of the imperial court.

*Kyūba no michi* [弓馬の道], "the way of bow and horse."

*Kyūjutsu* [弓術], "bow technique," archery.

*Masamune* [正宗], "honorable origin," Priest Gorō Masamune is widely recognized as the greatest swordsmith that ever lived, his swords possessing a reputation for extraordinary quality and beauty, the blades said to sparkle with pearlite forged like stars in the night sky.

*Menpō* [面頬], "face armor."

*Mikawa* [三河], "three rivers," a province ruled by the Tokugawa clan, famous for its *bushi* [武士], "warriors."

*Miso* [味噌], "flavor," fermented soybean paste.

*Mochi* [餅], "rice cake."

*Mochiyari* [持ち槍], "hand spear."

*Momijigari* [紅葉狩], "*Maple Viewing*," a *Nō* play by Kanze Nobumitsu.

*Momotarō* [桃太郎], "peach boy."

*Mon* [紋] "crest," a coat of arms; or [門], "gate;" or [文], "coin."

*Murakumo no Hoken* [叢雲の宝剣], "Gathering-Cloud Treasure Sword," the legendary sword hewed from a dragon's tail by *Susanō no Mikoto.*

*Musashi* [武蔵], "martial storehouse," a province, ruled by the Tokugawa clan, where Edo was located.

*Musubi* [結び], "binding (force)," the interconnective energy of the cosmos; or "rice ball."

*Naginata* [薙刀], "mowing sword," a long polearm, a glaive or lance with a handguard below the curved, single-edged blade.

*Nihon* [日本], "sun origin," Japan.

*Ninja* [忍者], also *shinobi* [忍び], "stealthy person," a covert mercenary trained in espionage, deception, ambush and assassination.

*No aru taka wa tsume o kakusu* [脳ある鷹は爪を隠す], "the wise hawk hides its talons," a proverb meaning a wise man does not show off but keeps his talents in reserve.

*Nobutora* [信虎],"trusty tiger," Lord Takeda's given name.

*Nō* [能], "skill," a form of classical drama.

*Noren* [暖簾], "warm screen," a split, cloth curtain used in doorways, windows, and as room dividers.

*Obi* [帯], "sash," used to tie the waist of *kimono.*

*Oda* [織田], "woven rice field," the family name of the preeminent 16th century *daimyō,* one of the three Great Unifiers.

*Odawarajo* [小田原城], "Small Rice Field Plain Castle," a fortified post on the *Tōkaidō.*

*Oiran* [花魁], "elder flower," a high-ranking courtesan.

*O-mikoshi* [お神輿], "god palanquin," a portable shrine.

*Oni* [鬼], "demon" or "devil," a legendary supernatural being, a species of *yōkai.*

*Onna bugeisha* [女武芸者], "female martial artist."

*Owari* [尾張], "tail stretching," a province ruled by the Oda clan.

*Oyoroi* [大鎧], "great armor," a type of armor, heavier and more expensive than *dō-maru*, generally for fighting on horseback.

*Raijin* [雷神], "God of Thunder (and Lightning)."

*Raku* or *raku-yaki* [楽焼], "fired delight," a type of hand-shaped pottery traditionally used in *chanoyu,* the tea ceremony.

*Rokurokubi* [ろくろ首], "stretching neck," a legendary supernatural being, a spirit with a neck that stretches or detaches, a species of *yōkai*.

*Rōnin* [浪人], "wave man," a master-less *samurai*, generally a derogatory term for a *samurai* with no lord, a drifter.

*Rosoku* [蝋燭], "wax light," a candle.

*Sake* [酒], "rice wine."

*Sakuramochi* [桜餅], "cherry rice cake," a confection made of pink-colored rice cake filled with sweet red bean paste and wrapped in a pickled cherry blossom leaf.

*Samurai* [侍], "one who serves," a knight of the warrior class.

*Saru* [猿], "monkey."

*Saru mo ki kara ochiru* [猿も木から落ちる], "even monkeys fall from trees," a proverb meaning even the most skilled can fail.

*Sashimono* [挿物], "insert," a small banner fitted to the back of *samurai* armor for identification and esprit de corps.

*Sekigahara* [関ヶ原], "barrier plain," site of a pivotal battle in 1600.

*Sengoku jidai* [戦国時代], "age of the country at war," a period of constant civil war from the middle 15th to early 17th centuries.

*Sensei* [先生], "ahead in life," elder, scholar, martial arts master.

*Sensu* [扇子], "folding fan," hand-held, usually made of bamboo and covered with rice paper or cloth.

*Seppuku* [切腹], "cut belly," ritual suicide by disembowelment; see also *harakiri*.

*Shakuhachi* [尺八], "one *shaku* [尺], eight *sun* [寸]," being units of measurements for an end-blown, bamboo flute of that size.

*Shamisen* [三味線], "three flavor strings," a fretless lute.

*Shiba inu* [柴犬], "brushwood dog," a small, alert and agile breed of hunting hound.

*Shima* [島], "island."

*Shinai* [竹刀], "bamboo sword," a sword made of split bamboo bound with leather.

*Shinkai* [神界], "god world," a parallel universe, the world of gods and demons.

*Shintō* [神道], "the way of the spirits," an indigenous faith in the connection between the natural and supernatural worlds.

*Shiro,* also *jiro* or *jo* [城], "castle."

*Shōbu* [菖蒲], "water iris;" [尚武], "martial spirit;" [勝負], "victory or defeat."

*Shōgun* [将軍], "army commander," a de facto military dictator.

*Shōji* [障子], "lesser screen," translucent, rectangular lattices, covered in rice paper, that slide from side to side on tracks to act as doors or redefine spaces within rooms.

*Shōtō*, [小刀], "small sword," a short sword.

*Shuriken* [手裏剣], "hand blade," a dagger, knife, or throwing star.

*Sōhei* [僧兵], "warrior monks."

*Sōjutsu* [槍術], "spear technique."

*Sumō* [相撲], "contest of striking," an ancient form of wrestling.

*Susanō no Mikoto* [須佐之男命], "tempestuous deity," the God of Sea and Storms, younger brother of *Amaterasu.*

*Tabi* [足袋], "foot cover," toe-divided socks worn with sandals.

*Tachisukashi* [立ち透かし], "light standing posture," a technique for maintaining stability in mounted archery.

*Taiko* [太鼓], "(fat) drum."

*Takeda* [武田], "martial rice field," the family name of the preeminent 16th century *daimyō*, the Tiger of Kai, father of Shingen (Tarō).

*Tanegashima* [種子島], "seed island," name for the matchlock-configured arquebus or musket; see also *teppō.*

*Tanuki* [狸], "raccoon-dog," a legendary supernatural being, reputed to be mischievous, bibulous, lecherous, and jolly, and capable of shapeshifting, a species of *yōkai.*

*Tantō* [短刀], "short sword," a knife or dagger.

*Tarō* [太郎], "big boy," a nickname for the eldest son.

*Tatami* [畳], "mat," a thick, rush-covered straw mat used as a traditional floor covering.

*Tengu* [天狗], "heaven dog," a legendary supernatural being, half-kite, half-human, a species of *yōkai.*

*Tenno Heika* [天皇陛下], "His Majesty the Emperor."

*Tenzaemon* [天左衛門], "heaven protection gate," a *Shintō* priest of Fuji Hachiman Shrine.

*Teppō* [鉄砲], "iron cannon," another name for the matchlock-configured arquebus or musket; see also *tanegashima.*

*Tessen* [鉄扇], "iron fan," a weaponized, hand-held folding fan.

*Tofu* [豆腐], "bean curd."

*Tokugawa* [徳川], "virtuous river," the family name of the preeminent 16th century *daimyō,* one of the three Great Unifiers.

*Tōkaidō* [東海道], "Eastern Sea Road," an important trunk road from *Kyōto to Edo.*

*Torii* [鳥居], "bird abode," a traditional gate that symbolically marks the transition from the mundane to the sacred.

*Tsunami* [津波], "harbor wave," a large forceful series of waves, sometimes called a tidal wave.

*Uchiwa* [団扇], "batting fan," hand-held, fixed (not folding), usually made of bamboo covered with rice paper or cloth.

*Ukiyo* [浮世], "floating world," a term referring to the urban lifestyle, especially its self-indulgent aspects, ironically alluding to the homophone [憂き世], "sorrowful world," the earthly plane of death and rebirth from which Buddhists seek release.

*Urashima Tarō* [浦島太郎], "(bay) island boy."

*Wabisabi* [侘寂], "rustic loneliness," an aesthetic of impermanence and imperfection.

*Wakizashi* [脇差], "side inserted sword," a short sword.

*Waraji* [草鞋], "grass shoes," sandals made of rice straw.

*Yagyū* [柳生], "living willow," the family name of the preeminent 16th century sword masters Munenori and his son Jūbei.

*Yamashiro* [山城], "mountain castle," a province, ruled by the Oda clan, where the imperial city of *Kyōto* is located.

*Yama Uba* [山姥], "mountain hag," a witch who eats her victims, a species of *yōkai.*

*Yari* [槍], "spear."

*Yogaiyamajō* [要害山城], "Strategic Mountain Castle," home of the Takeda clan.

*Yōjimbō* [用心棒], "protective staff," a bodyguard.

*Yōkai* [妖怪], supernatural creatures.

*Yoshiwara* [吉原], "lucky field," the red-light district of *Edo.*

*Yukata* [浴衣], "bath clothing," a light robe, an unlined, casual cotton *kimono*, usually worn in the summer or after bathing.

*Yumi* [弓], "bow," especially the long bow used in archery.

*Yūgen* [幽玄], "deep mystery," awareness of the universe evoking an emotional response too profound and mystical for words.

*Zabuton* [座布団], "sitting cloth mattress," a cushion.

*Zōri* [草履], "grass footwear," a thonged sandal made of straw, cloth, leather, or lacquered wood, more formal than *waraji.*

## THE AUTHOR

Born in Memphis, Tennessee, and raised in Atlanta, Georgia, Blue Spruell lived and worked in Japan for several years before returning to Atlanta. A trial lawyer and certified mediator, he runs his own firm, The Outlaw Firm, specializing in family law and civil litigation. An internationally recognized black belt instructor, he also owns Peachtree Aikikai, a *dōjo* for Japanese martial arts.

## THE ILLUSTRATOR

Born in Atlanta, Miya Outlaw graduated from Savannah College of Art and Design with a B.F.A. in printmaking and illustration. As an artist, her original works explore the psychology of nostalgia with whimsical characters. Japan is a second home, and her illustrations of *Tarō* are homage to her affinity for Japanese art and culture. She currently resides and works in Atlanta.

Printed in Great Britain
by Amazon

62248083R00163